OCT - 2 2017

31027007864339   **16.95**
HCLS-MD
F FRIEND
Friend, Catherine

Spark

SPARK

D0932705

FIC S- 00

What Reviewers Say About Catherine Friend's Work

The Spanish Pearl

"A fresh new author…has penned an exciting story…told with the right amount of humor and romance. Friend has done a wonderful job…"—*Lambda Book Review*

"The author does a terrific job with characterization, lush setting, action scenes, and droll commentary. This is one of those well-paced, exciting books that you just can't quite put down. …This is one of the very best books I've read in many months, so I give it my highest recommendation! Don't miss this one."—*Midwest Fiction Review*

The Crown of Valencia

"Her storytelling talent is superb and her plot twists continually keep the reader in suspense…"—*Just About Write*

The Copper Egg

"*The Copper Egg* by Catherine Friend is a modern day Indiana Jones style adventure. [It] has a bit of everything, adventure, kidnapping, double crossing frenemies and of course a romance. …Well written and an action-packed adventure of fun."—*The Romantic Reader*

Hit By a Farm

"*Hit By a Farm* goes beyond funny, through poignant, sad and angry, to redemptive: all the things that make a farm—and a relationship—successful."—*Lavender Magazine*

"A sweet and funny book in the classic 'Hardy Girls Go Farming' genre, elegantly told, from the first two pages, which are particularly riveting for the male reader, through the astonishing revelation that chickens have belly-buttons and on to the end, which comes much too soon. It has dogs, sheep, a pickup truck, women's underwear, electric fences, the works."—Garrison Keillor

Sheepish: Two Women, Fifty Sheep, and Enough Wool to Save the Planet

"As provocative as her reflections are, it is Friend's acerbic wit that keeps the reader turning pages. A perfect choice for book groups, this is a look at the road not taken with a guide who pokes as much fun at herself as she does at the world around her."—*Booklist*

"Friend details the challenges of balancing a writing career with sheep farming in southeastern Minnesota. ...Her voice is wry and funny; she's self-deprecating and thoughtful, and strikes a balance between teasing and kindness, whether her subject is pregnant sheep, yarn-loving 'fiber freaks,' or spirituality and nature."—*Publishers Weekly*

Visit us at www.boldstrokesbooks.com

By the Author

Bold Strokes Novels
The Spanish Pearl
The Crown of Valencia
A Pirate's Heart
The Copper Egg
Spark

Nonfiction
Sheepish: Two Women, Fifty Sheep,
and Enough Wool to Save the Planet

The Compassionate Carnivore, Or, How to Keep Animals
Happy, Save Old MacDonald's Farm, Reduce Your
Hoofprint, and Still Eat Meat

Hit By a Farm: How I Learned to Stop Worrying
and Love the Barn

Children's
Barn Boot Blues
The Perfect Nest
Eddie the Raccoon
Silly Ruby
Funny Ruby
The Sawfin Stickleback
My Head is Full of Colors

SPARK

by
Catherine Friend

2017

SPARK

© 2017 By Catherine Friend. All Rights Reserved.

ISBN 13: 978-1-62639-930-3

This Trade Paperback Original Is Published By
Bold Strokes Books, Inc.
P.O. Box 249
Valley Falls, NY 12185

First Edition: July 2017

This is a work of fiction. Names, characters, places, and incidents are the product of the author's imagination or are used fictitiously. Any resemblance to actual persons, living or dead, business establishments, events, or locales is entirely coincidental.

This book, or parts thereof, may not be reproduced in any form without permission.

Credits

Credits
Editor: Cindy Cresap
Production Design: Susan Ramundo
Cover Design By Sheri (graphicartist2020@hotmail.com)

Acknowledgments

My mom, Irene Friend, decided that if I was going to write a novel that took place in London, I should probably hang out there awhile. Thanks to her, we spent a marvelous week in a flat on Red Lion Square, joined by my sister Sandy and my aunt Gladys, and we had a blast exploring the city. Thanks, Mom, for all your support.

I'd also like to thank my patient and eagle-eyed readers Ann Etter, Carolyn Sampson, Irene Friend, Phyllis Root, Kris Ferguson, Brent and Karen Bjorngard, and Kathy Connolly. A special thanks to everyone at Bold Strokes, especially my ever-patient editor, Cindy Cresap, and cover designer, Sheri, for creating a gorgeous cover that far surpassed the one I'd imagined in my head.

Last but certainly not least, a big hug of thanks to my best cheerleader, my wife, Melissa Peteler.

Dedication

For my mom

Since I seem to have two personalities, perhaps I should donate my extra to someone who doesn't have one.

—Jamie Maddox

A Mini-Prologue, Sort of...

I, Jamie Maddox, must confess that until all this happened I'd never given much thought to my own sanity. I mean, really. Who stops every morning before leaving the house to take this inventory: Keys? *Check.* Backpack. *Check.* Sanity. *Oops. Left it on the kitchen table.*

But now, sitting in the doctor's office waiting for my shot, I get it. The journey to becoming a nutter, as the British say, is much shorter than we think. Sanity isn't a given. It's a fragile mix of hope for the future and an unwavering belief in yourself. Lose one of these two and you can probably limp along.

Lose both and you're pretty screwed.

Lose both *and* travel backward in time, and suddenly those people who've been taken by alien spaceships and operated on by little green men appear stone-cold sane next to you.

All of those things happened to me (except the little green men), so it should have been no surprise that my life ended up being truly fire trucked. That word was in my life because Aunt Nicole deplored the f-word and pleaded with me, "Jamie, dear, there must be another, less offensive word you could use." You'd think she was eighty instead of fifty. For her, I did find an alternative, which was harder than you might think. After she died, I continue to use it, even though I suspect it makes me sound a little...well...crazy....

Chapter One

I loved London. People there ate biscuits instead of cookies, had rows instead of arguments, and lived in flats instead of apartments. They also snogged instead of kissed, which just struck me as hysterical.

In London I inhaled history with every breath. It rose from a cobblestoned street polished to a sheen, and from the stones of the eighteenth century buildings that looked like faded blocks of soft butterscotch. Even the air felt laden with history as centuries of other people's breaths flowed into my lungs.

After eight months here I still hadn't tired of disembarking at random Tube stations to explore. I'd stumble onto a small, one-block park and sit on the cool iron bench as music blared from the Pakistani grocery around the corner and men argued good-naturedly outside a Russian teahouse. My partner, Chris, never came with me, since she thought a journey without a clear destination made no sense.

Today our destination—her choice—had been the National Gallery. So here I was, stuck inside staring at this "artwork," when all I wanted to do was flee to Trafalgar Square and find Bradley. This uninspiring exhibit left me speechless. Another five minutes and I thought I might lose my mind, ironic given what happened three days later.

The "artwork" was nothing more than twelve nearly identical brain scans. While the colors of each varied a little, I couldn't tell if the colors had been done digitally or if the neurology professor had just colored them in with a handful of Sharpies.

Chris squeezed my elbow, her blue eyes drilling into me. "What do you think? Aren't they *amazing?*" Chris was everything I wasn't—driven Type A, scientific, and crazy smart. My brother Jake once called her a computer with breasts, which wasn't very nice.

I smiled at her. "These images are unforgettable." *The Artistry of Neurological Scans,* by Dr. Anoop Rajamani had not been high on my list of must-see art exhibits.

Chris growled softly in her throat as we maneuvered around the packed room to the next brain scan. "Liar."

I struggled for something kind to say. In art school, they called me Switzerland because I couldn't stand giving harsh critiques. To me, if someone made art they loved, that was all the reason I needed to accept its existence. Loving what you did was infinitely more important than creating a piece that could hang next to a Degas or a van Gogh with pride. "Art should move you in some way," I said, "even if it's to hate it. But I'm not moved. I'm not anything." I cocked my head. "No, that's not true. I am curious why there is *way* more white in the scans for Subject Seven and Subject Twelve. Other than that, the art has failed to move me."

Chris shot me an impatient look and moved to the next piece, her blond ponytail swishing like a haughty horse's tail. I loved her hair.

I followed, checking my phone for the time. Bradley would be leaving Trafalgar Square in exactly thirty minutes. Because very little was certain in Bradley's life, he kept to his schedule with the precision expected of the ex-British Army officer that he was.

"I saw that," Chris whispered. "Why are you in such a hurry?" We stood at the far back of the crowd so we could whisper during the professor's incredibly boring speech. "How many art exhibits have you dragged *me* to?"

Hmmm. Good question. "Four here, two at the National Portrait Gallery, and three at the Tate Modern."

"What about *The Sounds of Art?*"

Our grimaces matched, the result of ten years together. "Yeah, okay, point made." I'd expected *The Sounds of Art* to present music inspired by art, but it had been an interpretive dramatic work sharing the shrieks and howls made by paint itself as it was cruelly smashed and slapped and dragged across the rough canvas. Fire truck, that was a painful two hours.

Chris turned back to the speaker still droning on. How could I get out of here? I shifted the straps of my heavy backpack, then froze when it rattled.

Chris shot me a confused look, then leaned closer as applause masked her voice. "What's in your pack?"

I shrugged. "Nothing." Actually, it was a small box of Burgess Excel Adult Rabbit Food with Oregano, to be exact. Sainsbury's had been out of the rosemary and thyme. Chris shook her head. "It's rabbit food for Annie, isn't it?"

I nodded, hoping my sheepish grin would buy me a little of Chris's patience. Call me a crazy optimist, but that's who I was.

I shifted, feeling hemmed in by the enthusiastic crowd in the small room. Someone behind me was wearing way too much lavender perfume. Perspiration slid down my back and soaked into my waistband, which made me feel sticky and cranky. The painfully microscopic details of this mind-numbing neurobiology exhibit were fascinating only to neurobiologists like Chris. When she shot me another "pay attention" look, I rolled my eyes.

"…to build this wiring diagram of the human brain, we are mapping all the structures and functions." Dr. Rajamani spoke with an endearing, singsong Mumbai accent. He wore a knee-length yellow jacket with a Nehru collar, and yellow slacks. When the image of a banana Popsicle zapped forward from my childhood, I bit my lip to cut off the chuckle.

"Descartes's notion that the mind and body are separate has been abandoned by most of the scientific world. As a result, scientists are studying how the brain creates our consciousness."

"Isn't he brilliant?" Chris whispered. She glared at me before I could come up with a sufficiently witty retort.

"My scans show brain connectivity by capturing myelin content around the nerves. The areas in red and yellow have higher myelin content, and therefore are more responsible for brain connectivity."

It was easy to get swept up in his musical accent; it was as if he were singing his speech. Then Dr. Rajamani waved his arms. "See those thin threads of white around the edges of the high myelin sections?" Chris's professor at University College London glowed with pride. "Our project does not yet have an explanation for these white areas, but I am conducting further research." He leaned closer to the microphone. "And this is what I have theorized. The white is the world's first visual image of a person's actual consciousness."

Luckily, the crowd's gasps were loud enough to mask my snort. I ignored Chris's dig into my ribs. Either the Gallery had been desperate for an exhibit, or Dr. Anoop Rajamani had forked over a double-decker bus full of money to buy himself the right to exhibit here.

I tuned out as the professor began describing with great enthusiasm something called "glial cells." Finally, polite applause followed the end of Dr. Rajamani's remarks.

"What is *wrong* with you?" Chris said. "As an artist, you should appreciate the creative value of these scans, even if you don't buy the science."

"That's true," I replied. "But as a scientist, don't you think this guy's a little wacky?" I lowered my voice, since neither of us liked PDAs—public displays of argument. "He believes he's located the site of human consciousness. That's like saying you've discovered what love looks like. How insane is that?"

But Chris had stopped listening and began leading me to the "artist." When he saw Chris, Dr. Rajamani's white teeth gleamed in his handsome face. He pushed through the others and reached for her hand.

"Chris, how are you feeling?"

"Just fine, Dr. Raj."

"No aftereffects?"

I frowned at my partner. Aftereffects of *what*?

"None whatsoever." Chris smoothly made introductions before I could ask. I had to look up to meet the man's eyes, unusual for me. His brow furrowed as if he were on the verge of some scientific breakthrough that I'd just interrupted.

"You are the artist, no?" The professor's childlike glee was infectious as he motioned to his scans. "Have you ever seen such colors?"

I attempted a supportive smile. "They are amazing. Thank you for sharing them with us." I checked my phone again, the niceties out of the way. "Chris, I'm sorry, but I need to get going. I'll meet you back at the flat like we planned."

"Jamie, wait. Dr. Raj has something to ask you."

Dr. Raj took my hands in both his large, smooth palms. "These scans are only the first step in locating consciousness, the *spark* of who we are. I need volunteers for the next, and most important phase, of my research. Chris thought you might be willing to be one of my subjects."

I fired an eye laser at Chris: *Thanks a bunch. Really appreciate it.* But my Minnesota Nice asserted itself. "I could probably do that. What's involved?"

"Ninety minutes of your time, no more. I will attach electrodes to your face and head, then ask a series of questions and record your brain scans as you answer."

"Sure, okay." I tingled with pleasure at Chris's beam of approval. I loved making Chris happy, especially since it was getting harder to do. I wasn't sure why our relationship seemed to be faltering, but I was confident I could figure it out and fix things.

Dr. Rajamani clasped his hands together and bowed. "This Monday at nine a.m.?"

I nodded.

"Excellent. Please eat nothing after nine p.m. the evening before. You will need three hours after the experiment before you should drive. It takes the GCA that long to reduce in strength."

"GCA?"

"The magic serum!" he crowed. "GCA, or glial cell activator, is the drug that will help me locate your consciousness by providing a slight electrical charge to cells that normally do not conduct electricity."

I failed to hide my grimace. "Okay, first, I'm not big on drugs. Second, not wild about the idea of electrifying my brain. And third, is this GCA administered orally?" Chris stiffened at my question and glared at me. Her anger, however, was less important than my suddenly sweaty hands and crazy heartbeat.

"GCA is not oral," Dr. Rajamani said. "One simple shot is all you will need."

I stepped back, palms up. "Uh oh. Needles are my kryptonite."

Dr. Raj threw back his head and laughed. "Ha! You are making a joke with me! Superman, no?"

"Jamie, it's just one shot," Chris said. "It doesn't hurt. I've particpated in the experiment myself. There's nothing to it."

I lived to give Chris what she wanted, but I didn't know if that included a shot. I shook the doctor's hand. "Let me think about it." I turned to Chris. "I'm late for an appointment. Gotta go. See you at home."

I jogged up the stairs from the basement level, then detoured over to the lobby's polyurethane collection box and dropped in a fiver, something Chris always refused to do. "It's a free museum, she'd say," and I'd always respond, "That's why it needs our support."

I moved with the crowds through the National Gallery's wide glass doors out onto the landing. The crisp air brought relief from the stuffy exhibit room. A needle. Crap. After a nurse in college had clumsily taken a blood sample from my arm with a needle the size of a garden hose, I'd sworn off needles. I sighed. Sometimes I wondered if Chris had been paying attention these last ten years. How could she not remember that I hated needles? I knew *everything* there was to know about her.

When I started at the University of Minnesota, I'd been unwilling to live at home, so I rented an apartment over Midwest Mountaineering, where I worked part-time. Because both apartment and work were only a short walk to the U's art department, my world narrowed to the West Bank campus, the bars gathering like lonely sheep at Seven Corners, and the Somali coffee shop that got me hooked on sambusas.

For twenty hours a week, I sold Midwest canoes, skateboards, skis, and mountaineering crampons with the confidence of someone who'd done it all, ridiculous since my riskiest sport was walking around Lake Calhoun. My knowledge came from watching weekend sports shows and Netflix documentaries.

During undergraduate and grad school, I went through girl-friends with the speed and recklessness of a world-class ski flyer. Then the week before I received my master's in art education, a gorgeous blonde with high cheekbones and awe-inspiring grace came shopping for a pair of inline skates. Nearly tongue-tied by her slight dimple, I managed to croak out my usual spiel about skates and which brand I preferred and why. When I sputtered to a triumphant finish with the words, "Um…they're, um, great," the woman's languid grin melted my remaining brain cells.

She leaned closer, smelling exotically of eucalyptus. "Has anyone told you that you're full of shit?"

My eyes widened.

"You've not skated once in your life, have you?" Her voice was playful, not angry

I met her eyes. "*So* busted." When I held out my wrists for cuffing, she circled them with warm, strong hands, and I fell in love with Chris.

Applause for the juggler performing on the plaza below snapped me back to the present. The National Gallery, with its dramatic central portico and impressive facade, formed the northern boundary of Trafalgar Square. In my free time, I was drawn to the Gallery, spending most of my time with my favorite artist, Vincent van Gogh, in Room 45. The most compelling painting, however, was in Room 41—Paul Delaroche's *The Execution of Lady Jane Grey*. I'd stand, transfixed, at the image of the sixteen-year-old girl, Queen of England for only nine days. Lady Jane was blindfolded, dressed in a flowing white gown that seemed made of polished pearls, and was reaching out a slender hand in search of the chopping block where she was to lay her head. Painting with oils wasn't in my skill set, so a well-executed oil never failed to astound me. Delaroche's layers of thin paint created flesh so real I was tempted to feel for a pulse.

I descended the Gallery's front steps, then crossed the pedestrian plaza to the upper level of Trafalgar Square, scanning the main plaza below for Bradley's faded military jacket. It still took my breath away to realize that just south of the square, in an area now filled with gray office buildings, was the former site of Whitehall Palace, home of King Henry VIII and his doomed wife Anne Boleyn. When their daughter Elizabeth became queen in 1558, she moved to Whitehall. The palace was gone now, but no matter. I drank up Elizabethan history like Chris drank up brain science. Soon after I began teaching at Carleton, my colleague Mary spent an evening entertaining me with the story of the Tudors. This family was the ultimate reality show, with its intrigue, adultery, hangings, and the occasional beheading. I was hooked, and after reading dozens of books and watching movies, I soon became weirdly conversant in Tudor England.

It didn't hurt that every child in my dad's family had been baptized in a christening gown said to have been given to the family by Queen Elizabeth I. Even though the story was just family lore gone wild, I loved to fantasize that Elizabeth might have actually touched the gown. The poor little dress was now yellowed with age, and almost all the tiny pearls from the gown's front were missing.

Noise rose from the impatient traffic curling around three sides of the square. Where was he? Was I too late? Another scan found the aging Bradley sitting on the pavement against a short wall, with Annie on a slender leash by his hip. I hurried down the central staircase and past the western fountain as the spray cooled my skin. "Hey, Bradley."

"Jamie Maddox! My very best American friend." His gray dreads flashed almost silver in the sun. His worn eyes radiated a kindness that always drew me in. This was a man who'd been knocked down and dragged behind the pickup truck of life, yet could still love.

"I'm your only American friend, big guy."

We bumped fists and I sank onto the warm pavement beside him, opening my pack. "More food for Annie."

Bradley's hands were scarred, the fingers curled with arthritis. It was a fire trucking crime that this veteran was living "rough" at his age. He'd fought for the British in the Falklands in the early 1980s.

Bradley's worn, mahogany face glowed as he opened the box and fed Annie a few pellets. "Brilliant," Bradley crooned. "She's chuffed over this new flavor."

I ran my hand over the brown-and-white rabbit, then scratched behind one floppy ear. I'd been trying for months to get Bradley off the streets, but he resisted at every turn. St Martin-in-the-Field Church, not twenty paces from the eastern edge of Trafalgar Square, had both day and night centers for the homeless.

"Won't let Annie in," had been Bradley's excuse for St Martin's. "Too claustrophobic," had ruled out the shelter at the north end of Drury Lane. So I did what I could, buying food for Annie, granola bars and toothpaste for Bradley, and listening to his favorite stories from British history. In Minneapolis, I'd never stopped for the homeless, but for some reason in London I couldn't *not* stop. That was why last winter, as Chris and I were learning how to be Londoners, and Chris was starting special degree classes in cognitive neuropsychiatry at University College London, I had befriended Bradley, a fixture in Trafalgar Square. I'd been drawn to Bradley because of his rabbit, and we'd found in each other someone willing to listen to whatever crazy thoughts invaded our minds. The only secret I'd kept from Chris was that on six of the coldest nights in February, I'd let Bradley and Annie into the locked vestibule between our inner door and the second floor hallway. Chris, not a fan of the homeless, never knew that Bradley and Annie were rolled up inside a sleeping bag thirty feet from her bed.

"I love this square," I said. Talking with Bradley had different rules than normal society. We could switch topics without warning.

"It's the heart of London," Bradley intoned. "Did you know that this whole area used to be the Royal Mews? They were the stables for centuries of royal horses."

I did know that, since Bradley had told me three times already, but I didn't want to discourage him. When he'd been stationed in the Falklands years ago, before cell phones and e-readers, the only two books he had access to were the Bible and a history of London. Too poor to actually travel by Tube, now he would walk to a station and establish a command outside, shouting all the history he could remember, hoping that donations would clank into his worn tin box.

Traffic banged on around us. Kids shrieked as they tried but failed to climb the four reclining lions guarding the base of Nelson's Column at the southern edge of the square. Tourists chattered on in Japanese, German, and French. Twice, I climbed to my feet and fulfilled requests to photograph tourists in front of the nearest fountain. Perhaps selfies were finally losing their appeal.

I closed my eyes as Bradley and I sat in silence, feeling all of London swirling around its beating heart. Political protests, New Year's Eve celebrations, rock concerts, announcements, everything happened here. Victory Day at the end of WWII brought Londoners to the square. The premiere of the final Harry Potter movie had Emma Watson walking a red carpet across the square.

We watched Annie nibble at her pellets. "Much obliged," Bradley whispered.

"No worries," I replied, then checked my phone. "Time for you to head for Charing Cross?"

Bradley nodded. "There is so much history to share."

"I wish you'd use one of the shelters. And there are programs to help vets like you." Bradley's answer was to gently lift Annie and press his face into her lush side.

"I know," I said. "Annie is your love and you want to keep her, but I worry about you." How did he get up every morning, from whatever doorway or park bench had been his bed, and keep going?

"Life is a constant battle not to lose yourself," he said.

"Amen," I replied with appreciation, but really, I didn't have any experience with that. I'd never really lost myself, since my parents, two brothers, my aunts and uncles, and Chris had always supported and accepted my choices. My mom called me "spunky" because I was such an optimist. Sometimes during parties in college I'd try to play the jaded pessimist, but my friends would end up laughing because I couldn't pull it off.

Quietly, we began transferring the goodies from my pack into Bradley's, which was patched with grimy duct tape.

"I hope to see you soon," I said.

Bradley jumped when a shadow fell across our laps.

Chris.

"It's okay," I said as I shot to my feet. "Chris, I'd like you to meet Bradley. Bradley, my partner, Chris." Chris knew about Bradley and Annie but had never met them.

Bradley scrambled to his feet, much faster than you'd expect from a guy his age, then held out Annie for Chris to pat. "This is my rabbit, Annie," he said. I held my breath but needn't have, for Chris's Minnesota Nice was as automatic as my own.

When she reached out and lightly touched Annie's head with one finger, her flinch was invisible to the untrained eye. Chris wasn't an animal person. "Hello, Bradley. Hello, Annie. It's nice to meet you." She looked at me. "I'm done at the Gallery so I thought we could ride home together."

After one last stroke of Annie's silky back, I told Bradley I'd find him again. Then Chris and I walked across the main plaza and up the stairs. As we followed the sidewalk toward Leicester Square, I lightly touched Chris's arm. "Slow down. No need to run."

Chris's usually rosy cheeks were carved marble. A muscle twitched along her jaw, but she slowed down. "I know. I'm sorry. Homeless people push some weird button in me that I don't understand, so I flee. I'm not proud of it, but there it is."

I slid my arm into Chris's to avoid being separated by oncoming pedestrians. "Are you afraid of him?"

"No, not at all. But right now, Bradley's not important. I'm just so disappointed that you didn't say yes. Dr. Raj really needs help with his experiment."

"He's a prof. He has dozens of students to experiment on."

"Students are a little afraid of him. He's sort of considered, well, on the fringe."

"No kidding. Locating our consciousness? He's not *on* the fringe, he's hanging from the very frayed end of it."

We crossed the street and fed our Oyster cards through the turnstiles just inside the Tube station. "I'm not just disappointed *with* you," she said. "I'm disappointed *in* you."

I swallowed. "What?" Instead of heading down the stairs, I pulled her aside into a small alcove. The unspoken rule of the Tube system was not to bring conflict down those stairs. Conflict created tension, and tension created a desire to flee. But when you descended crowded stairways, were trapped on crowded escalators, or stood along the narrow, crowded platforms, there was no way to escape. PDAs were highly frowned upon in the underground.

"You're afraid of needles, which are sanitary and safe. Yet you'll cuddle up right next to a homeless guy and his germ-infested rabbit."

"How is it fair to be disappointed in who I am?"

Chris worried her upper lip. "I'm not saying this right. The last thing I want to do is hurt your feelings. You are so kind and diplomatic and creative, but I worry that sometimes you let your fears define you. Instead of stepping outside your comfort zone, you hide inside it. You don't seem to take many risks in life."

I felt as if I'd been slapped. "I took a sabbatical from teaching to come with you to London. That's a risk. I often propose radical art classes. That's a risk. I'm paying my half of the bills with work-for-hire that could disappear at any second. That's a risk."

"But you make no effort to conquer your fear of needles."

People had begun to stare as they passed, no doubt noticing the hurt look twisting my features. "Chris, my dad is so claustrophobic he can barely get onto an airplane. It's not a conscious choice. Do you judge him because he can't will away his fear?"

"No, but—"

"One year my family rented a cabin in Itasca State Park. Marcus opened the door and came face-to-face with a spider the size of his fist. The little guy whirled around and climbed me like a tree. He's still terrified of spiders. It's a *fear*, Chris. Fears aren't logical or defensible."

Chris watched the crowds streaming past us. "I just wish you would try harder. It feels kind of cowardly not to step outside your comfort zone."

My jaw dropped. "Cowardly? Remember your sister's meltdown when I put a dirty knife in the sink? She started shaking like a leaf, yelling at me to get it out of there because she hated to reach in and touch the bottom of the sink. How cowardly is that?"

"Yeah, she is a freak." Chris sighed. "Okay, I get your point. It's just…it's just that facing our fears builds strength of character."

"And you think I need to build character?"

She shot me an odd look.

"Chris, this is who I've always been. I can't just run over to Harrod's and buy a new personality."

She turned and headed down the stairs. Stunned, I followed.

We said nothing when we reached the platform. A few minutes later, a low rumble announced the approaching train. It whooshed to a stop and the doors slid open.

Chris took the first open seat, but I strode to the very end of the car and sat down. This problem between us was bigger than I'd thought, much more serious than me loading the dishwasher wrong, or not being on time, or falling asleep in front of the TV.

I closed my eyes, feeling a little sick to my stomach as the train rattled around a curve. No, I would not despair. We loved each other. We could figure this out. I just needed a little time to nurse my wounded pride.

Once I'd recovered from this latest shock, I would do whatever was needed so Chris would continue to love me, to love *us*. We had four months left in London, and I would make each moment count. I was not a quitter.

And even though just the thought of a needle made me wince, I knew what my first step would be: Letting Dr. Rajamani experiment on me.

Chapter Two

When the train stopped at Holborn, I exited without looking back, then hurried up the left side of the escalator and out the building onto High Holborn Street. During the two-block walk to our flat, I knew Chris had to be no more than twenty paces behind me. Half a block before our flat, I turned to face her. "I'm sorry you're so disappointed in me. I need a few hours to myself."

She nodded, so I veered off to the right and entered The Bountiful Cow. Sam, a black Swede working the bar, looked up and grinned. I loved Sam for his sense of humor, and because every time I saw him it was a refreshing slap in the face. He reminded me that not all Swedes were blond, an easy stereotype to develop living in Minnesota. He was as tall and slender as the bottles of vodka lined up behind him.

One of Sam's eyebrows shot up. My reply was to nod, meaning *Yes, send up a Bounty Burger with the works*. Now *that* was taking a risk, consuming a massive burger with chopped onions, gherkin, bleu cheese, bacon, and a fried egg.

Two more flights of stairs brought me to my studio, nothing more than a small room with one window. The room held my drawing table and stool, as well as a long table with books, supplies, and printer. The only bit of comfort came from the green overstuffed chair left in the flat across the hallway by the tenants evicted for nonpayment. Chris had vacuumed it for over an hour to lift out every speck of anything living in the fabric.

While I waited for my heart attack burger, I paced the perimeter of my studio. City sounds rolled through the open window. Even though I was two floors above the pub, the smell of roasting meat and beer somehow wafted up through the floorboards. The family living in the flat between me and the pub must gain weight just by breathing.

Coward? Comfort zone? Chris's labels stung. But I wasn't a coward, and I wasn't afraid to step outside my comfort zone. However, when I considered the eight light and airy watercolors tacked to my board, paintings for the most recent Mr. Froggity book, a shiver ran down my spine. Was Chris right? The book publisher's art director had requested pastel colors, so the blandness wasn't my fault. Still, Mr. Froggity easily fit within my artistic comfort zone.

I'd worked hard all my life and achieved more than I'd hoped, yet I was cowardly?

Chris had still been a graduate student when we met, so we needed to live in the Twin Cities. While she attended the U of M, I got a job teaching art and art history at Carleton College, a private college fifty minutes south in the sleepy river city of Northfield. I loved the slower pace of life there and had nurtured an unspoken dream of the two of us becoming Northfielders one day.

In addition to art department classes, I also taught an art class for non-majors called Art Isms: How to Sound Smart at Parties. The course proved to be one of the most popular on campus, so my star rose high enough to be short-listed for tenure. My brothers, Jake and Marcus, said I was the family's go-getter, the super-ambitious one who fought her way up the academic ladder. But they also both held wonderful jobs. Jake ran an anti-poverty nonprofit, and Marcus was a computer programmer. We were all three pretty happy and content with our lives.

Then a few years ago, Chris discovered an obscure branch of psychiatry called cognitive neuropsychiatry and decided this was her future. She suspended her therapy practice, went back to grad school, then decided she needed to attend the University College London for one year. Our options? We could lease our house while Chris was in London and I'd take an apartment in Northfield and keep working. Or I could take a sabbatical and join Chris in London. After nine years together, the prospect of twelve months apart was too painful, so even though I was next in line for tenure, I convinced my department head to release me for a few semesters. Hopefully, I'd still be at the top of the list when I returned, but it wasn't a given. Putting my career at risk to support Chris's was brave. I didn't deserve the "coward" label.

I texted my brother Jake. He was my Bullshit-O-Meter. No one got to the heart of a problem quicker than Jake. *Do I lack courage? Stuck in comfort zone?*

Too impatient to await his reply, I texted the same questions to Ashley. Our friendship was cemented the day in third grade when we both stood up to a kid bullying a second grader. She was my cheerleader. No matter what I wanted to do, Ashley supported me unconditionally. She thought I was the smartest, bravest person in her life. I didn't agree, but whenever I felt a little falter in my step, Ashley made it disappear. Stout and fierce as a bulldog, Ashley defended me without hesitation.

I waited five minutes. Nothing. Then I texted Mary, my art department colleague at Carleton. The tall, outspoken black woman stood out in the mostly white river city of Northfield, but she wasn't self-conscious. In fact, she loved playing the inner Chicago kid shocking the rural white folks. Mary was my go-to party girl, but she was also my analyst. When I had a problem, she expertly deconstructed it until we could see all the pieces and make sense of what had befuddled me.

I moved my easel to better see the view outside my window—the roofs of surrounding buildings, a few tall trees adding color. Then I jammed earbuds in and turned on my music.

I would show Chris. I primed the canvas with black acrylic, then when it was dry, I attacked with color. In a fever, I gave no thought to matching color with reality, but only matching color to emotions. The heavy bass line in my ears set the rhythm for my brush.

I took a break to eat my Bounty Burger. Soon all my fingers but one pinkie were covered in melted cheese so I used it to open and read my texts.

Jake: *Don't be stupid.*

Ashley: *You are much braver than I am!*

Mary: *Sounds like you need wine. Even if you have a comfort zone, who the hell cares? Fire truck anyone who says otherwise.* Blinking back tears, I finished my burger and cleaned my hands. I didn't tell any of them that the words had been Chris's, since protecting her came so naturally to me I hardly gave it a thought.

It was eight p.m. when I finally stepped back. A thread of cadmium red dripped down onto the black border, adding an edginess I could feel in my teeth. Red buildings, green sky, blue trees all crashed together in a riot of color that made my heart ring like a Caribbean steel drum. Instead of delicate watercolor lines, the painting vibrated with thick slashes and broad splashes of color. Black glowered around the colors, an angry outline to the ragged buildings.

"Oh, my God."

I jumped. Chris stood behind me, two glasses of lemonade from downstairs in her hands. "That is fucking amazing," she continued. She'd never spent much time with Aunt Nicole.

I pressed my lips together and shrugged. I accepted the glass, then perched on my stool and waited. The only other chair in the room was the green saggy chair that sat much lower than the stool. Chris took it.

"I'm sorry about this afternoon," Chris said.

I sipped the sharp lemonade, enjoying the cool slipping down my throat. "You called me a coward because I don't want to let your Dr. Raj shoot me full of his GCA."

Chris bent her head, nodding. "Yes, that was really inappropriate. I've been thinking this evening about why I did that, and I think it's because I've been wanting to talk to you about something kind of hard, and it came out sideways."

My heart thumped up into my throat. "Hard?"

Chris rested her head back on the chair and flashed her dark blues at me. "I've been trying to find the courage to ask you what you want."

"What I want? Right now? I want you to apologize for being such a jerk. Then I want us to make up and move on."

She smiled weakly. "No, not right now. I mean what you want out of life. What do you *yearn* for, Jamie?"

Because it was obviously important to Chris, I took a moment to consider, then shrugged. "I don't really feel any deep yearning."

"Everyone yearns. There has to be something you want that's bigger than you, unattainable even, something that drives you."

"Chris, I'm happy. I'm content. I have a great job at Carleton, at least I think I still do, where I love the faculty and the students. My life is full of art. And now? I'm living in London, for God's sake, and most of the people we love have come to visit. I'm healthy. My brain works. And most of all, I have you. I have nothing left to yearn for except world peace and a rational plan to combat climate change."

Chris pressed her lips together. "I can appreciate that you're content. That's not a bad thing. But…but you seem to lack ambition."

I could feel my eyes double in size. "Chris, I work hard. I learn something new about myself, and about the world, every day."

She struggled out of the chair and began pacing in a circle around me. "Don't you want a painting of yours to hang in the National Gallery some day?"

"The Gallery only shows Western European art, thirteenth to nineteenth centuries."

"Okay, then, the Tate Modern."

I nodded toward the board on the wall. "I suppose, but it's highly unlikely the Tate is going to devote much wall space to Mr. Froggity."

"So that's why you're not trying?"

"Not trying? Chris, I'm painting nearly every day. I'm proud of these paintings. Yeah, the Froggity thing is getting old, but it's paying my bills."

"But you could be so much better than this."

"Why must everyone push for the best job, the best body, the highest position? Why must you take something wonderful, like contentment, and turn it into a horrible weakness?"

"Because it's important to me." She stopped pacing.

I tipped my head back and drained my glass. "Well, okay, then what do *you* want?"

"I want to break open the field of neurobiological psycho-therapy. I want to conduct history-making research." She hesitated. "I also want *you* to want more than you want."

A surprised chuckle bubbled up my throat and slipped out. "Let me get this straight. Your ambition is that I get more ambitious."

"Yes."

"Chris, I've loved you with every fiber of my being for ten years. I care for you when you're sick. Every day I look for new ways to make you laugh. For ten winters I've filled your hot water bottle." One of the strange things that had glued us together was a hatred of electric blankets, and a love of snuggling our feet up to the spreading warmth of a hot water bottle. Filling each other's bottle had become a symbol of our love and devotion. I drew in a shuddering breath, not afraid to show her I was upset. "You think I'm unambitious, that I'm wasting my life. That's really, really hard to hear."

Chris's face softened and she took my hands in hers. "Good. Maybe it will get you thinking about your future and what drives you."

"What drives me is love and beauty and the feel of a brush on canvas. Isn't that enough?"

We stood facing each other. Chris's eyes were shaded in the poor light. "Not for me," she whispered.

So. Now it was out. Chris didn't want a contented me. She wanted an ambitious me.

Chris hugged herself. "I don't know what to say. I can't help wanting what I want. You are so smart and talented that I just wish you would push yourself harder." She waved toward my painting. "Like that."

I filled my lungs with air. "You want to know what I want? One, I want us to hold hands and be okay. Two, I want us to figure out a way through this by talking more about ambition and see where it might take us. Three, I also want all six original My Little Ponies and an Easy Bake-Oven and a Crocodile Dentist game that works. Four, I want directions to Rajamani's lab so I can show up Monday morning at nine a.m."

Chris's face crumpled into tears. "I want all of that too," she said softly. "Except for the Crocodile Dentist game. It scared the pee right out of me, literally."

I pulled Chris into a hug and held her tightly enough that her crazy expectations about ambition couldn't fit between us. Finally, she pulled away and blew her nose. "Let's go home. I'd be happy to give you directions to Rajamani's office."

Home was a two-bedroom flat in a four-story building of brown brick that faced a small park called Red Lion Square. The view outside our windows wasn't the park, but the apartment building next door. The narrow street between the two buildings was a shortcut for commuters walking to and from the Holborn Tube station two blocks away, so the sound of feet scuffling and pedestrians talking came with the flat.

The flat had worn mustard carpeting, cream walls, glass door handles, and white fixtures. My favorite was the faucet in the tub— the shower head rested like an old-fashioned phone in its cradle. The first time I took a bath and tried to wash my hair with the "phone," I managed to spray everything in the bathroom but my head.

That night I lay awake for hours, puzzling through all that had been said. I'd never really stopped and analyzed my life. What if I *had* stopped trying? What if I'd let complacency look like contentment?

Fire truck.

CHAPTER THREE

I smoothly navigated around the parked cars on Hampstead Road, pleased with the used bike I'd bought from Sam at the pub. A warm mist brushed my skin, soft as the caresses Chris had offered last night but which I'd declined, surprising us both. I pulled up at the red light and checked my watch. Plenty of time. Steadying myself against the curb, I inhaled the city smells—hot streets, gasoline, and fresh naan being sold by a street vendor.

The first few months we'd lived in London, I'd been overawed by the city's heady mix of history and architecture and royalty. Gradually, I transformed myself from London tourist to London resident, learning to take out the rubbish instead of the trash, grousing about the prime minister, and accepting that the rain would, eventually, ruin all my leather shoes and boots. And it had.

I'd learned that exploring London meant getting lost, an unusual experience for someone with a great sense of direction. Yet getting lost was a rare treat I cherished. Chris would reach for her phone's GPS app, but I'd stop her. "No, let's figure this out on our own."

The traffic light changed, and I surged ahead until the Wilkins Portico, the iconic image of University College London, rose up in front of me. I turned right, then left, weaving my way deeper into the compact but bustling campus. I slid into the last free slot of a bike rack and snapped the lock shut.

Traffic noise from Euston Road drifted between the buildings, but the campus itself was wondrously quiet. I inhaled the moist air, still marveling that approaching rain smelled the same here as it did in Minnesota. A few drops plopped on my face, and the clouds overhead seemed to thicken and swirl with sudden rage. In the distance, thunder rolled like a bass drum on parade. I ran for the door.

Dr. Rajamani's office was in the Alexandra House, home to the UCL Institute of Cognitive Neuroscience, and one of the older and shabbier campus buildings. Much of London was either new or very renovated. Old buildings such as this one created a sense of how layered the city was. For generations, buildings had been built, used, torn down, and replaced with others, which were used and then torn down for new ones.

I took the stone stairs two at a time until I reached the top floor, out of breath but not wanting to admit it. Clearly, I needed to spend more time biking and less time painting to stay in better shape. My body was an average size ten, maybe a twelve in winter when bread became my food of choice, but my muscles were going to mush here in London.

I knocked on Dr. Raj's door, unable to see through the frosted glass. The door swung open. "You are here!" Dr. Raj clasped my shoulders and pressed one of his cheeks against mine, then the other.

"My lab is at the end of the hallway. Come, come." He stepped out ahead of me, the sides of his white lab coat flapping like wings. Dr. Raj seemed to lean forward when he walked, as if he were pushing himself through water. From what Chris had told me of his career, that made sense. When everyone around you resisted, you pushed harder.

Dr. Raj hurried us down a gritty linoleum floor that buckled and bent in places from water damage. The bare fluorescents running down the dim hallway were either out or flickering like in a homemade scary movie. The walls needed a coat of paint fifty years ago. A small prick of alarm tickled the base of my skull.

The lab itself was no better, boasting a vintage look, sort of an Early Frankenstein. The walls were a puke green and could have used a good scrubbing. The floors, covered in what once must have been a snappy black and white tile, were gritty and dull.

I sat down on the cold folding chair Dr. Raj set up, then watched as he wheeled over a cart of really old equipment, stuff that hadn't been dusted since the war, and I don't mean Afghanistan or Iraq or even Vietnam. There were a few laptops, but the main instrument was a huge green metal box with twenty small gauges that looked like car speedometers. Dr. Raj opened a box of electrodes and began peeling off the plastic wrap. At least those things were new.

"So," I said, "how many people have gone through this experiment?"

He tipped his head. "I think you are the tenth person, in this round at least."

I licked my lips. Even though Chris and a handful of others had gone through this and were fine, the whole setup was making me nervous. "This round? You've done this before?"

"Last year I was perfecting my GCA."

I jumped as a crack of thunder rattled the window. "And now it works perfectly, right?" I watched as he opened another electrode wrapper, knowing the needle would be coming out soon. Apparently, I hadn't left my fear of needles behind in Red Lion Square. It had stalked me and now shivered up from the soles of my feet. *For Chris, for us*, I mentally chanted.

I looked out the rain-streaked window and listened to the quality of the thunder—some were faraway booms, others so close and deep you could feel them through your feet.

"Yes, yes, I learned much from the experiment, even though a few subjects dropped out," Dr. Rajamani said.

I attempted a laugh, but ended up coughing. "So GCA makes people disappear?"

Dr. Raj smiled. "Faulty reasoning, my dear. No, even though the man never returned my phone calls, I am sure he is just fine. But do not fear. The GCA is flawless now. Everyone in this study has returned for the follow-up." He frowned.

"Everyone?" I jumped as the professor attached a cold electrode to my forehead.

"One other woman did not return, but she was having relationship problems, so I believe she moved from London."

The electrodes continued around my face, then Dr. Raj attached some to the base of my skull, moving my hair aside. His dark brown eyes gleamed as he worked. Here was a man obsessed. "I am most appreciative that you are volunteering. Others will follow. I am sure of it. This work is too exciting to be ignored." He picked up another electrode. "I am close. I feel most certain of this fact. I will locate the consciousness."

"Why are you interested in this anyway?"

"It is one of the last great mysteries of the body," he crowed. "I want to solve that mystery."

"Yeah, but that's the beauty of the whole thing. It *is* a mystery. Shouldn't it stay that way? Why do I need to know what part of my brain is *me*?"

Dr. Rajamani sat back suddenly. "Why would you *not* want to know?"

"Because I'm more than just my body. My personality, my thoughts, and my dreams are created by my conscious mind. It's magic how our brains do that." To be honest, before that moment I'd never given much thought to this topic, but I *liked* that one part of the human mind was still a mystery. I *liked* that my consciousness was all mine, and was housed in my body, and that it ran the show. "Besides, if you locate this part of who we are, won't people start treating it like other organs, to be studied and fixed?"

"Oh, yes, all that and more. But I am interested in something much greater, something most radical." He patted my knee confidentially and leaned forward. "Once I locate the conscious mind, then I can transplant it."

"Transplant it?" My words came out as a squeak.

Dr. Raj placed the last electrode. "What if your body is dying? Why not transplant your brain and its consciousness into a storage vessel? You could live forever."

"That's a freaky idea."

"No, no. Did you not watch the old *Star Trek* TV shows? I saw one when I was a child that created in me the desire to do this. The explorers find a race of people whose bodies have died, so they stored their consciousness in these oval eggs that flashed with color and light." He shook his head, face aglow with the memory. Another crack of thunder surprised us both and he smiled. "I love storms."

"I thought thunderstorms were rare in London." I watched as Dr. Raj fiddled with his equipment.

"Not in the summer," he replied.

A flash of lightning was followed almost immediately by crashing thunder directly overhead. I considered the old equipment, now plugged in. The only step left was to connect my electrodes. "Is it safe doing this in the middle of a thunderstorm?" Surely the answer had to be "no."

Dr. Rajamani considered my question, then waved dismissively. "Yes, yes, of course. These buildings are old, but they have been grounded sufficiently to protect us. Not to worry!"

Dr. Raj then connected each electrode to the big green box with all the speedometers. "I built this equipment myself," he said. "It may not be beautiful, but it will do the tricks and treats, since I am making do with a most pathetic budget."

A tiny shiver of fear slid up my spine. I'd assumed the university had sanctioned the experiment, but what did I know? Maybe a professor could conduct crazy-ass experiments without getting approval. I closed my eyes briefly, trusting that Chris would not get me into anything dangerous.

"My experiments are less orthodox, shall we say, than most. But you are not to have fear. Now I ask you to describe the experiment so I know *you* know what is going on." Another crack of thunder seemed to come up through the floor.

"You're trying to locate the consciousness in the brain. You've hooked me up to a machine that will record the activity when I use various parts of my brain. And just to clarify, you are not, at this time, attempting to remove or in any way transport my consciousness."

Dr. Rajamani laughed, a short seal bark. "That is most correct. Our brain is made up of lobes and cells and dendrites, but it also contains *you*, the person that exists within your body, the spark of your consciousness. I am not transporting that today because I do not know where it is. To isolate the location of our thoughts, of our consciousness, the core of who we are, I will activate…" He waited.

My mind spun as I tried to recall his words from the National Gallery lecture. "My glee cells?"

Dr. Raj smiled. "Your glial cells. I believe the secret to our consciousness lies with the millions of glial cells in our brains. Glials were once considered nothing more than bubble wrap for the brain, but now we suspect they do so much more. Your glial cells might, when electrically charged, reveal their secrets about our consciousness."

"Electrically charged?" My mouth felt dry.

"That is what the electrodes do—deliver a minuscule electrical charge enabling us to better see what is going on inside there." He knocked gently on my skull. "I am telling you, glials and electricity are the key to everything. Imagine the various parts of your brain as an orchestra tuning up. It is chaos until the conductor steps up and sets the beat. The conductor is your intralaminar nuclei, which set up an electrical oscillation. When the oscillation reaches forty hertz, consciousness happens! Is this not amazing?"

He lost me at intralaminar nuclei. I nodded. "Totally."

Dr. Raj opened a small flat box, pulled out a syringe, and ripped open the plastic wrapper.

My throat tightened. Damn it. Chris had better appreciate the sacrifice here. I strained to see the size of the needle. Thank God it was small. "I see it's time for your magic serum." Dr. Rajamani patted my arm reassuringly. "It is most certainly nothing to be frightened of. It will simply heighten the responses of your consciousness so we can see the results more clearly. The GCA, or glial cell activator, is necessary for the experiment because it provides a slight electrical charge to cells that normally do not conduct electricity."

I forced myself to return his smile. One GCA injection, twenty electrodes, and a thunderstorm. Nothing to worry about.

The injection was swift and painless. By the time I opened my eyes, Dr. Raj was tossing the needle into a biohazard waste bin.

"How are you feeling?"

I blinked. "Weird. Very weird."

"That is normal," he said. "The effects will wear off soon."

The hair on my forearms stood straight up. "Dr. Raj, I feel *really* weird, as if I'm...." I couldn't find the words. "As if I'm full of static electricity."

He frowned. "Really?" He glanced at his big green box and shot to his feet, muttering something in what I presumed to be Hindi. He began checking the electrode connections.

The little speedometer needles had all sprung to life and were reaching nearly all the way to the right, as if a car were pushing one hundred miles per hour. "But the equipment's not on," I said. "How can that be?"

Dr. Raj unplugged the machine, disconnected it from the three laptops, then reconnected everything. The needles shot up again. "I do not know. The electrodes must be faulty. I will replace them."

I shivered as he applied the new electrodes, hoping we'd exchange a spark of static to drain the electricity coursing through me, but no. And when I closed my eyes, it was as if a door had blown open somewhere. How did I know that? If you were sitting in a room with your eyes closed and someone opened a door, you'd feel the air currents change; a breeze would brush against your skin. Smells would enter; sound would change. I felt all of that sitting on the folding chair in Dr. Raj's lab. A door had opened, and I wanted it closed.

The new electrodes behaved the same way—they measured an electrical current coming from my brain even though Dr. Raj wasn't sending any current through them. It was as if I were generating the current myself.

After a few minutes, my vision cleared and my alarm faded. The freaky feeling receded, even though the needles remained in the red zone. "Dr. Raj, I'm feeling better. I'm okay."

Dr. Raj leaned close. "Are you sure?"

"Everything seems more…intense, but I'm okay."

"Good," he said. "We will proceed. You might have had a slight reaction to the GCA." He turned on the machines, clicked a few keys on the computers, then began asking me questions from a thick stack of papers. I sighed. I was going to be here a while.

After some questions, Dr. Raj scribbled in his notebook, then asked more questions—about the weather, some math problems, about movies, books, names of British prime ministers, of which I knew only one—for another thirty minutes. Thunder still boomed outside; after a particularly bone-rattling clap, Dr. Raj's gaze swung toward the indicators. His eyes widened. "Good gods, your glials are lighting up like fireworks."

I licked my dry lips. "Is that why the electrodes are kind of tingling now?"

Dr. Raj looked at me in alarm, which wasn't very reassuring. "Tingling?" he said. He tapped the keyboard, muttering to himself. "You should not be feeling the electrodes. You say they are tingling?"

I cleared my throat. "Maybe we should stop now, since there's such a huge storm. Maybe the lightning—"

"I have never seen glials react this way. I wonder if I am misdosing the GCA."

Okay, that was the last straw. Between the thunderstorm and Dr. Raj's confusion over the GCA dose and the electrodes burning my skin, it was time to leave. *I* knew it, my consciousness knew it, and since we were one and the same, the decision was unanimous. "I'm no longer feeling comfortable doing this. Please unhook me."

Still entranced by the data on his screen, the professor nodded but didn't look up.

"Unhook me *now*."

I finally got his attention. As he reached for the dial to shut everything off, the loudest thunderclap yet sent an earthquake of a tremor through my Birkenstocks. Sparks flew from the old equipment with a sickening snap. My entire body buzzed, and I clutched at an electrode, trying to rip it off, but suddenly everything moved in slow motion. All sound faded. The world disintegrated into a black sea of nothingness as I was yanked upward, drowning in an upside-down ocean. I fought the current, but it was too strong. The sky sucked me in.

CHAPTER FOUR

Itried moving, but my legs resisted, as if bound by ropes or heavy fabric. With my eyes squeezed shut against the nausea, I tried again, this time succeeding in rolling onto my side. Something musical hit the floor nearby; must be rain given the smell and the mist settling across my skin. Voices spoke to me, but from behind a wall too thick to penetrate.

"Dr. Raj?" I managed to whisper. "Chris?"

The storm. The huge spark. Had the equipment exploded? Was I dead? Hands tugged on my arms, tugging impatiently. "I'm trying," I muttered. "Have you called an ambulance?" I opened my eyes a crack to see a woman bending over me.

"Are you unwell? What manner of play is this?"

For an emergency technician, the woman was unusually abrupt and impatient. I forced my eyes open. "Please call Chris Johansen. Her cell is…." My brain struggled for the number. "Use my phone. It's in my pocket."

"You are making no sense at all. Her majesty sent you to complete a task, and she expects you to return quickly. You may be her pet, but you can still incur her wrath."

As I sat up, I realized my legs had felt bound because of yards and yards of a heavy fabric were lying across them. A dress. Blue brocade with silver trim. I groped at my waist, chest, and hair. Someone had changed my clothing and dressed me in a wig and headdress. The woman pulling on my arm was dressed in the same manner. I clutched at my aching head. How had I gone from Dr. Raj's lab to an Elizabethan costume event?

"Come, you must return to the Queen." The woman helped me stagger to my feet, but the wet dress slowed me down.

Shocked at the weakness in my legs, I leaned back against the wall. "Damn, that GCA crap really packs a punch. Who brought me here? Does Dr. Rajamani think this is funny?"

We were under the covered edge of a small, outdoor courtyard. Rain pounded the cobblestoned floor and bounced off two wooden chairs. Was it still Monday morning? How much time had passed? Surely Chris must be worried about me, since we'd planned to meet at the Wilkins Portico for lunch.

When I inhaled deeply, a sharp pain burned across my ribs. I clutched at my body and discovered I was bound by some sort of corset. Then I bent over and vomited onto the cobblestone walk, spitting out as much of the acrid taste as I could before I wiped my mouth. Damn it.

Clucking in disgust, the woman once again grabbed impatiently for my arm and managed to pull me down the walkway. "Her majesty sent me to find you, and I have done. I am not going to endanger my own position here for one of your childish pranks." Shorter than me, and quite stout, the woman looked about forty, with deep fissures along her mouth and nose that were unsuccessfully hidden under a layer of chalky cake makeup. "I will deliver you back to her chambers and then you are on your own."

We entered through a thick, planked wood door, then hurried down a dark corridor, lit only by candles on wall sconces every ten feet or so. We passed through a number of richly decorated rooms, and I thought at once of the sets for *The Tudors*, the Showtime series about King Henry VIII and his six wives. Was I on some sort of movie set?

But when the woman hurried us past a window, I yanked myself free and peered through the mullioned glass. I was too stunned at the sight to even gasp. I was in a building that rose a few stories directly above the Thames. To the left was the familiar curve in the river, and beyond it rose St. Paul's Cathedral, only the spire was taller and more slender. I could just see the roof of the White Tower, the central feature of the Tower of London. Dozens of white swans floated in the river, despite the rain. When I pressed my left cheek to the pane, I could see Westminster to the right. But everything else about the London skyscape was wrong. Where was the Tower Bridge, the Gherkin building, the London Eye?

I stepped back, rubbing my eyes. What the hell was going on?

"Make haste," the woman snapped. She latched onto my wrist and pulled me into a warm room lit with a gilded candelabra suspended overhead that blazed with candlelight. Six women, all dressed in some version of the costume I wore, sat on stools or on the floor, each bent over a sewing project. With their skirts spread wide, the women looked like elegant flowers that had collapsed into themselves. The room smelled of burning candle, body odor, roses, and cloves.

I stumbled over the hem of someone's skirt as the woman yanked me one more time, then released me. The woman sank into a deep curtsey. "Ma'am, as you requested I have found Lady Blanche and brought her to you. She was in the eastern courtyard."

A woman sat on a wide chair, its wooden back elaborately carved into a scene of battling lions. She leaned over the table beside her, eating the last of some sort of meat. Dressed in green fabric shot through with silver, the woman was younger than me—mid twenties?—yet she practically vibrated with the same sense of privilege I'd seen at my uncle's country club years ago. She wore an excessive number of ropes of pearls around her neck, as well as a ruff of delicate white lace. Her sleeves ended in matching ruffs. A pearl headdress held back pale red hair tight with curls.

Judging by the red hair, pale skin, and long, slender fingers, the woman was obviously playing the role of Queen Elizabeth I, and since the actor was young, she must be playing the period shortly after Elizabeth had taken the throne at age twenty-five. In the United States there were murder mystery parties. Did the UK hold Life in Elizabethan England parties?

"Dear Blanche, how lovely of you to grace us with your presence," said the woman in the broad chair. "You have been gone so long, we thought that perchance you had decided to seduce one of our courtiers."

The women in the room laughed.

I scowled. Why were they calling me Blanche? And why did they think this was some sort of joke?

"Although, from what we hear about most of the men, very little time would be required to consummate the act." The actor grinned wickedly, as if hoping to shock me.

I stepped forward. "Listen, you all look lovely. Your costumes are stunning, and you—" I motioned to "Elizabeth." "You even bear a remarkable likeness to the Queen, at least from the paintings I've studied in the National Portrait Gallery. So congratulations." I gave a slow, insolent clap. "But I'm done. Point me toward the exit. I have no wish to keep playing your games. And my name's Jamie, not Blanche."

Both of "Elizabeth's" brows arched. Her smile frosted over. "Games? Hell's gate, we see no games being played at the moment. And your name is certainly Blanche and we sent you on an errand. Has our Master of the Horse yet returned from his hunting trip?"

From my Tudor obsession, I knew that Elizabeth's Master of the Horse was Robert Dudley. Elizabeth had loved him her entire life, but no one knew for sure if they'd ever consummated the relationship. I admitted to being a little curious to see the actor portraying Dudley, since he'd been considered one of the most handsome men at Elizabeth's court—tall, dark, and broad-shouldered.

I rested my hands on the fabric flaring out from my hips. "Much as I'd love to meet your Dudley, I'm serious. Where are my real clothes? My cell phone? I intend to call the authorities and have you all arrested for kidnapping. And I'll have Dr. Raj arrested for reckless experimenting."

The tittering laughter turned to murmurs. "Arrest us? For kidnapping?" The room seemed to hold its breath until "Elizabeth" threw back her head and roared. "Ah, dearest, you are amusing us again. Lord Cecil is our Spirit, Dudley is our Eyes, and you are our Spark, the flash of humor and soul in our life."

The woman who had dragged me to the room stepped forward. "Ma'am, I found Lady Blanche on the ground, with a bruise on her head." When the woman motioned to my forehead, I reached up and touched what was indeed a tender lump. "Blanche is not amusing you," the woman said, "but is perchance injured in some way from her fall." The look the woman shot me made it clear she hoped for major brain damage.

The Elizabeth actor rose to her feet and gracefully crossed the room with more speed than seemed possible in these restrictive dresses. She lightly probed my forehead with long, cool fingers. "Poor dear, you might be befuddled after all. Here, you shall sit until you have fully recovered your senses." The woman urged me down into another carved wooden chair and then tucked a shawl across my shoulders.

I remained in the chair, surprised at how good it felt to be still. Perhaps I had fallen, or been dropped, when being transported from Dr. Raj's office to this…whatever this was. While I should seek medical attention, I didn't seem to be in any immediate danger, so I relaxed into the chair. Activity in the room returned to normal as the women picked up their work, talking quietly among themselves. The Elizabeth actor returned to her chair, sipped something from a jewel-encrusted goblet, then picked up a small book and began to read. With the women's dresses sparkling like constellations and the warm air, and the quiet voices, the setting was almost peaceful.

My eyelids closed, but I forced them open again. Falling asleep with a concussion could be bad news. Instead, I examined the room in which we sat. Large windows behind "Elizabeth" were gray with the storm. Heavy drapes hung at the windows and large, dark tapestries had been draped across the remaining three walls. A few small dogs rested on some of the women's laps. The ceiling was dark as well, carved into deep wells that arched over our heads.

I picked up that the woman who'd brought me to the room called herself "Lady Mary," and the older woman who seemed to be in charge used the name "Kat." Kat Ashley was Queen Elizabeth I's dearest friend, so at least these women were accurate in their role-playing.

Then an attractive woman across the room caught my eye. Her black hair was pulled back and up into a sleek bun, and the small cap on the woman's head matched her blue dress, which was the same dress that I wore. The costume shop must have run a discount on it. I smiled shyly, and she answered with an equally shy smile, as if to acknowledge we wore matching gowns.

But when I brushed a lock of hair back off my face and she did the same, my throat constricted. I straightened the lace dripping out my left sleeve. She did the same. *What?*

When I rose and approached her, she did the same. I reached out to touch her, but instead touched something smooth and cool.

A mirror.

I stared at the unfamiliar woman staring back at me, then ripped off my cap and tried to remove the wig, but it wasn't a wig. I winced as I pulled the hair free of its constraining pins. What the hell was going on? My own hair was reddish brown, not black, and this face was all wrong. Dark blue eyes instead of light hazel. Fine eyebrows instead of thick ones. Wide forehead, high cheekbones.

I probed my face. Was this a mask? Prosthetics? Where were my cheekbones or my chin? My dainty ears?

Sudden fear squeezed my chest even tighter than the corset. "Off!" I yelled, and I began clawing at my dress. But there was no visible way to get it off—no buttons, no zippers, no Velcro. I yanked the nearest woman to her feet. "Off! Take this off!" With shaking fingers, I helped the woman untie and tug and unlace until I stood before the mirror wearing nothing but a thin white chemise. Stunned, I ignored the concerned murmurs that rippled through the room.

I lifted the chemise over my head, aware of the gasps and "Elizabeth's" loud guffaw. This wasn't my body. The breasts were large and full; mine were much smaller. The waist was thick, where mine was narrow. The thighs pressed against each other more than mine did. I wore a consistent size ten, but this body surely wore a size with an X in it, if not two. I stared at the body in the mirror, then touched it, feeling my hands on my body as I did so.

Fire truck.

Not only was I wearing someone else's dress, but I was wearing someone else's *body.*

CHAPTER FIVE

The sound of Chris puttering in the kitchen pulled me out of the sinkhole of sleep I'd fallen into. I stretched, rubbed my ear in a futile attempt to get rid of a high-pitched whine, then shot out of bed. I raced for the window. Twenty-first century buildings! Honking cars. Barking dogs. Wailing police sirens. When I bent double, clutching myself, I realized it was *my* body I held, not some stranger's.

I was back. It'd been a nightmare, nothing more. Other than this irritating hum in my ears, life was back to normal.

I dashed into the kitchen, inhaling strong coffee, and flung my arms around Chris. "Thank God," I murmured into her neck.

"That I've made the coffee already? Poor baby, you were really out. Guess you need this. Here." She stepped back and handed me my favorite mug, the one with an image of the mosaic floor in St. Paul's Cathedral.

My hands shook as I held the mug against my face. The warmth was reassuring.

"Are you okay?"

"No, I've got to give your Dr. Rajamani a piece of my mind. That stupid GCA really messed me up."

Now dressed, my coffee mug empty, I ran down the apartment steps and hailed a cab, too impatient to bike to campus. The cabbie let me off in front of the Alexandra Building and I dashed up the stairs. Dr. Raj's office door was closed, but that didn't stop me. I burst in to find him on his cell.

Angrier now than I'd ever been, I tore the phone from Rajamani's hand and flung it across the room. It shattered against the wall.

"What are you doing?" Raj leapt to his feet.

The humming in my ears became the roar of a chainsaw so I had to shout. "Your GCA gave me hallucinations. I thought my mind was in the body of some chick in Queen Elizabeth I's court. Can you imagine what that felt like? All your talk of transporting my consciousness into another vessel started it, but I'm sure the GCA made everything worse. I can't remember anything from yesterday after that last clap of thunder, but I somehow managed to get myself home safely, all the while thinking I was in some sort of Elizabethan costume drama."

Hot rage spread like wildfire through my limbs. I wrapped my hands around Dr. Rajamani's neck and squeezed until his eyes widened in fear. His hands clawed ineffectually at mine, but I was too strong. I shook him so hard his head snapped forward and back. "I'm going to shake you until your head comes off," I yelled. "You're a lunatic! You're dangerous!" Dr. Rajamani's lips began to turn blue, so I closed my eyes and squeezed harder.

"Blanche! Stop!"

I tightened my grip even though hands now tried to pull me off of Rajamani.

"Blanche! You must stop!"

Blanche?

With a shuddering gasp, I opened my eyes to find my hands wrapped around the throat of the woman next to me in bed. I let go, allowing the hands to drag me back. The room was dark, the only source of light the sputtering candle held by "Kat Ashley." White candle smoke rose into the oppressive dark. The woman next to me struggled to sit up, coughing and clutching her throat.

"Blanche Nottingham, have you lost your senses?" "Kat Ashley" hissed. I held my pounding head and struggled to remember. I was sharing a lumpy bed with "Lady Mary," while "Lady Charlotte" slept on a pallet on the floor. Across the room were women in two more beds. Ahh, the ladies chamber. All their shadowed faces looked haunted. "Mary" still clutched her throat.

I covered my mouth to cut off a scream. I'd had a nightmare within a nightmare. The room's darkness weighed on me like a thick tapestry. My marvelous sense of direction was no help to me now. When you were trapped in something you didn't understand, it was almost impossible to find a way out.

"Mary, are you able to breathe?" "Kat" drew the stunned "Mary" into her arms.

Finally, the woman nodded, croaking out her assurances.

I licked my lips. "Lady Mary, I am so sorry. I was having a nightmare." Tears welled up, but I refused to yield. Instead, I leapt from the lumpy bed. "I will find somewhere else to sleep so you don't need to worry."

"Lady Charlotte" waved me toward her pallet, then she slid into the bed beside "Mary."

I lay down on the pile of straw covered with a blanket and pulled a dirty fur rug up over my shoulders. The end of a goose feather poked through the pillow cover and scratched my cheek, so I punched the pillow down and tried to get comfortable. Despite the straw, cold rose up from the wooden floor and shackled my ankles, knees, hips. Thank God this wasn't truly a straw bed from Elizabethan times, for that would have been crawling with fleas and lice.

A small brown and white spaniel with long silky ears and serious brown eyes trotted over and sniffed at my face. When I offered a finger and was rewarded with a sandpaper lick, I lifted the covers in invitation, and the little thing hopped in. He circled a few times, a doggy trait I'd always admired, then curled up against my chest. I adjusted the covers so he could breathe, then began gently stroking his ears. My reward was a small sigh of approval.

I looked around the room, remembering now that "Lady Charlotte" had brought me here last night and taken pity on me. "This is your room. This is your trunk of gowns." While a quiet-as-a-mouse actor playing a servant undressed me, the woman droned on about my shocking behavior. After the servant left, the woman pushed me toward the bed. "This is your bed. I suggest you use it."

Despite the soft warmth of the dog, loneliness pierced me like a thousand tiny arrows. But was I alone only in my mind, or in reality? I could only come up with three options for my situation. Perhaps I was collapsed on the floor of Raj's lab, locked in a drug-induced dream or nightmare. Or I could be in a coma at University College Hospital, locked in the same dream or nightmare, with Chris at my bedside, my frantic parents and brothers flying across the Atlantic to join me. With both of these options, my knowledge of London and my fascination with all things Tudor were providing the details. So far everything I'd seen could have been culled from the books I'd read, the movies and shows I'd watched.

The third option? That the freaky Rajamani had actually located my consciousness and somehow transported it into the body of a woman named Blanche Nottingham sometime in the mid sixteenth century. But this was too bizarre to believe.

No, the more logical answer was a coma.

I scratched a few itches on my calf, then curled around my only friend, grunting at the uncomfortable straw. I was still Jamie Maddox. I'd been born in 1984 at Abbott Northwestern Hospital in Minneapolis, Minnesota. My parents were Rick and Julia Maddox. I had a younger brother, Marcus, and an older brother, Jacob.

I was still the girl who had fallen while running down the sidewalk and cracked open my chin on the head of the antique doll in my arms. There'd been no plastic surgeon on duty, so an inexperienced resident had stitched me up. Thank God the eight stitches were out of sight on the underside of my chin, but I knew them intimately, for I often ran my thumb over the bumpy ridges when nervous.

I reached for my chin and felt nothing but skin smooth as a peach.

No. I was still the girl who'd fallen while trying to skateboard down the low brick wall at the Beautiful Savior Lutheran Church a block from our home. I reached for the resulting scar but touched only flawless skin on a plump knee.

As I shifted on the straw, I winced at the waves of body odor escaping the covers. I'd read that Elizabeth used scented rose water to both mask her scent and the scent of others, but this was a perfect example of a detail my mind could have conjured up while I rested in a warm, pristine hospital bed, deep in a coma, instead of on a dry, rustling pile of straw that attracted cold rather than repelled it.

I needed help. I needed to ask Chris for advice. Call Ashley and Mary and Jake. Maybe they could help me figure it out…but apparently nightmares didn't come with cell phones.

The candlelight jumped wildly as the wick began drowning in melting wax. Then it went out. I closed my eyes as the dog's paws twitched in his dreams. If only my dreams could be as pleasant.

I stroked the soft fur. I would figure this out in the morning.

Chapter Six

The next morning, I couldn't think of how to escape this nightmare. My only solution was to remain in bed, in retrospect a pretty cowardly choice, but I hoped each time that I awoke I'd be home where I belonged.

Several times a day someone brought me bread and broth. Perhaps to punish me they forced me to use a chamber pot, and scowled in confusion when I demanded a flush toilet. I slept and slept.

Each day I made a small mark with my thumbnail in the soft leg of the wooden table next to my bed. After seven marks it was clear the nightmare wasn't actually a nightmare, but some sort of reality, so I arose on the eighth day to the dawning awareness that this body I inhabited, either for real or in my coma fantasy, needed a bath. My skin looked drab and my head itched as I imagined an army of lice on patrol. My ankles were red with bites. These people might have been taking the whole realism thing just a bit too far, for there had been fleas in the bed.

While "Lady Mary's" maid, Rosemary, helped her dress, I cleared my throat. "Lady Mary, once again, I'm sorry for hurting you the other night."

The short woman shrugged it off. "My brother and I would fight like dogs when we were small, so I am used to it."

"Speaking of dog," I motioned to my sleeping companion for most of the week, now sitting on my left foot. "What's this guy's name?"

She shook her head. "You know perfectly well his name is Vincent." She frowned. "What is odd, however, is that he suddenly appears to like you. He has never had any love for you before."

I scooped Vincent up into my arms and kissed the white blaze streaking down his forehead. He looked up at me with those liquid eyes, brow furrowed as if he were as confused about his feelings for me as "Lady Mary." I bumped my nose against his, pleased his owner was also a fan of van Gogh's. I stopped Rosemary as she turned her attention to me. "Before I dress, do you think we could find a basin of water somewhere? Clean water? I'd like to bathe."

"Lady Mary" looked at me down her long nose, her brown eyes small and close together. "God's teeth, you are irritating today. I am glad you are recovering from your fall, but it has only been a fort-night since your last bath. The queen will call for the tubs when she is ready for us to bathe. Until then, the wash basins are where they have always been."

When I didn't respond, she sighed and took me into a sort of closet in the next room. I thanked her gratefully and washed myself as well as I could without taking off my chemise and robe. The hair would have to wait.

Getting dressed left me exhausted and humiliated because I needed so much assistance. First, Rosemary helped me step into two skirts, one stiff brown taffeta, the other a brocaded orange. Then she slipped a sleeveless tawny-orange bodice on, lacing it together in back, then tying it to my skirts. What followed was a short, stiff white collar. Next was the padded, triangular corset thing, which came to a point well below my navel. This was the dreaded stomacher.

Rosemary then tied the stomacher to the bodice. Next she at-tached the sleeves, which were brown with long slashes lined with orange silk. Tiny beads lined the slashes, the fitted wrists, and the edges of the stomacher.

I looked down at my chest. The snug bodice and even snugger stomacher had turned my breasts—or rather, Blanche's breasts—into rosy, rising bread dough, threatening any second to overflow their container. "Lady Mary," I said, "let's cover up the girls a bit." I motioned to the fabric that covered her own décolletage.

She laughed. "I swear you have lost much of your mind. You know perfectly well your bosom remains bare until you marry." Right. Gotta advertise the goods.

Rosemary brushed my hair back, expertly twisted and pinned it to the back of my head, then topped it off with a soft velvet cap trimmed in more beads, work detailed enough to require bifocals of even the youngest seamstress.

I thanked Rosemary, then followed "Lady Mary" to the outer chamber where food was to be served. In doing so, I banged against two tables and the doorframe. It wasn't just the heavy skirts, it was the hips. Wearing someone else's clothes was awkward enough; wearing someone else's body was insane.

I helped myself to a thick slice of grainy bread and a plate of cut apples and pears for breakfast. I poured myself a mug of the brown liquid from a glazed blue jug, took a drink, then spit it back into the mug immediately. Wine, spiced with cloves. I searched the table for water. A servant refilled the blue jug. "Excuse me," I said, "but is there anything to drink besides wine? Perhaps some water?"

The woman's eyes bulged like a fish's. "Water? You would die of some horrible sickness, m'lady, if you drink water from the Thames or any other river."

"Could you boil me some water to drink?"

Now the servant looked worried, as if I might be dangerous. "M'lady, everyone drinks the mulled wine. Why would you *ever* want to drink water?"

I licked my dry lips and resolved to hold out for water as she hurried away, even though dehydration surely lurked in my future.

The other women bustled in and out of the room, clearly occupied waiting on the "Queen," but I didn't dare participate. It was as if I walked across a thawing lake, with the ice cracking and melting. No matter where I placed my foot, it would be wrong.

The sounds of musicians drifted down the corridor—a flute and some sort of stringed instrument, and a woman singing. I peeked into the room but did not enter. This must be the Queen's presence chamber, for it was dominated by a huge carved chair raised on a dais, and decorated with dozens of flags and emblems. "Elizabeth" sat in the chair with an older man dressed in heavy robes at her side. The room was filled with men and women pretending to be courtiers in elaborate Elizabethan dress. The air was thick with perfume that couldn't hide the musky, moist smell permeating the room.

I slid back against the wall into the hallway. It was getting harder and harder to convince myself this was all in my coma-fied imagination. But yet, it had to be. The alternative was beyond impossible. I even managed to chuckle at creating two levels of impossible: the regular impossible and the beyond impossible. But my chuckling didn't change the fact that a high-pitched scream of terror crouched at the base of my throat, desperate for release. I breathed in through my nose and out through my mouth, which was supposed to be calming. It took many minutes of inhaling and exhaling before Terror's little sister Anxiety arrived to take Terror's place. I still didn't feel calm, but I preferred a little anxiety to terror.

With one more inhale, I pushed myself off the wall and began exploring the palace, which I assumed was meant to be Whitehall Palace in my waking nightmare. Cardinal Wolsey had built Whitehall then gave it to Henry VIII and his second wife, Anne Boleyn. The palace became one of the homes of Henry and Anne's daughter, Elizabeth, when she became Queen.

Some hallways were dark and narrow, but others were wide, lit by windows and capped with beautiful arched ceilings at least three stories overhead. I walked and walked, bewildered by the maze of corridors and galleries. Some of the rooms had fresh rosemary scattered across the floor, which made them smell as good as you'd imagine.

I wandered from room to room, undisturbed by servants as they went about their business. Apparently, they either knew "Blanche Nottingham" or respected the quality of my dress. "M'lady," someone said behind me. "Is there anything you require?"

I turned to face a tall, kind-faced man.

"No, I....I'm just a bit restless so feel the need to wander." I considered asking him how someone got a bath around here, but I doubted he'd be in charge of cleaning the ladies-in-waiting. The man bowed and slipped away through an open door.

As he walked away I wondered—if I ignored everyone around me, refusing to respond, would that release me from this dream? Another turn of the corridor brought me up short. There, hanging on the wall, was the *Coronation Portrait of Elizabeth*. The colors nearly leapt off the canvas, creating an ache in me that the version hanging in the National Portrait Gallery did not. The Gallery's painting had been copied from the original, which had gone missing centuries ago. Could this be the original, the one lost to history? Don't be ridiculous, I scolded myself.

The next door I passed led into a small library with towering walls lined with books.

On an easel in one corner was another portrait, also of Elizabeth, revealing the same soulful, deep-set eyes as the woman I'd met yesterday, the same expressive mouth. Either this was real, or my imagination was being very thorough in creating a believable fantasy. Suddenly, creativity seemed a curse rather than a gift, and I thought of van Gogh. Poor man had some major brain issues that historians now believe had their source in some sort of epilepsy. Was I losing touch with reality as Vincent sometimes had?

I pulled a book off the shelf at random, running my fingers over the well-worn velvet binding. I flipped through the heavy parchment pages, unable to read its French contents. But the book fell open to the first page, which held a handwritten inscription:

To the most high, puissant, and redoubted prince, Henry VIII, of the name, King of England, France and Ireland, defender of the Faith.
Elizabeth, his most humble daughter.
Health and obedience.

I began running my fingers through my hair, but they caught in the tight locks. I missed my loose hair swinging gently against my cheeks. I reread the inscription. How could I have created this in my mind? I had no idea what "puissant" meant. I'd never even seen the word. Was I clever enough, in my coma, to make up words to confuse myself?

And then there were the names. My support system was Jake, Ashley, and Mary. Already I'd met "Kat Ashley" and "Lady Mary." All I needed was a Jake or Jacob to confirm this was all in my imagination. And then there was the dog named after Vincent van Gogh.

I replaced the book, then stroked the jewel-encrusted spines of a long line of books. I would return to this room later and search for books in English.

"You do not belong here."

I whirled around to find a woman crouched in the corner of the room, wrapping the tie of her grungy apron tighter and tighter around one hand. "I'm sorry," I said. "I'll go."

"You are not of this world. Neither am I. We are all weary travelers looking for home." The woman burst into tears as I approached. "Why can I not find my way home?"

My throat constricted. "Are you lost?" I managed to croak out through dry lips.

"I do not belong here. I do not belong anywhere," the woman wailed.

I grasped the woman's hand. "Who are you? Do you know Dr. Rajamani? Did he give you a shot of GCA?"

"The doctors cannot help me. I have no future. It is gone, all gone."

"Are you from the future?" I choked, stunned I'd actually voiced that possibility. "Do you know what's happened to us? Is this real?"

The woman clutched at me. "We cannot get back. We can never get back. All we have known is lost. The doctors took it all away."

"Oh, Margaret, there you are." A servant dressed in blue with a white cap scurried into the room, a horrified look twisting her plain features. "I am so sorry, m'lady. Please do not tell Her Majesty." The woman gathered Margaret in her arms. "My sister is not well. We got her out of Bedlam, a wicked, wicked place, but she is still not herself. I will not let her escape her room again."

"Bedlam?"

"The madhouse. Bethlehem Hospital. My sister lost her wits two years ago, but Bedlam only made it worse. Come, Margaret."

The woman stopped for a shallow curtsey. "Please, m'lady, if the Queen—"

"I won't say a word," I replied, forcing my voice to stop shaking. What had just happened? I watched the woman lead her sister away. Was the woman truly mad? Had she been driven mad by the same circumstances that now trapped me? And if I spoke to anyone about where I'd come from, asked anyone if they were from the future too, would I be bundled off to some private facility called Bedlam? I shivered in the warmth of the sun filtering through the tall library windows. On the table beside me was an elaborate clock with a man riding a rhinoceros, with another four men standing on the ground around him. The clock gently chimed nine times while the four attendants slowly bent at the waist then gracefully returned to their original positions. The last chime echoed in the room.

Desperate for air, I ran down the corridor, turning and doubling back until light ahead led me out onto a second floor balcony. I gulped the fresh air in relief, clutching the railing as I surveyed the grounds. The rosy red brick of the palace was used in most of the buildings that lined a narrow street running from this building to the edge of a forest. Rooflines dipped and climbed, with dozens of chimneys creating a ragged horizon. Courtiers entered and exited the buildings, calling to each other and talking in small groups.

The palace grounds were a maze of pebbled paths and streets, brick walls with arched gates, narrow alleys, and great swaths of green. Roughly dressed men worked in an orchard, and others tended a small rose garden. Off to my right, someone was chopping wood, and smoke arose from some sort of oven. The smell of baking bread was so strong and so familiar it brought tears to my eyes.

The garden below had two reflecting pools and a fountain. It was a knot garden, broken into four large sections, each featuring an elaborate pattern of thick green hedges. That I knew about knot gardens told me I'd recently been diving too deeply into the Tudor pool. The green hedges wove in and around themselves, forming knot-like patterns nearly as complicated as embroidery. The green hedges were set off by exploded pinks, pansies, and grape hyacinth.

Scattered throughout were poles topped with carved lions, dragons, and other beasts, each holding a flag. It was a cheerful garden. Outside the four knot squares were rows of hollyhocks and damask roses. Beyond these was a raised walkway that must allow strollers a better view of the patterned garden, then three rows of cherry trees.

I sighed softly. Chris would be so proud. When we'd purchased our 1898 home in Powderhorn Park, Chris was determined to turn our backyard into a horticultural masterpiece. I suspect she was motivated less by a love of gardening than a desire to outshine the neighbors. One couple to the east had turned their entire front and backyards into a chaotic wildflower garden, a haven for bees and butterflies. The women to the west had gone crazy with their water feature, stacking granite slabs into an elaborate set of waterfalls cascading into shallow pools. The monstrosity so dominated the backyard that the couple's two poor labradoodles could barely find space in which to do their "business."

I'd helped Chris move soil and create beds and rock pathways, but she had been in charge of design. For two years, our living room, kitchen counter, and bed overflowed with plant catalogs and garden design books. That I could recognize the plants in this palace garden meant some of Chris's constant garden talk must have stuck.

In the distance, I could barely see the tips of what must be lances, then the lances disappeared and hooves pounded the ground. I scanned the entire area for the laundry building, since surely that would have a way to heat water. Perhaps I could bathe in some lukewarm wash water…that's how desperate I was.

Directly across from the garden was a large gatehouse next to a stone wall. Beyond that was a massive arch topped with another tower. Horse-drawn carts rumbled by under the arch.

Off to the left was a bowling green, with one of three men rolling a small ball toward the pins. A huge forest rose up at the edge of the grounds. The whole thing was less a well thought out palace and more just a mishmash of buildings and narrow paths and lush plants.

As my gaze returned to the bowling green, I froze. The tallest of the men waved at me impatiently, as if he wanted me to join them. Ha. Not likely. Then one of the men ran toward the palace and disappeared. A few minutes later, that same man showed up at my elbow and proclaimed, "Lady Blanche, there you are. Lord Winston has asked me to escort you to the bowling green." I had no choice but to let him place my hand in the crook of his elbow and follow. The man, dressed in hose and velvet coat and bloomers, rattled on about how lovely I looked this morning, and how the orange dress brought out the brilliant blue in my eyes. I rolled my brilliant blue eyes but he didn't notice.

I was suddenly so weary I actually needed the man's support. I wanted to close my eyes, sleep for a week and then wake up with Chris's familiar face next to mine.

When we reached the green, the tall man, apparently "Lord Winston," looked at me as if I were a bug he'd found in his soup. "Finally," he snapped. "What have you learned?" He carried himself as you'd imagine a lord would, with the complete confidence he'd be obeyed.

My mind spun. "Learned about what?"

Winston jammed his fists on his velvet-coated hips. "God's bones, woman, this is no time to play games." His fury only emphasized how poorly I understood the situation in which I found myself. And I was also noticing that a pretty decent curse around here consisted of one of God's body parts—bones, teeth, blood. If I hadn't been so confused by my situation, I could have admired the clever cursing system.

The "lord" scowled. "What have you learned of Dudley's habits?"

Dudley. Him again. Controversy had always swirled around the man, for he seemed to control and influence the Queen more than a commoner should. Dudley fully expected to marry Elizabeth and be King. Inconveniently, he was already married to Amy Dudley.

"His schedule?"

"Is this woman totally daft?" one of the other men snapped. "Winston, you said she would help our cause."

Winston grabbed my arm and pulled me against the tall hedge to hide us from the palace windows. "We need to dispatch Dudley here, in the palace. When does he visit the Queen next?"

"I don't know. He comes and goes as he, or as the Queen, pleases." What else could I say? I reached for anything from *The Tudors* TV show that could help. "But he always sends a request through his squire that he would like to visit, so we have several hours' notice."

"Good." One of the men handed me the heavy, smooth ball, which fit snugly in my palm. "Now pray take your turn so we appear naturally engaged to anyone observing us."

I moved away from the wall, took a few steps and rolled the ball toward the pins, missing every one of them.

Winston tucked my hand into his arm. God, it was getting old being dragged around by men's elbows. "The next time Dudley sends notice of his intent to visit the Queen, you will contact me in the usual way."

The usual way? That would be fine, if I actually were Blanche Nottingham and knew what that was.

Winston gripped my hand too tightly. "England's future, its safety, and its honor are all at stake, Lady Blanche. Do not fail us."

With that, each man executed a slight bow, then disappeared down the garden path.

Winston's words were over-the-top dramatic, but still alarming. No matter where I was, clearly, having nothing to drink but wine might be the least of my worries.

CHAPTER SEVEN

After "Lord Winston" and his entourage left, I dropped onto the nearest marble bench. What the hell was I supposed to do next? A few years ago, I'd watched a BBC show called *Life on Mars*, about a detective hit by a car and transported thirty-three years into the past, to 1973. It was an hysterical vehicle for laughing at the men's wide shirt collars, the big hair, and the lack of computers or cell phones, but the detective had struggled just as I was struggling. He didn't know if he was in a coma from the accident and imagining everything, or if it was real. From time to time he would hear medical people talking to him, as if trying to rouse him from a coma. Season two revealed he was in a coma, but when he came out of it, he missed the people in 1973 so much that he jumped off a building, hoping he'd go back to 1973 when he died. Kind of a creepy ending.

Instead of jumping off a building, I would figure this out. I scanned the bustling palace grounds. Everything I'd seen I could have culled from books or movies, even down to the public King Street that cut through the palace grounds, and the massive, two-story arch above the street. I stood, flush with hope. If I walked as far away from this spot as I could, surely my imagination would run out of details. Things should get more vague and fuzzy the farther I was from the palace.

I gathered up my skirts and marched toward the entrance to King Street, heart racing as I neared the street crowded with carts and horses rattling by. But just at the entrance, one of the guards stepped forward. "M'lady, is there something you require?"

I looked into the man's kind but determined face. "Yes, I need to leave the palace for a while. I am going to walk the street."

The guard's eyes widened in alarm. "Walk the street? Lady Blanche, if you need to get somewhere in the city, pray let one of the palace barges take you."

"That's not what I want. What is your name?"

The man's dark eyes snapped with amusement. "You well know my name, for I served your father those three years."

I drew myself up in what I hoped was a haughty snit. "Your *name*, guard."

He gave me an insolent bow. "Jacob, my lady."

Crap. Ashley, Mary, and Jacob. It was official. I was fantasizing all of this.

"Well, Jacob, I appreciate your concern, but what I need now is to walk."

"Then perchance in the park." He nodded over my shoulder toward the forest. "I recently saw you walk there with Lord Winston." Jacob's voice tightened with what might have been anger, but I didn't care.

"No, it's the street for me." I dipped my shoulder and smoothly slid past him, turning right onto the street that would follow the Thames north, then east into the heart of London. Jacob's voice barked in frustration as he called for replacement guards, and suddenly, he and one other guard were walking at my heels, armed with swords and carrying long, iron pikes.

"Go away, damn it," I tossed over my shoulder as I tried to avoid a large pothole filled with murky water. I could hear the guard muttering to Jacob something about picking me up and carrying me back. Jacob's reply helped me understand the Blanche I was supposed to be. "The lady will gouge out your eyes and see your head put on a spike. She is astonishing."

Soon I forgot Jacob's appreciation of the "astonishing" Blanche in the focus needed to navigate the street. It was in horrid condition, deeply rutted in places, slick as snot in others. Within one minute, my skirt hung heavy with muck. I held it up as best I could, but dropped it whenever I stumbled. My feet began to ache in these stupid, thin-soled slippers. Yet still my mind created detail after detail. And the smells! Damn, they were bad. My nostrils could have sued the city for assault and battery.

We hadn't walked five minutes when, up a slight incline to the left, we passed a series of long buildings with soaring roofs. Was that north? The sky was thick with clouds, so the sun couldn't help me. I rubbed my temples. I always knew my directions. Horses whinnied from within the buildings, and the air glittered with dust and pulsed with the shouts of men and the creaking of carriage wheels. The rich smell of horse manure joined the party in my nose.

I stopped in my tracks, heart pounding. The royal mews. Just twenty-four hours ago I'd been standing at the top of that slight hill, looking out over Trafalgar Square. A vise began tightening around my head. I was just creating an image of the mews in my mind.

I forced my feet to keep moving. Along the next stretch of street, regal mansions rose from the banks of the Thames. Each house had at least one dock with numerous boats on the river. On the left—north?—past the mews, were more modest houses but still grander than I'd imagined there would be in Elizabethan England. One well-dressed gentleman hopped into an open carriage and was driven across the street and down a narrow path to the Thames, where he must have kept a boat at a neighbor's dock.

The closer to London we walked the rougher the buildings appeared. We passed an open market of timber-covered stalls with chunks of meat, mounds of vegetables, and small, square cloths piled high with spices. A trader called to me, "Come! I have the best mutton you'll find!" A side street was filled with laughter and women dressed with enough abandon that they were clearly prostitutes. Two boys passed me carrying leather water vessels, their faces screwed up in such concentration they must have been lectured not to spill.

In the distance, at least four church bells chimed. In fact, there were lots of bells chiming. I could easily create this detail because I knew there were over 120 church parishes in London, many with exquisitely toned bells that young people chimed for amusement. The gray sky reflected off the glass in the upper story windows as I passed; in one a little girl looked down at me and waved.

The people were clean and filthy and fat and razor thin. I kept expecting to see people I knew since my brain must eventually run out of facial features and begin relying on my memory. Soon I would see Chris and my parents and my brothers, and my entire senior class. I would see old teachers and Carleton students and neighbors and my dead grandparents. I would soon see Ashley and Mary.

But no. Every face was new. Familiar, but new.

Shops, pubs, inns. Signs for glassmakers and shoemakers and astrologers. Food stands, dogs and children running loose. Massive piles of horse manure steaming in the middle of the street. A man in a long black coat stood on one corner waving a handful of leaflets, shouting, "Repent, England! Repent!"

The buildings ranged from brand new to barely standing. After an hour, Blanche's body was ready to turn back, but I pressed on. There was no way my brain could keep supplying these details.

I came to a halt when we passed a dark building with bars on the open windows. Filthy hands and weak voices reached out for food. "What fresh hell is this?" I muttered.

"Debtors' prison," Jacob said. "Lady Blanche, I beg you to let us take you back."

"Debtors' prison? And doesn't *that* make sense. If a person can't pay his debts, you throw him in prison so he can't earn anything to pay off the debts so his family starves. That is *beyond* idiocy."

I stomped away, only to be brought up short by the sight of a man sitting on the ground with a cap in front of him, waving for attention with arms that both lacked hands.

"Sweet Jesus," I said, turning to my friendly guard.

Jacob shrugged. "Thieving gets your hand cut off. If this cutpurse has lost both, he is one of the worst."

"Maybe he was thieving to feed his family," I snapped.

I ran up a side street with second and third stories looming out over the street like giants. The city was growing more crowded. I'd seen the spire of St. Paul's Cathedral, so I knew I was close to the heart of London, and still my brain kept creating more. The weirdness of the last week threatened to overwhelm me. I had no one to turn to, no one to ask for advice. And I wasn't running out of details. My brain, or this world, just kept presenting more and more information.

Jacob ran up behind me, panting slightly. "My lady, this street continues up to Holborn. There is nothing for you there."

My first thought was amazement that Holborn Street had existed in Elizabethan times, but then I got a grip. This wasn't real, and believing it was would only make things harder.

Anger at Dr. Raj and confusion at my own inability to figure this out sent me stamping back to the main street with my two guards huffing to keep up. Then I lost it. "You're the only ones who seem to care what happens to me. And I don't even know if you're real, or if I've just made you up!" I actually smacked poor Jacob on the chest of his red wool uniform. "I'm not supposed to be here. Do you understand that? I don't belong here, not in the palace, not here! It's the wrong time. It's even the wrong damn body. What am I supposed to do?" My voice rose in panic, but I couldn't stop it. "Where's Dr. Rajamani? Why doesn't any of this make sense?"

One of the men shook his head. "You are sounding just as crazy as the man in the Tower." He looked at Jacob. "Remember him? Wild-eyed bloke kept trying to get onto the palace grounds, going on and on about this doctor, named Raja or something."

"The Tower?" I squeaked. "You threw him in the Tower because he was sounding just like me?"

"No," Jacob said. "The bloke got thrown in for sorcery. Her Lady, Bess of Hardwick, claims he used witchcraft on her."

"That's ridiculous," I sputtered, but I forced myself to calm down. Funny how just the mention of the Tower of London could do that. Chris and I had toured the landmark our first week here, and I'd been awed by the history within the 800-year-old walls, but also horrified at the pain and torture that had taken place there. I faced my guards. "I'm not crazy, you know." The men looked at each other. "So you don't need to throw me in Bedlam, but I need to see this man. Is he still in the Tower?"

"Last I heard they got him salted away in the Salt Tower." Jacob grinned at his own pun.

I was too freaked to appreciate his wit as I whirled to examine the horizon. The Tower was located on the Thames near St. Paul's Cathedral "Could you take me to him? Then afterward, perhaps we could take a barge back to the palace." My bribery worked, for none of us wanted to repeat the torturous walk.

Jacob's companion squinted at me, then nodded. "We are almost there now, but we cannot stay long."

The walk took longer than it should have because the streets were clogged with carriages and wagons, but eventually, the White Tower rose into sight above the fort walls. We stopped at the guard station, and Jacob explained Lady Blanche Nottingham was here to see the sorcerer.

"Aye, Hew Draper be here. Cozy little setup the man has got." He nodded to me. "Best be quick about it, and do not be letting him tell you any tales about how we been treating 'em. Him's got a cushier life than me own."

The Tower of London, basically a walled fort, looked considerably different than when I'd toured it. In this version more wooden buildings filled up the green space and the roar of a lion reminded me there'd actually been a small zoo here, with a lion, lynx, tigers, and an ancient wolf, an animal as scarce in Britain as any of the other zoo inhabitants. Rising high from the middle of the grounds was the White Tower, a building that housed the Queen's armories and most of its gunpowder. The basement contained torture chambers.

Missing from this version of the Tower of London was the glass sculpture in the Tower Green marking the site of the beheadings that occurred there over the centuries, Elizabeth's mother Anne Boleyn being the most famous.

The Tower guard, busy chatting with my own, led us down a cobblestone street that ran alongside the Thames. We passed the Traitor's Gate, a wooden lattice set into a stone arch above the water where prisoners were brought into the Tower via boat. Princess Elizabeth had entered the Tower this way when her sister, Queen Mary, was so worried about an uprising that would put Elizabeth on the throne that she imprisoned Elizabeth in one of the corner towers for months.

When we climbed a narrow staircase to a walkway that ran along the top of the wall, I looked out over the Thames. To the right was the London Bridge, packed with houses and shops lining both sides of the bridge. I followed the guard through a number of small round towers, then he came to a halt at the corner tower topped with a slate-roofed turret. "Here we are," the guard said gaily. He pulled out a set of heavy iron keys and clanked one into the lock. "Master Draper, ye got yourself a visitor, and a lovely one at that." He swung open the heavy door, and I followed him inside, shaking with excitement. If this man had mentioned Dr. Rajamani, he had to know what was going on.

The tower cell was round and two narrow slits let light in from the south. A hearth was set for a fire but did not burn. There was a narrow bed, a small table and chair, and books piled everywhere. Seated at the table was a stooped man with thin gray hair resting listlessly on his shoulders. While his body looked so weak I knew I could easily knock him down, his eyes burned with interest.

We stared at each other. He stood and gave a wobbly bow. "M'lady," he said.

I turned to the Tower guard. "Please leave us alone."

"Are you sure she will be safe?" asked Jacob. Of all the people I'd met so far, he was the only one who seemed to care about me other than "Elizabeth" herself.

"You're sweet," I said. He blushed red as his uniform. "But I'll be fine."

"There is no exit but this one," the Tower guard said. "Your lass will come to no harm."

"I still do not think—"

"Jacob, look at his size. Look at mine." My brain reached for a twenty-first century reference. "Besides, I'm really strong. I'm almost Wonder Woman."

The imprisoned man inhaled sharply as our eyes met. We exchanged cautious smiles. Shrugging, the three guards left, assuring me they would be right outside. "Let us have us a drink, shall we, boys?" said the Tower guard.

The stone room seemed to absorb all the sound. A little noise from river traffic drifted in, but the only sound was Hew Draper's breathing. He moved his chair for me to use, then he sat on his bed. Nervous now, I took a minute to look around. Carved into the wall closest to me was an elaborate graffiti of an astrological chart. I did a double take because I'd seen this very graffiti on my tour, but then it had been preserved behind a sheet of Plexiglas.

"I know what you're thinking," the man said softly. I waited. "You've seen that graffiti on your tour of the Tower, no? And you're wondering where you are and when you are, and if your mind is creating this scene from memory, or if it's a real scene in 1560."

"Did you say 1560?"

"When are you from, Wonder Woman?"

I took a deep breath. "From 2017."

Hew smiled. "How is Manchester United doing?"

I shook my head. "Sorry, I don't follow sports."

"Bugger all. It would have been nice to know." He seemed calm, but then I noticed his hands shook.

I reached for one of them. "How long have you been here?"

He pressed his thin, chapped lips together. "I arrived last year on May fourteenth."

"Oh, my God. You've been here over a year."

"Were you part of Rajamani's experiments?"

"Yes, and you?"

He nodded. "I've had lots of time to think, and I'm sure it was that blasted drug he gave me. There was a devil of thunderstorm going on at the same time as the experiment, and suddenly, I woke up in the gutter of a London I didn't recognize, in the body of a man I didn't know."

I leaned forward. "This is real? I'm not just making it up in my head? I'm not in a coma somewhere?"

Hew barely moved, but his voice sank an octave with his reply. "This is real."

"But what about coincidences that my mind could be creating?" I told him about Vincent, Ashley, Mary, and Jake, and how each name had appeared here.

He shook his head. "Don't get so wrapped up in your fear that you forget that simple coincidences can happen in 1560, too. This isn't something your mind has created. This is very, very real."

I shivered. "I'd hoped it was a nightmare."

"That's what I thought at first, and then I went a little mad. I had no skills, no home, no food. After a few days of living in the filth of the street, having to steal what I ate, I lost it. I began dancing around on King Street, inside the palace walls, cursing and spitting at a carriage passing by me. Out pops ol' Bess of Hardwick, sure I'd just cast a spell on her." He sighed. "I've been here ever since."

"That's horrible. We have to get you out of here."

Hew threw up his hands. "No, absolutely not. Look at me. I'm a thirty-year-old man in the body of a sixty-year old one. I was born in 1985, for Christ's sake. My only skills are programming computers, kicking a football, and drinking with the boys down at the pub. I can't survive out there on my own. At least in here they feed me, give me a bit of wood for warmth in the winter, and bring me books to read." He smiled. "You seem to be doing much better."

I snorted. "At least I'm living in the palace, but I've already found myself part of some stupid plot." I stuck out my hand. "My name is Jamie Maddox. This overstuffed dress belongs to Blanche Nottingham."

With a grin, Hew shook my hand. "Name's Ray Lexvold, Covent Gardens, London. This bloke you're looking at is Hew Draper."

I rubbed my forehead, suddenly weary. "I want to believe this is real because the alternative is that I'm dead or in a coma, but I still don't trust it. I could be making you up in my head."

"Do you know anything about masted sailing ships from the sixteenth century?"

I laughed. "Not a damned thing."

He shuffled over to one of the window slits. "If you stand right here you can see the activity on the Thames. It's why I love this cell so much."

I pressed my cheek against the cold stone. "Okay."

"See that three-masted boat with the red hull?"

"Yes."

"Look at the riggings running up and down the masts. Watch the men making oakum over in the corner. Did you know any of this?"

Hungry for proof, I squeezed into the opening as far as I could without getting stuck. Rough stone pressed into my shoulder. Men were unloading the ship with wheeled carts. Three horses waited on the dock, each harnessed to a cart. Men scampered through the masts and rigging doing mysterious things with ropes. I watched for a few minutes, then sighed.

I pulled back and touched Ray's arm. "Thank you."

"No use having you go bonkers and end up in a cell, or Bedlam. You at least have a safe place to stay."

I nodded but couldn't stop thinking about Winston and the other men, and what they had planned. "Okay, I have to ask. You're still here, which means you haven't been able to find a way home."

Ray slumped back onto his bed, which creaked alarmingly even at his slight weight. "I thought it was the storm. Summer brings a fair number of thunderstorms to London. I'm kind of the guards' pet—don't know why—so I talk them into letting me walk along the top of the wall during storms. They think I'm batty. I kept hoping to make a return 'trip,' if that was what it was, but no luck. I'm still here." He squeezed my hand. "There's no going back, luv. There just isn't."

I pushed down the panic. I couldn't be stuck here. Impossible. "What do you suppose is going on with our bodies back in our present?"

"I've had plenty of time to puzzle that out as well, and I came up with two options. Either we're in hospital in a coma while our minds are back here, or...." He winced.

"Or what?"

"Or there was some sort of exchange. When my mind traveled into this decrepit body, what if Hew Draper's old mind ended up in my body?"

"You mean Hew Draper's walking around in twenty-first century London?"

"If you accept that this is real, then why not?"

My blood ran cold. "You mean someone I don't even know is wearing my body?"

"You're wearing hers. It's only fair."

"Sleeping in my bed? That's not right." I found myself unable to swallow. Was Blanche sleeping with Chris? No, that couldn't happen. Chris would know that Blanche wasn't me.

"I know how you feel," he said. "I'd just bought a brand new Mercedes. Imagine what must have happened when a bloke from 1559 got behind the wheel." He shuddered. "Makes me sick to think of what he's done to my car."

I sat down hard on the chair. "What am I going to do?"

Ray patted my knee. "You're going to accept where you are, and when you are, and who you are, and get on with it."

"On with what?"

"That's the question, isn't it?"

Jacob's voice came through the thick door. "Lady Blanche, the barge is ready to take us back to the palace."

Ray gave me a weak hug. He clearly wasn't a well man. "Could you visit me again?"

"Of course. Anything you need?"

"Another blanket would be grand, and maybe some of that rich palace food would put some meat on these stupid old bones."

I held Ray by his thin shoulders. "I'm going to figure this out. I'm going to get *both* of us home."

Ray's laugh turned into a cough. "You got spunk, Jamie."

At that word, homesickness hit me so hard I gasped. I missed my family and Chris so badly I teared up. "Thanks, Ray. I'll be back."

Within minutes, I was seated on a thick cushion in the small cabin of the palace barge. This really was the past. My mind, in someone else's body, was existing in the year 1560. My reality check was the Thames, usually fairly clean. The smell of it now, however, brought on several dry gags that irritated my throat. Jacob opened a small chest and moistened a handkerchief with something and passed it to me. Rose water. I held it under my nose to mask the river.

"There are so many wharfs," I said, struggling to distract myself from the pain of missing everyone I loved.

Jacob gave a surprised snort. "You speak as if you have never seen London, yet you have been here as long as I have." Jacob looked at me with a familiarity that made me uncomfortable. He and Blanche clearly had some sort of history.

"Indulge me," I said. "Pretend I am new to the city."

"That is the Old Wool Quay, where they ship wool, obviously. That is the Bear Quay, used by Portuguese traders. Gibson's Quay has your lead and tin." He continued listing the more than twenty quays between the Tower and the fast-arriving London Bridge.

We passed under one of London Bridge's stone arches, which were built on flat pillars of stone shaped like boats. I asked Jacob about them.

"They act as cutwaters to protect the bridge when the tide goes out since the water moves quite fast."

That was the only bridge. Yet in the London I knew, there were at least thirteen bridges crossing the Thames in the heart of London. My favorite was the Millennium Bridge gracefully arching from the area south of St. Paul's over to the Tate Modern, housed in an old power plant. Second favorite was the pale blue Tower Bridge, with its soaring towers and graceful arches.

The boat bobbed in the river, choppy from all the traffic. After at least an hour, when the sun had sunk behind western London, I saw the palace walls ahead and could hardly wait to get safely behind them again.

But then it hit me that I should never feel safe. Once I did, I might give up, as Ray seemed to have done. I wouldn't do that. I would help Ray get back to his Mercedes. I would get back to Chris. I would get back to my parents and my brothers. I would bring Bradley more rabbit food and get him off the street. I would finish those damned Froggity paintings and return to Carleton. Or maybe I'd apply to a larger school. I would be the risk taker Chris wanted. I would become the most ambitious person on the planet.

Once we docked, Jacob hopped from the small barge and extended a hand. He held me a little too long, and a little too tightly, as he helped me ashore. Uh oh. Poor Jacob clearly had the hots for Blanche Nottingham. I would have chuckled but for a terrible thought: What if I was actually crazy and none of this was true, not even Ray?

I pushed myself away from Jacob and ran up the grass toward the palace. But then I slowed and focused on sending calm breaths deep into my belly and down to my toes. No. I was not insane.

I would not give up hope, since hope was kind of my thing.

Hope made you spunky.

CHAPTER EIGHT

That evening after I performed one of Blanche's responsibilities—refilling the Queen's perfume pan with fresh rose water and cloves, I was so parched I had no choice but to guzzle down three mugs of wine. As a result, an unfamiliar warmth quickly spread all the way out to my fingers and toes. Feeling a bit tipsy, I lowered myself onto a cushioned stool in the Queen's private chamber where the other women talked and sewed.

While Elizabeth sat reading in her thickly padded velvet chair, I drank in every detail of her—her face, her dress, and her fingers, pale and straight as rulers. After my visit with Ray, I was convinced. This woman wasn't an actress, but the real Elizabeth Tudor, Queen of England, who would rule for another forty-three years. Her navy would explore the globe and defeat the Spanish Armada. She would invite Shakespeare to her palaces to perform his dramas. Her reign would produce such a burst of art, music, and science that history named the period after her—the Elizabethan Age.

When Lady Charlotte handed me one of the Queen's collars that needed repair, I sputtered something inane while staring at the needle and thread she'd also given me. I had no idea what to do and couldn't even thread the needle to get started.

But when my fingers—or rather, Blanche's fingers—picked up the needle and spool, they acted of their own accord, folding the end of the thread over the needle, moistening it in my mouth, then slipping the folded part expertly through the eye of the needle. I bit off a gasp as I then tied some sort of knot at the other end of the thread and began to sew. Holy crap. I knew little about the brain, but the part that performed familiar functions must still be under Blanche's control. In this case, it was a relief, but it worried me. How much control did I actually have over this body? If I came across someone who'd been hurt, my instinct was to run toward them. What if Blanche's were to run away from them? Could I stop that?

My ignorance ate through me like battery acid. Did this mean that Blanche was in my body, using my skills? Painting, texting, navigating the Tube system? My thoughts returned to that idea that Blanche was sleeping with Chris. Chris would certainly know it wasn't me, right?

As I stared at the threaded needle, the delicious surprise of an unfamiliar action in 1560 feeling natural reminded me of my first middle school art class when I'd picked up a paintbrush and a tube of Golden's Cerulean Blue. The feeling of sliding the thick paint across the canvas felt so right, I'd gasped. Then I'd picked up some Red Oxide, some Cadmium Yellow, and proceeded to turn my sea of Cerulean Blue into a painting of what you'd see while looking down into a shallow pool of clear water.

"Lady Blanche."

I rose and approached Elizabeth, shuddering over my earlier statements to her, amazed that she hadn't thrown me from the palace on my heavily-skirted butt. I was hesitant to try my first curtsey, but Blanche's body took that over as well, for I sank gracefully, then rose back up without a wobble to my ankles or knees.

"We are wondering if you feel better. How fares the blow to your head?"

Tongue-tied, I could only mumble that I was fully recovered. But then I found my voice. "Your Majesty, I—"

"Ma'am will do fine. You know that."

"Ma'am, I wish to humbly beg your pardon for my earlier behavior. I was not myself." Truer words were never spoken.

Elizabeth dipped her head. "An apology gracefully given is graciously accepted."

As I returned to my stool, Elizabeth clapped her hands. "We have spent the day being pressured by our councilors to marry and provide the realm with an heir. How sad that we must waste a day on such an inconsequential matter. To shake off the dry words of dusty old men, let us dance. Someone call for the musicians."

To the accompaniment of lutes and flutes and a woman's soft soprano, I spent the rest of the evening dancing something called the cinque pas, a dance of five steps that I somehow knew.

Finally, when I was so exhausted I couldn't keep my eyes open, I asked the Queen's leave, and she, flushed from dancing, waved me toward the exit. I gathered Vincent to my chest and retired to my room with the little dog's tail beating happily against my side. Before closing my eyes that night, I made another notch in the table leg.

❖

The next day, I walked into the Queen's bedchamber, determined to blend in so I grabbed her silver brush. "Sit still, ma'am," I scolded her as she squirmed under my vigorous attentions. After brushing the Queen's red-gold hair to a sheen, I struggled to pull it up into something resembling her usual look, but soon even the Queen dissolved into laughter, and I had to give up. Lady Clinton, a sharp-faced woman with teeth too large for her mouth, did the hair, then I pushed my way back in and arranged the headpiece, which was a small crown with six long bobs of jewels that rested forward of the crown, lying across her hair as if they'd come down in a gentle rain.

"You have done well, my Spark," Elizabeth said as she contemplated her image in the thick, heavy silver mirror. She winked at me. "But it will be quite some time before you do our hair again."

I followed Elizabeth and the others into the Whitehall Chapel, a square room lined with marble columns and a ceiling that soared at least two stories above us. I settled into the nearest box with three other women, not wanting to presume that Blanche belonged with the Queen. When we sat on the narrow bench, our skirts filled the box. I watched the service with interest, knowing that the Protestant Elizabeth had already issued many proclamations that reversed her sister Mary's Catholic reformation.

Yet as I looked around the elaborate gold and white room, it was clear Elizabeth had retained some of her favorite parts of Catholicism—the beauty of the church, the soaring music, and the act of kneeling during parts of the service. Even though no heavy incense clogged the air, the heat of the worshippers crowded into the room made my eyes feel heavy. It might also have been the minister droning on about misguided Catholic beliefs.

I distracted myself by thinking of other times I could have visited. Why couldn't I have been transported back to 1890 in Auvers, France, where I could have saved Vincent van Gogh from the gunshot wound that would kill him. The "romantic" version of his death—artist in anguish takes own life—was bullshit. Who shoots himself in the stomach? And the doctors said he'd been shot from a short distance. I lost myself imagining coming to van Gogh's rescue as he likely confronted the teenager who'd bullied him for months.

A jab in my side from Lady Clinton snapped me to attention. "Cease snoring or the Queen will hear you."

I wanted to suggest she try living in the body of another person and see if she wasn't a little worn out.

Once the service finally ended, with Kat Ashley's permission and Lady Mary's grumpy help, I put together a small care package for Ray—wool blanket, feather pillow, sausages, two wedges of cheese, and a jug of ale. These I took to the guardhouse, where I knocked and found three men. Luckily, one of them was Jacob, whom I beckoned to step outside, which he did. "I am so happy to find you," I said.

When he blushed violently, I smiled to myself. I'd been correct: Sweet Jacob had a crush on Blanche.

I explained that Hew Draper, the man in the Salt Tower, was someone who needed my help and that I'd gathered some things for him. "Would you be so kind as to deliver them for me?" I rested my hand lightly on his chest. "You're the only one I dare trust, especially with this ale."

He dragged his gaze from his feet to Blanche's bountiful chest, finally reaching my eyes. I tried not to make a face, as feminism wouldn't take hold in England for at least another three hundred years.

"Why are you being so kind to me?"

"Aren't I always?"

"You used to snap and scold and command me. I wonder, where is *that* Lady Blanche?"

"She's gone. I don't like her," I said.

"Well, I do," he replied.

"Fine, you want to be commanded, I'll command. Deliver this package to the Tower." I pushed the package at him and left.

My next need was to wash my hair. With Vincent at my heels, I strolled through the working parts of the palace grounds and found the laundry. Vats of madly boiling water hung over open flames. If I could get some of that water before the laundress added soap, I could drink it. But I saw no place to take a bath or shower, only rows of servants' dresses hanging in the morning sun.

As I walked the garden, I found leaves in the shade that still cupped the morning dew, but the few drops of precious liquid did nothing to quench my thirst. Mild nausea had plagued me all morning, so I suspected I might be dehydrated.

By noon, the only place I hadn't explored was the park itself. It wasn't what we'd call a park, but more a thick forest that pressed in against civilization, such as it was. I found a foot trail and followed it into the woods, where the late summer day was just as lovely in the garden. Bright green ferns unfurled at the base of trees. Leaves fluttered softly overhead as the sun filtered down and warmed the top of my head. Some sort of red berries flashed through the underbrush. The path widened until it could easily accommodate five or six horses across. I listened for any sign of water but heard nothing through the calls of warblers and jays.

I was about to turn around and head back when I flushed hot and began to sweat. I dropped to my knees and vomited in the grass. Not fun. I remained there until I stopped trembling. God, what had I eaten? I managed to get back on my feet despite the three hundred pounds of dress, then noticed that Vincent was sniffing at a narrow opening in a stand of bushes. Was that a trail? If so, it wasn't advertising itself.

I pressed through, holding the bushes away from my dress, and found myself picking my way carefully down a moss-covered slope. I stepped lightly around a large tree and felt joy for the first time in days. A small, kidney-shaped pond, lined with ledges of stone, wrapped around a thick stand of oak trees. I dipped my hand in the water—cool, but not frigid. The water was clear enough I could see the clean bottom. I didn't dare drink it, but I could still take a swim.

I stopped. This stupid straitjacket! I couldn't undress without help. Grunting against the tight stomacher, I managed to drop to my knees and lean over the pond. I splashed off my face, my parched skin reveling in the wetness. Damn it. I wanted to jump in fully clothed but the yards of wet skirts would be so heavy I'd probably drown.

I dangled my hand in the cool water. Shadows flickered across the pond as birds swooped overhead, scolding me for violating their privacy. For the first time since being zapped into 1560, a hint of contentment settled over me. I thought about my parents and brothers. Would they even know I was gone? Was Blanche Nottingham trying to fit into my life, as I was trying to fit into hers? Was she instead making waves? What if she said something so horrible to a friend or family member that I could never repair it?

Aunt Nicole's voice filled my head. *If it's not within your control, don't waste your energy worrying about it.* That had been her mantra those last months. She focused on what she could do to fight off the cancer that had begun in her breast then gone on a major walkabout through her body until it finally settled into her bones. The path the cancer took, its ferocity? She chose not to worry about those. I helped Mom care for Nicole and treasured every moment spent with her. Even though her bones were brittle as cold glass, her mind was strong. She had made a decision a few years ago to slow her life down, to really appreciate what she had, and to allow herself to be content with that rather than fussing over what she lacked. I wish Chris had been able to spend time with Nicole during those months. She might not have been so harsh about my horrible "lack of ambition."

Vincent snuffled the ground by my feet, then climbed up onto my dress. I looked into his eyes of melted dark chocolate and played with one of his ears. This was a real dog living in 1560. I was really, truly here. Time travel was something I'd read about in novels— *Outlander*, *The Spanish Pearl*, Octavia Butler's *Kindred*, and almost anything by Connie Willis. When reading a novel, it was so easy to believe that time travel was real, but given all that scientists knew of physics, time travel was totally impossible. Yet here I was. Or at least here *part* of me was. In the novels, time travelers took their bodies with them. Why couldn't I have done that?

After I'd exhausted myself thinking about family and time travel, I returned to the problem of bathing. By the time I pulled myself back onto my feet and began walking back to the palace, I had a plan.

I needed a servant's dress, for they were simple, without corsets, so I could easily don—and remove—one without assistance. I strolled back through the laundry. The women working there ignored me, so it was a quick matter to reach up, unpin a dress and apron, a cap, swipe a small chip of soap, then scurry around the corner.

CHAPTER NINE

That night, after Rosemary had unpinned and deribbonned me, I slipped under the covers and waited until Mary's snoring rattled the bed. Because they drank ale or wine all day, everyone slept as if on Ambien. Even Vincent snored like a mastiff. I rose like a ghost, pulled on the comfortable dress, then headed down the hallway. Moonlight lit my way through the palace; I couldn't have picked a better night. Leaves glowed almost blue in the garden.

Low voices from the main gate reached me as the guards talked softly, but I managed to slip past the knot gardens and cherry trees without being seen. I ran across the bowling lawn toward the dark forest. Once inside, the moonlight dimmed, creating deep shadows that followed me. I should have brought Vincent with me, but the night was filled with so many frogs croaking that I wasn't afraid. As I picked my way down the path free of bodice, padded stomacher, and heavy skirts, I was as agile as a dancer, as graceful as a cougar. Now and then a twig snapped or something snuffled in the dark, but the thought of clean hair and a clean body kept me moving.

As I walked, my thoughts kept wandering back to the obvious, that Rajamani was messing with the mind in ways he couldn't control. His drug had somehow made me and Ray Lexvold sitting ducks for the electrical surge that must have come with the lightning strike. If Rajamani thought he had funding problems now, he was in for a big surprise. Once I found my way home again and into my own body, I'd sue the professor's ass off.

It felt good to think things like that. Yet how could I possibly duplicate the conditions of a risky experiment? I had no GCA, but perhaps it still flowed in my veins. And the only source of electricity I'd find in 1560 would be a thunderstorm. I didn't think I needed to actually get close to a strike of lightning, but I certainly had to be in the vicinity.

By the time I reached the pond, the silence had encouraged me to be as stealthy as a shadow. I stepped so lightly no one could have heard me approach. I leaned against the rocks to take off my shoes, then slipped the dress off, hung it on the rocks, and lowered myself into the water.

"Ahh," I murmured as I sank in up to my neck. I considered sipping the water around me, but knew I'd pay with diarrhea, unfun even with a flush toilet. But with a chamber pot and twenty pounds of skirt? Fire truck.

I swam around the pond's curve.

"Oh my God!" shouted a woman. Heart pounding, I shook the water from my eyes. A naked woman stood on the side of the pond, a candle burning at her feet. She clutched her rough muslin dress to her chest. Her eyes were red, and tears streaked her face.

"Hell's gates!" I cried. "I'm so sorry. I didn't know you were here."

The woman calmed down when she heard my voice, no doubt relieved I was a woman. "I thought I was alone."

"Me too. Come on in. There's plenty of room."

The woman dropped her dress and slid into the water. She had a strong, sturdy body, and suddenly, I was so lonely for Chris that my throat closed up. It's not that I was attracted to this woman, but that I hadn't been held or hugged for days and days.

"My name is Harriet Blankenship," she said. "I come here every week to bathe so I don't pass out from my own stench." Her plain face, visible in the faint moonlight filtering through the leaves, was softened by the warmth of her dark eyes. She wasn't beautiful in the usual sense of the word—her eyes too wide-set, her nose too small for her broad face—but every feature, no matter how plain, sparkled when she smiled.

"You don't like going weeks and weeks between baths?" I returned her smile.

"I would rather be poked with one thousand pins. Or attacked by one thousand dogs."

I laughed as we began swimming side by side. "My name is.... Nicole," I said.

Harriet's eyes flickered up to my servant's dress hanging on the rock. "I have never seen you before," she said. "Where do you work?"

"All over the place." If she knew I was one of the Queen's ladies, everything would get awkward.

"I am new to the palace," she said.

"How long have you been here?"

Harriet rolled onto her back and floated, a plump mermaid with silver breasts. "Too long, too long." She held up nine fingers. "Nine weeks and three days."

"I don't mean to pry, but you were clearly crying before I startled you."

"I...I am from the country. The life here in the palace, with the Queen and her court, is very strange to me. Crying helps."

I nodded. "I know exactly how you feel."

She stopped swimming. "My life here is not what I'd hoped. Sometimes I clean the palace, which is interesting, but I spend most of my days in the laundry."

"That would be hard work." Without a Maytag and a bottle of Era Plus, I'd be lost.

She sighed. "I can handle the work. It is just the boredom I despise. I used to...back in my village I performed many different activities. I was never bored."

I let my feet float to the surface so I could scrub my toes. "Maybe you could find another job in the palace. Do you have other skills?"

She grunted in frustration, eyebrows fierce as she frowned. "I can read and write, which none of the others I have met can do. But no one believes me. Even when I pick up a stick and write in the dirt outside the laundry, they say I am just writing gibberish. When

I read out loud a leaflet dropped in the street, the women say I am lying."

"It's unusual for a servant to read and write?"

"Yes."

"Maybe I could help."

She reached for my hand. "I would be so grateful. This can be such a lonely place."

I answered her squeeze, wanting to pull her close for a hug but unsure if she'd be comfortable hugging a naked stranger. "We must help each other through this."

"Absolutely."

We said nothing more as we swam for a few more minutes, then each retrieved our soap. I knew I shouldn't be putting soap in the water, but I was desperate to be clean. Harriet, however, had brought a bucket, so she soaped up out of the pond, and then rinsed herself with the bucket. Note to self: bring bucket next time.

At first, I was self-conscious as I pulled my naked self out of the pond, but then it hit me: This wasn't even my body. Why should I be embarrassed to be naked?

Talking softly about the families we'd left behind, Harriet and I toweled off, then dressed. We wove our way back to the palace. As we reached the spot where we needed to part, I gave in to my need for physical contact and hugged her. "I'm so glad I've met you."

She hugged back. "And I you. One can never have too many friends. Let us bathe again in a week."

I smiled and headed for the palace, but at the same time my stomach sank to think I might still be here a week from now.

Chapter Ten

The next morning I awoke smelling of soap and ran my hands through my hair. It was thinner than my own, and the wrong color, but it was mine for now, and it felt damned good to be clean. And it felt really good to have made a connection with Harriet. For the next few days, I watched but never saw her. Instead, I sat on a stool for endless hours as men with woolen capes draped over their arms bowed before Elizabeth and requested certain lands or that she punish a new neighbor for the harm he'd done to someone else's livestock. I watched women in elaborate, filmy headdresses glare and gossip about other women in elaborate, filmy headdresses. The whole court charade was less entertaining than TV's worst reality show, which in my opinion included all of them.

The morning I gouged my sixteenth notch on the table, sounds of an awakening palace drifted into my room, but they seemed muted, as if coming from a distance. The louder noise was a persistent beating.

I shot up. Rain. I threw on my robe and raced down the hallway to the nearest window, Vincent clicking softly at my heels. I loved that the little guy was so devoted to me. Chris didn't really like dogs, so my only chance for Dog Time was here at Whitehall.

Outside, deliciously gray and ominous clouds emptied themselves onto London. Lightning flashed in the distance. Thunder boomed. I counted the seconds between light and sound. My heart soared when I realized the lightning was close.

I raced back to the room. Lady Mary had already left, so there was no one to help me dress in my Blanche clothing. I dug out my servant's dress from under the mattress and slipped it on. I would give some serious money to see the look on Blanche Nottingham's face when she found herself back in 1560 wearing such a low class dress. All her dresses were embroidered with beads and intricate stitching.

I put on my heaviest slippers and a thick cape. No use giving Blanche pneumonia as we switched bodies.

Shaking now, I dashed through the palace for the nearest stair-well, then made my way to the center of the knot garden near the fountain. Vincent stood in the open doorway, whining and pacing.

The lightning had reached me in Dr. Rajamani's office, so I should be in good shape outside. Cold rain smacked my cheeks as I threw back my head and opened my mouth. Water, blessed water. After two minutes, my slippers and skirt were soaked, but I'd drunk enough water I no longer felt like a wilting plant. With one last glance at Vincent, whom I would miss, I moved west to the large lawn of open space. I could see people inside the palace gathering at the windows to point at me. Apparently, a walk in the rain wasn't a standard 1560 activity. I waved, unable to contain my excitement.

My mind spun with what to do when I got home. First, find Chris and hold her until my arms ached. Second, find Dr. Rajamani and tell him I was going to sue his ass off for mental anguish and torture. Was there even such a category?

Lightning silently reached down somewhere on the southern shore of the Thames, miles away, and my vision dissolved in a rush of speed and blue, and I was blind. I was Dr. Raj's ideal of a freed consciousness, untethered to a body. It was frightening, and it was freeing. I was not myself, and I was *only* myself.

❖

When the spinning stopped, I opened my eyes and nearly fell over, but I managed to stop myself by grabbing a rack of books. I looked around and nearly shouted with joy, then I glanced down. This was my body! I was back!

I stood in a Waterstone's Bookshop holding a book about Queen Elizabeth I. Slowly, I returned the book to the shelf. Two seconds ago, Blanche Nottingham had been in this body, in this bookstore, holding this book. Now she was back in 1560, standing out in the rain with the entire palace watching, wearing a servant girl's dress. The thought was more satisfying than I'd imagined, even though I had no idea what Blanche was like, and none of this was her fault (except for the stupid plotting with Winston.) I listened for the hum that had been in my dream but there was none. I was really home. The nightmare was over.

My head spun with all the information rushing at me at once, as if too many trains had arrived at the station simultaneously. I was obviously not lying in a coma in a hospital, with my family and Chris at my side. I was functioning. I looked around for Chris but couldn't see her. That Blanche was comfortable enough in my body, and in this time, to be browsing a bookstore on her own, spoke volumes.

Something pinched at my waist. I looked down and gasped. I was wearing a black push-up bra under a black velvet cut out blouse. I blushed from my navel to my breasts, the whole route far too visible. The blouse was tucked into a lime green skirt, which was so tight a muffin top bulged out. Hell's gate. What had Blanche been eating?

Still unsteady, I wandered through the bookstore to make sure Chris wasn't there, then I made my way out onto the street into a steady drizzle. Passing headlights reflected off the wet pavement as I popped open the umbrella in my hand. When I determined I was at the Waterstone's near the London School of Economics, I scooped up a discarded issue of *Metro* and checked the day. Wednesday. Chris should be at school.

I fumbled for my phone, found it in my skirt pocket, then called Chris.

"Hey, babe. What's up?" Her smooth voice flowed over me like warm syrup.

"Holy shit, Chris. I'm back. I'm really back."

She snickered. "I know you were worried about making the trip to Waterstone on your own, but it's not as if you've traveled around the globe or anything."

"No, worse than that. I've been gone for almost three weeks. God, baby, I miss you so much."

Confusion thickened her voice. "Blanche, are you okay?"

"Why are you calling me Blanche?"

"Because you begged me to!"

"Seriously? Oh, that *bitch*. What else has she screwed up?" I clenched my teeth. "Look, it's a very, very long story. Are you at your office?"

"Yes, but—"

"Don't go anywhere. I'll be there in fifteen minutes." I was only a few miles from school, so after making sure I carried a wallet with cash, I flagged down a taxi. I was not going to spend any more time than necessary away from Chris. Images blurred through the windshield as the wipers failed to keep up with the downpour, but I didn't care. The city had never looked more beautiful. Even the squeaking of the wipers, the scratchy radio coming from the front seat, the smell of old, wet leather....all were precious to me.

I called my mom.

"Hey, Jamie! So good to hear from you. We've been worried sick."

At the sound of my mom's cheerful voice, tears began streaming down my face. "Why have you been worried?"

"Chris told us about that freaky accident, but she said you were too upset to talk. Your dad and I nearly bought tickets to show up at your apartment—sorry, your flat. I love that word. But Chris kept insisting you'd be fine. Then when you finally did call us, you just didn't sound like yourself."

I ached to tell her the truth. "I'm doing better," I choked out.

"Doesn't sound that way. I can tell you're crying."

I wiped my face. "It's just good to hear your voice."

"That's it. We're coming. Your dad can get a few days off, and I can get a sub for summer school."

"No, it's okay. I'm okay. Just really, really tired."

In the silence I could hear my mom comparing my voice with my words. "You're sure."

"Absolutely." What if another storm were to whisk me away and return Blanche while my parents were here? Would she be kind? Would she pretend she was me? Somehow I doubted it. "I'm sorry you've been kept out of the loop. I'll call more often, okay?"

"We'd love that," Mom said. She filled me in on my brothers' lives and my dad's latest home repair calamity.

By the time we were done talking, I finally felt at home. I was here, in the twenty-first century, and I needed to make sure that's where I remained.

I tossed the driver the fare plus a huge tip and stepped out into the rain right in front of Chris's building. I splashed through a huge puddle, black water reflecting the gray day, and ducked when thunder boomed overhead. I only had time to cry "No!" before darkness descended again.

❖

I staggered a few steps, nearly thrown off balance from my drenched skirts and looked around. I stood just inside one of the arched entrances to Whitehall Palace. Furious, I threw back my head and howled at the world through clenched teeth. The sound shivered through me and sank deep into my soul. Such rage pounded through me that I wanted to hit someone.

Rosemary stood in front of me. Judging by her hand cradling a pink cheek, and the horrified way she stared at me, I might have already done that. Vincent barked at me, his lip curled back in a snarl.

"Hush, Vincent," one of the women snapped.

"Rosemary was just trying to help you," said another. Damn it. Blanche must have slapped poor Rosemary. How did I apologize for something I hadn't done? I tore off my soggy cloak and flung it across the room. It knocked over a small carved table against the wall; candles and brass holders clattered across the stone floor.

Vincent now approached me, stiff-legged and growling. The soft fur along his back stiffened with rage.

"Vincent, it's me," I said.

I turned and stormed down the hall, up the stairs, and into my room. Lady Mary was being helped into a dress for that evening's performance by a theater troupe. Her eyes widened at my servant's dress, which I yanked off and fired against the wall. It hit with a hard, wet slap and slid to the floor. I changed into a dry chemise and climbed into bed.

"My, we are moody this day," Lady Mary cooed.

"Bite me," I muttered. How could life be so unfair?

Chapter Eleven

The next day I felt thick and unresponsive, as if a poisonous evil sludge ran through my veins. The thought of being Blanche Nottingham for one more second sent waves of nausea sweeping through me. And food didn't help. Midmorning I sat at a long, dark table with the other women and glared at them as they ate. The woman across from me pawed through her food with her hands, and then belched so forcefully I felt the gust. Apparently, forks and table manners had not yet reached England. Next to her, another woman was enthusiastically picking apart a goose leg, grease staining her sleeve all the way up to her elbow. Forks and table manners and napkins. I nibbled delicately at a piece of blackberry tart. Without a fork, I ended up with berry-stained fingers and bits of seeds on my generous bust. I longed for the days when food that missed my mouth could drop directly into my lap.

Feeling slightly woozy from two glasses of wine, I knew I couldn't sit through hours in the presence chamber with courtiers, nor in the private chambers no matter what the Queen wanted. Pissing her off wasn't a good idea, since Queen Elizabeth had a temper that flamed hotter than a solar flare. Last week when one of her ladies revealed she'd married without Elizabeth's permission, the Queen confiscated the woman's gowns and jewels, then had the guards deposit the poor woman in the middle of King Street. Another day, a servant's clumsiness so enraged Elizabeth that she'd flung the entire soup tureen at him.

So instead of waiting on the Queen that morning, I slipped out during the after-meal confusion and wandered the palace, as if the answer to my problem might be lodged in one of the dozens of rooms, perhaps on a huge whiteboard that said, "Jamie, here's your pathway home." Or, "Jamie, it will be all right." I would even accept a faint note written in the dust coating an unused table: "Jamie, don't despair." I found nothing, of course.

Vincent now trotted happily at my side. I didn't know if he'd been so fierce because Blanche had struck Rosemary, or because he'd just been responding to Blanche and couldn't instantaneously detect our switch.

From an empty room, I moved closer to the window to catch the refreshing breeze and watch two gardeners working down below. I'd been so close, so damned close. Four weeks of 1560, and less than thirty minutes of 2017.

I'd been here nearly four weeks. I did the math. Blanche's body would be getting a period soon. How on earth did women in this time deal with that? Could I ask Harriet without alarming her? Blanche was in her mid-twenties, so she would be expected to know what to do. When I left that room and stopped in the main corridor to examine a painting, Elizabeth's voice, raw with fury, blasted from another room. "Blanche Nottingham, show yourself. We demand you come to us at once." The voice echoed down a nearby hall, which meant Elizabeth would soon round the corner.

I froze. Should I flee or stay? I forced myself to move and slipped into the nearest open door, then stopped. Harriet dusted the massive desk dominating the room. Her head jerked up in alarm.

"Nicole?"

"Hark, Blanche Nottingham, where are you? God's blood, you will stand and face us."

I waved a hand toward the approaching voice. "Harriet, she's really steamed at me."

Her pale skin whitened even more. "*You* are Lady Blanche?"

"I'm sorry I lied. But please help me hide. I need to give the Queen time to cool off."

Giving me a look that said helping me was the last thing she'd planned to do today, she motioned me closer. "Here, under the desk."

She helped me crawl under the desk, not an easy task when you're wearing miles of skirt. I pulled Vincent up against my chest, and he sighed happily. Then when Elizabeth's bellow was nearly upon us, Harriet bunched up her skirt and joined us.

We said nothing to each other. Harriet smelled of soap and lemons. My nostrils drank in the scents with a thirst that surprised me. Vincent, however, stank of meat and sweat so I resolved that my next trip to the pond would include a dog bath.

"Blanche! We are vexed to the limit with you. Are you in here?"

While skirts bustled against furniture, Elizabeth's shoes clicked on the polished wooden floor and her entourage whispered assurances to the Queen that Blanche would indeed be found.

A number of skirts swept past the desk under which we hid. Vincent's eyes were huge, but he remained silent. The absurdity hit me and began bubbling up my chest, threatening to explode like the cork from a shaken bottle of Brut champagne. I caught Harriet's eye, and she covered her mouth so no laughter would escape.

One Sunday when I was ten, and once again forced to attend church with my family, the stomach of a woman in the pew ahead of us growled like an angry cat. My brothers and I began to giggle behind our hands but didn't dare look at each other or all would be lost. To this day Mom still told the story of how the pew literally shook with the power of her three children's repressed laughter.

That same uncontrolled hysteria now infected me as my shoulders began to shake. Tears leaked out, even though the consequences of being discovered while Elizabeth was in high anger could be devastating.

Luckily, Harriet reached over and sharply pinched the back of my hand. I winced and glared at her, but the pain derailed my mirth so effectively that I could relax.

A minute later, we were once again alone in the room.

"Thank you," I whispered.

Harriet just glared at me. "You're a horrible person. Why did you lie to me?"

I raised an eyebrow.

"You're not Nicole, you're Lady Blanche Nottingham. And I swam and talked with you as if we were equals. Not only could I lose my job for such familiarity, but I feel like an idiot."

I reached for Harriet's hand and when she tried to tug herself free, held on. "I'm sorry for lying to you, but who cares if I'm Lady Blanche? We're just two women who need to wash our hair more often than others. I really had a good time the other night, and I want to do it again. It won't be as frightening walking through the park if we're together." I squeezed her hand. "I really need a friend."

Harriet's white skin stood out in the shadows under the desk. She pursed her lips, such a cute look I wanted to reach over and caress her cheek, but she was still too angry for that. Even though we were crammed together under the desk, she held herself apart. "Apology accepted, but you understand that you and I cannot be friends."

I smiled as wickedly as I could. "Just try and stop me."

She laughed in spite of herself. "I should leave now."

I stayed her with a touch. "I'm not ready yet. In fact, hiding here with you like a couple of naughty children has been the most normal I've felt in too many weeks."

Harriet nodded, eyes dark in the shadows beneath the desk. "But the others told me that you have been with the Queen since she took the throne, that you are her favorite."

My throat tightened. How I wished I could confess everything to Harriet and not have her think me insane. "Yes, well, I am telling the truth when I say that my life is as foreign to me as if I'd found myself living on the moon."

Harriet's appreciative laughter fed my relief at finding a palace resident who didn't hate Blanche or fear her or expect her to conspire against the Queen. "No more lies," she said. Then she rolled onto her knees and crawled out from under the desk.

Grunting with the effort and hampered by my blasted stomacher, I did the same, wondering if not mentioning that I was from the future constituted a lie. By the time I stood, smoothed down my skirts, and adjusted my breasts so they weren't in danger of popping out like two rosy Jack-in-the-boxes, Harriet was gone.

Vincent and I stayed out of Elizabeth's way for a few more hours, then we decided it was time to face the music. I inhaled for courage, then strolled into her chamber, where the room was aglow with a fire and the women were gathered around sewing. Elizabeth was eating a slice of some sort of fruit.

Everyone looked up, faces alarmed at my arrival. Elizabeth raised her eyes from her book. "Ah, here is our Spark, come to entertain us. Sit beside us and play. We are tired of councilors and courtiers and battles over our matrimonial state. Why will these bloody fools not leave us alone?" She tossed Vincent a treat from the small table beside her. Whatever had gotten her royal knickers in a bunch earlier had obviously been forgotten.

I perched on the nearest stool and picked up the stringed instrument with a shaking hand. The only music I knew how to play was an old Beatles song on the piano. Blanche Nottingham needed to take over again because the more time I spent with people less easily fooled, like Elizabeth, the greater the risk that I would lose my position.

But when I placed one hand on the neck and the other against the strings, intending only to strum tunelessly, my fingers took over and played something soft and light. I couldn't take my eyes off my hands. I was playing the lute! Clearly, Blanche's body remembered.

I cleared my throat as I played. "Someone mentioned that you sought me earlier."

"Yes, and when we could not find you, it put us in a terrible temper."

"You weren't angry with me over something else?"

"No. Do not repeat this, but we do recognize that sometimes our royal person can get too easily piqued when events do not go precisely as we wish them to. We could not find you so we grew angry."

"I'm sorry to be the source of such emotions," I said. "But if I'd heard you I certainly would have responded. It's not as if I were hiding from you under a desk or something."

Elizabeth laughed. "Ho, that is an image to make us smile, that someone dare hide from her sovereign under a desk."

It felt good to make Elizabeth laugh. When she finally stopped chortling, she laid a hand on my shoulder. "Ah, our beloved Spark, we cannot recall the reason we sought you, but we are sure it was to lighten our heart." She sat back in her chair. "Kat tells us you sent comfort to one of the Tower prisoners. That was unusually thoughtful of you."

"Thank you, ma'am. I have another friend I would help as well. Harriet Blankenship works in the laundry, but her skills are wasted there. She can read and has an excellent speaking voice. With your majesty's leave, I thought she might join us of a night and read to you when you grow weary."

The queen narrowed her eyes, then nodded. "We would enjoy that. But, Blanche, all your caring for these people marks you a changed woman from the Blanche we knew but a month ago. Perhaps it is time for you to direct such love toward a husband. You are well past the age."

I blinked, and Elizabeth laughed. "Fear not, dear Spark. We have no plans to marry you off just yet, but I think it is time to begin considering a husband for you."

The ladies murmured in agreement. I cleared my throat. "Ma'am, while I appreciate your concern, I do not think I am yet ready to marry. I would prefer to continue serving you."

"You can do that as a married woman." The queen motioned me forward, then clasped my chin and pulled me so close our noses touched. Her breath smelled of venison and ale. "Dearest Blanche, when the time comes that we want you to marry, you shall do so as a devoted citizen of this realm. Do you understand us?"

"Yes, ma'am." She released me and I retreated to my stool. Crap. I was getting pulled deeper and deeper into Blanche's life.

CHAPTER TWELVE

The days blurred into weeks as the line of notches on my table leg lengthened. We were always required to be close at hand should Elizabeth want to do something. We all crowded into coaches when she wanted to go out and be seen by her people. We went with her when she watched a tilting or tennis match. Tennis in 1560. Who knew? And most of the time, Dudley was there with us. The center of attention most of the time, the tall, straight-backed man had an easy laugh. He sported a trim black beard and gray eyes that sparkled. Three times now, when the Queen was busy talking with someone else, he'd caught my eye and winked.

Robert Dudley, the man Elizabeth yearned to marry. I struggled to dredge up details from the books I'd read. He was *not* nobility, but he'd pissed off many nobles with his arrogant habit of inserting himself into decisions without being asked. He wasn't on the Queen's council, yet he acted as if he led it, as if being the Queen's favorite placed his opinions above all others. He also acted as Elizabeth's lovelorn suitor and she lapped it up like a kitten lapped cream.

Elizabeth's eyes almost always followed him, no matter where the activity, and her face softened whenever he looked at her. Note to self: Do not encourage Robert Dudley. It would be an excellent way to get kicked out of the palace. Life was bearable only because I had food and a place to live. But if I displeased Elizabeth and she "fired" me, I'd have nowhere to go. Maybe I'd have to knock on Ray's cell door and ask to bunk with him.

The more I encountered Dudley, the more I agreed with Cecil and Winston. The country didn't need an ego-driven Master of the Horse swathed in ermine to be its king.

At least our activities involved movement and being outdoors. My least favorite time was sitting in the presence chamber, mingling as Lady Blanche Nottingham was expected to do. Being a courtier was like playing a card game without knowing any of the rules. Certain men smiled politely, others gave me such cold looks I even shivered once. Blanche had obviously alienated many people at court, and I was stuck with whatever she'd done. While the room hummed with voices and laughter, it also vibrated with tension. People were fearful of making a misstep, while at the same time hoping to witness the mistakes of others.

It felt a bit like the scene my roommate Mary and I used to take in Friday and Saturday nights at our favorite campus bar. Mary called it visiting the zoo, maintaining that if you spent enough time perched on the corner bar stools you could witness the full range of human interaction—falling in love, falling out of love, awkward conversations, money fights, jubilation, depression. Mary was a great student of human behavior, and I wish I'd paid more attention to her pearls of wisdom so I could better "read" this crowd of courtiers.

I'd been here long enough to know that the man in the ermine cape in his late thirties, who often bent his head in consultation with Elizabeth, was William Cecil. Elizabeth's trusted secretary was also her spymaster until he died an old man. He might be someone I should befriend, so when he passed me early one afternoon, I stood and smoothed out my skirts. "Lord Cecil," I said, my mouth dry. "You're looking good this day…I mean, you're looking well."

No one had yet commented on my English, which would have sounded like a foreign language, but there must have been enough of Blanche still in this body for communication to work. I probed my mind gently but could not feel any mind but my own.

The man's gaze chilled me to the bone. "Do not expect your wiles to work on me, Mistress Nottingham. Your father, the earl, was no friend of mine, nor the Queen's. That your head still rests on that pretty neck is a surprise to me. Our Queen is generous to a fault."

I forced a laugh. "Come now. Let's forget the past. No hard feelings, whatever happened. Friends?"

Cecil leaned closer, so I did the same, imagining he could see down my gown all the way to my navel. "Step lightly, girl. You may find yourself up to the neck in quicksand and none in this room will lift a finger to save you." In a swirl of brown velvet cloak, the man stalked away. Damn it. Besides the Queen, was there anyone who liked Blanche?

After he left I spent some time fuming about my gowns. They made women so dependent on everyone around them. Were I to fall in this gown, I would be like a turtle stuck on its back, unable to right itself. The stays and boards were too stiff to allow any natural movement. It struck me that the gowns were the sixteenth century equivalent of S&M chains and tight black leather. Apparently, restraint was erotic in any century, at least to some people.

Late afternoon of an endless day filled with stupid courtly activity, someone pinched the back of my arm. I whirled to face Lord Winston wearing an unpleasant smile. "We meet again."

I scowled. "Another perfectly fine day ruined."

Now his smile was real. "The more I disgust you, the deeper runs my desire. It has been six weeks since I took you in the park. I wish to do so again."

Hell's gates. I growled low in my throat when it hit me that he'd said "take you *in* the park," not "take you *to* the park." I didn't know who to be more disgusted with, Winston or Blanche.

Winston dismissed my anger with a wave and leaned closer. "Why have you not sent me word? We are tired of waiting."

I twisted free. "Dudley comes and goes from the palace without warning."

"We must create the moment we want."

"Yeah, I've been thinking about that. I've decided to bow out, since—"

Winston moved in so close others might have thought he was about to kiss me, but I could see the flint burning in his eyes so knew differently. "You are not going to bow out, my sweet little cunt. What would the Queen do if she were to learn that her virginal Blanche could no longer be sold off to a bridegroom as pure? When I reveal what you and I have done, you will lose all prospects of an advantageous marriage. Your father's debts have left you existing solely on the Queen's good graces."

"God's teeth, you are such a prick." One eyebrow shot up, but he looked amused rather than threatened. God, I hated this man. "I'm not going to help you murder Dudley."

"Perhaps we will proceed without you, but you will be implicated nonetheless." Winston bowed, a movement dripping with sarcasm, and moved to another cluster of courtiers.

I closed my eyes for just a second, willing the tableau to change when I opened them. It did not. I retreated to the nearest window bench and leaned back against the wall, welcoming the cool against my steaming back. When Vincent hopped onto my lap, I spread his ears out across my skirt and began picking out bits of leaves he'd picked up outside. I wished he could come with me when I returned to my own body, but that was impossible. When Vincent sighed with contentment, I sighed with boredom and a smidgen of worry. I had friends in Ray, Harriet, and, I think, Jacob, but none were as powerful as Lord Winston or William Cecil.

I flexed my hands and straightened my back. Hope. Don't lose hope, Jamie Maddox.

I imagined that hope was a balloon floating by that I could reach up, grab, and hold tightly to my chest.

Chapter Thirteen

The next day, the sky darkened wonderfully, and I spent a great deal of time out on a west balcony watching the storm approach. Would this one contain lightning? Could my ordeal soon be over?

I'd always loved storms. My friend Ashley and I would stand inside my open garage and perform song and dance routines with umbrellas to Queen, George Michael, and Uncle Cracker. We'd leap out into the rain and sing as loudly as we could, punch drunk with the knowledge that no one could hear us.

But this storm refused to land. Instead, I spent most of the day stuck inside with the other women listening to the buzz about the attempt someone had made on Robert Dudley's life the night before. As a result, security had increased throughout the palace. I hung back at the edges of the different groups, managing to piece together that at dinner Dudley had put a piece of meat in his mouth then spit it out when he tasted something off. He tossed the chunk to the nearest dog—thank heavens Vincent had been with me—who foamed at the mouth and fell over dead one minute later. Dudley laughed it off as a mistake, but that afternoon Cecil took all the ladies-in-waiting into the Queen's chamber and warned us not to accept any gifts on behalf of the Queen, especially none that she might wear next to her skin since gloves and scarves and elaborate lacy collars could have been soaked in poison.

Lord Winston was not in court that day, the coward. But I spent hours worrying the inside of my cheek. If Winston managed to kill Dudley—with or without my help—it could change the path of history. With Dudley dead, Elizabeth would likely give up hope of marrying for love and yield to the pressure from her council to marry, especially to England's advantage. If Elizabeth married, her husband would rule as king, and she would never become the ruler she was meant to be. History would be altered forever. I hated being the only one who knew that.

After an evening meal of venison soup in a bowl of fresh bread, which was more edible than lunch, we sat around the Queen's chamber stitching, which I hated. When my full stomach gurgled loudly enough that the Queen snickered, I prayed my earlier nausea wouldn't return. The storm still hadn't hit, but I would find a way to get outside once it did.

Kat Ashley entered, leading Harriet straight to the Queen. I'd expected Harriet to be intimidated, but she held her head high as she looked around the room to take it all in. Unexpected pride warmed me as Harriet's eyes shone with interest and excitement, not fear. Her hair was pulled back and covered with an ivory kerchief. Her brown dress was a bit worn but clean and well made.

She curtsied deeply before the Queen.

"Rise, my dear. Lady Blanche has informed us that you are skilled at reading."

"Lady Blanche is very kind. I am passable, but I do love books."

Elizabeth pulled a book from the stack on the table next to her. "We are ready to hear some Latin poetry this evening."

The women around me tittered and my jaw tightened. While a country girl might have learned to read English, it was extremely unlikely that she would know Latin. Then I remembered reading that Elizabeth enjoyed putting others on the spot.

But Harriet curtsied once more, then graciously sank onto the tapestry stool nearest the Queen. She opened the small, leatherbound book, flipped through several pages, then began speaking Latin in a clear, confident voice.

The Queen stared, a bit slack-jawed, then threw back her head and laughed. She began to clap, and we quickly joined her. "Read on. We must confess we are astounded. Our prank has come to naught thanks to your abilities."

We all returned to our stitching as Harriet read. I had no idea what the words meant, but her voice held me spellbound. The Queen rested her head back on the chair, now and then mouthing some of the words.

As she turned the page, Harriet caught my eye and winked. I was so charmed I wanted to throw my arms around her but managed to keep the needle going instead. While I'd been impressed with the women I'd met—for the most part, kind and intelligent—Harriet intrigued me like no other.

Thirty minutes later, when out of the corner of my eye I saw lightning streak across the sky, I was ready for the thunder that cracked overhead, but a few of the ladies yelped and Harriet stood up so fast she dropped the Queen's book. Her face had gone splotchy red. "A storm," she said, her voice no longer strong but quavering.

"We are safe here," I said, my mind racing for a way to leave the room without angering the Queen.

Thunder rolled through the palace, rattling a few candlesticks. "Oh no!" Harriet gathered up her skirts and fled the room.

We all turned toward Elizabeth, tense as patients awaiting the bad news. No one left the Queen's presence without permission. No one.

"Well, the poor girl seems to have lost her head." Elizabeth's face softened. "But our dear brother Edward had the same fear of storms, so the girl is not to be punished for her abrupt departure. Lady Blanche, make sure she isn't cowering under a dusty desk somewhere."

Perfect. I curtsied and left as quickly as Harriet had. While I should have sought out Harriet to comfort her, I needed to take advantage of the storm.

I hurried down the stairs and out into the garden. Rain needled my face, my chest, the backs of my hands. I closed my eyes and lifted my face up to the storm. The warm rain ran down my arms, and my skirts grew heavy with water; it felt as if gravity were trying to suck me into the earth. Vincent stood under the arched doorway with his forehead wrinkled in worry and his ears back.

"My lady!" a male servant called from the open door. "Please come in. Think of your health."

I turned and waved to him. "I'm fine," I called. "This is just something I need to do." Once I returned to the future, Blanche could deal with convincing the entire palace that she wasn't insane.

After another ten minutes of rain, I was soaked to the skin but still here, still in 1560, still stuck in Blanche's plump, unwieldy body. Why didn't the lightning take me? Exhausted, I dragged myself back into the palace. Damn it, damn it, *damn it.*

My skirts clung to my legs and threatened to trip me at every step. It didn't help that Vincent danced in a circle around me. Distracted, I managed to take a wrong turn somewhere and was in a hallway I didn't recognize, having to squint because the two candle sconces were losing the battle against the dark.

Then a door flew open at the end of the hallway, and a woman stumbled in from the rain. When she passed the first candle, I could see it was Harriet.

"Hell's gate, Harriet, you're soaked."

She stood before me, her face buried in her hands, her shoulders shaking. I pulled her close. "There's no need to be afraid, but surely you know that running outside makes you less safe, not more."

She sobbed against my shoulder.

"What's wrong?" I asked.

Harriet pulled back to look at me. Her hair had come undone and was plastered against her face and neck. "Believe me, I would tell you if I could."

"Has someone hurt you?"

"No, no. I must go." She jerked free and disappeared down a side hallway, her wet slippers slapping against the tile. I sagged against the wall for a minute, then retraced my steps. What an awful night. Harriet had been driven mad with fear by the storm, and I was still in 1560.

I finally found my way back to a familiar hallway and encountered Rosemary dusting a painting. "Oh my," she said, scanning the soggy me.

As she helped me up to my room, getting herself wet in the process, I apologized once again for slapping her days earlier, but she tutted as if it were nothing. She untied and unlaced me while I stood there shivering, then she lifted the wet chemise over my protesting head. She toweled me down, then helped me into my linen nightgown and robe.

My heart hurt from my failure. Why did one storm sweep me back into my real life, and another leave me here? Rosemary left as Kat Ashley appeared in the doorway. "The Queen has requested you share her bed this evening."

"I share her what?"

"Do not be ignorant. You know you are her favorite. It shall be you and Lady Clinton."

"Three of us?" I squeaked.

"Why have you begun lately to play the idiot? Off you go. And this time, try not to be so entertaining. The last time you slept with the Queen, you made her majesty laugh so hard she nearly choked."

Great, just great. If there were any situation in which I would be revealed as not Blanche, this would be it.

I made my way to the Queen's bedchamber. The stone floors were frigid, and by the time I reached my destination, so were my feet. Lady Clinton was already there undressing the Queen, so I hurried to help. I knew how to perform this task, since it was all about undoing laces and ties. The dark room was lit only by four candles. Even thought it was August, a fire raged in the fireplace, and it felt good.

The Queen sighed as I unlaced her incredibly tight stomacher. "Ah, Blanche, dressing like a queen can be wearisome."

"Yes, ma'am," I said dutifully as I searched for the ties holding up the skirts.

Elizabeth peered down her nose at me. "That is all you have? Yes, ma'am? You have no biting comment about the unfairness of parading our narrow waist before our prospective suitors?" Her voice was light, but the tightness around her eyes revealed her worry for Dudley's brush with death by poison.

"No, ma'am."

The skirts dropped, and I gathered them in my arms. Outside, as rain blasted the window, I prayed for lightning even though I was uncertain it would do the trick since I'd already been rejected once by this storm.

Lady Clinton folded back the bedding while Elizabeth seated herself on a flowered upholstered stool and looked at me. On the table next to her were a massive silver-handled brush and a series of combs. I grabbed the brush and began searching Elizabeth's head for the pins holding up her hair. I managed to take it down and begin brushing the glorious red locks without appearing too inept, but my hands shook. Elizabeth's hair was lush, glistening with red-gold highlights. I stopped, sick when I remembered that Elizabeth would fall gravely ill from small pox only two years from now. Near death, she would name Dudley as the "protector of the kingdom." She would recover, but the disease would leave her skin pocked, her hair thinned, and her scalp entirely bald in spots. I swallowed hard as the thick, red waves slid through my palms.

I blew out the candles, then climbed into the bed with Elizabeth and bit off a shriek at the cold, hard mattress. With the Queen in the middle, I lay on my back, goose down quilt pulled up to my chin, while Lady Clinton chatted about something that had happened in the gardens this afternoon. I racked my brain for a story I could share with the Queen, but all I had were 1) I was from the future; 2) I was not really Blanche Nottingham, but only inhabiting her body; 3) Winston and I were conspiring to do something treasonous; and 4) Robert Dudley had flirted with me. None of these would make a royal bedtime story.

When Lady Clinton fell silent, Elizabeth sighed and cuddled against me. "Tell us something funny, or even better, outrageous. We must divert our thoughts from useless worry."

My head was only inches from the woman considered to be the greatest queen England had ever had and possibly the greatest ruler. In the firelight, her green eyes were tired but bright. The bed had begun to warm, but when Elizabeth planted her icy feet against my legs, I gasped. "God's *blood*, your feet are cold."

It was a girl who chuckled in delight, not the Queen of England. Who would ever believe that I would be cuddling up with Queen Elizabeth I? I felt so comfortable that I could have been at home with Chris on the sofa, both of us huddled under the big floral comforter we kept by the TV.

My throat tightened. "I seem to be fresh out of outrageous tonight."

She sighed, nestling deeper into her pillow. "Then tell us a story, any story."

I could think of only one. "Once upon a time there was a boy named Harry. He lived in the cupboard beneath his uncle's stairs. His aunt and uncle and cousin treated Harry horribly, like a servant, because they were afraid of him. They were worried Harry might be a wizard like his parents."

Elizabeth smiled. "Ah, a wizard story. Our favorite."

I had gotten Harry to Diagon Alley and was deep into a description of this hidden part of London, when there was a commotion outside the door. Men's voices, then laughter. The door burst open and in strode Robert Dudley and a servant, both bearing torches. Lady Clinton shrieked and pulled up the covers, but Elizabeth sat up in her nightgown, nipples hard against the linen. Dudley swept off his hat and bowed with an elaborate flourish "I am unable to sleep tonight until I steal one more glimpse of Your Grace's face." He straightened, eyes sparkling at Elizabeth.

"Oh, Robin, I have been so distraught—" She stopped, pressing the back of one hand to her mouth until she could gather herself back into the Queen. She plumped up her pillow and sat back against the wall. "Well, Robin, we would hate to be the cause of your insomnia. Perhaps you should ride your new mare if you are unable to sleep."

Robert gave a sly smile and sat on the foot of the bed. "Oh, thoughts of...*riding* would make it even more impossible to sleep."

Elizabeth roared with laughter and flung her pillow at him.

My heart raced. First, this was wrong. Rumors about Elizabeth and Dudley would plague her reign. Second, what if Winston found out that Dudley had been here, and I hadn't told him? But I'd had no warning.

What would Blanche do? I wanted to cower under the covers with Lady Clinton, but instead I leapt out of bed, grabbed my own pillow, and began beating him back toward the door. Everyone laughed as I managed to finally get Dudley out of the room. "And don't return until your thoughts of riding involve only horses." I slammed the door in his grinning face.

Elizabeth lay back in the bed, still laughing. "Oh, Blanche, there is nothing like a good pillow fight. Let us fall asleep with Robin's smile in our eyes."

I crawled back into bed. Within minutes, Lady Clinton was snoring softly from the other side of the bed.

Elizabeth sighed. "He is a wicked man to burst into our room, is he not?"

"Very wicked," I said. Thunder boomed in the background, making me think I should try the storm again.

"But oh, so wickedly handsome." Silence settled over us, then the Queen sighed again. "'Tis a cruel twist of fate that we must love a man whom others insist we must not take as our husband."

I propped myself up on an elbow. "Why do they resist him?"

The bed rustled as Elizabeth turned. "He is a commoner, and the people would never accept a commoner for a king."

"Can't you, well, make him a noble? Make him Sir Robert Dudley?" Elizabeth would do precisely that in a few years.

I could feel her turning the idea over in her mind. "Yes, we could do that. But there is much opposition to Robin as our consort." Her voice softened. "We wonder why, in this world, we have so much sorrow and tribulation and so little joy. Robin brings us joy, yet many men, Lord Winston amongst them, speak foully of him even though they know it upsets us."

I stiffened. "Do you know why Lord Winston objects?"

"He believes it would be bad for the realm, yet Robin has a good head on his shoulders and we enjoy having him around." Her voice slowed as sleep began to take her. "And we do love him so...."

I felt sick to my stomach as Blanche's life tightened around me like a noose.

"Blanche?"

"Yes, ma'am?"

"Will you tell me more of poor Harry's story tomorrow?"

"Certainly. Pleasant dreams."

"And you as well." She snuggled closer. "We love that you can both make us laugh and, with your stories, make us think. You are our beloved Spark."

The Queen's breath lightly brushed my hands as sleep approached. I liked this woman and would be sad to leave her. I would wait another ten minutes, then slip from the bed and into the storm. But as I lay there, listening to the Queen breathe, thunder boomed directly overhead and suddenly I was *yanked*—hard, rude, lightning fast—up into a darkness blacker than night and colder than ice.

Chapter Fourteen

The sense of zooming faster than light came to an end. I opened my eyes and inhaled Chris's scent—Aveda shampoo, Obsession perfume. We were in bed, spooning, with my arm flung over her. I held my breath, waiting for the hum of my earlier dream, but it didn't come. I lifted my head, then kissed Chris's neck, choking back a sob. I was back!

Despite my joy, the sense of disorientation gave me a headache. To instantaneously exchange one set of sights, sounds, and smells for another was insane.

"Blanche, you are frickin' amazing," Chris whispered. My eyes widened. "It's been over five weeks since your accident. I thought we'd never make love again. But these last few nights have been unlike anything I've ever known." She pulled me closer as I tried to sort this out. Chris just had sex with Blanche. Jealousy flared, and I wanted to wring Blanche Nottingham's neck.

"So everything feels…normal again?" Except that Chris had just called me Blanche, which was anything but normal.

Chris kissed my wrist. "Nothing feels normal, and that's why I love it. You were pretty out of it those first two weeks, but you've really popped back. In fact, you're better than ever. You have energy. You have drive. You really took what I said to heart. You're bubbling over with ambition. I *love* that."

I needed to watch a movie of the last five weeks. How had Blanche adjusted so well? I, at least, knew something about 1560 from my studies, but there was no way Blanche could know anything about the future. She was obviously better at adapting than I was.

"So you think I'm doing okay?" I asked.

"Are you kidding me? You've stopped working on those stupid Froggity paintings. You're starting to write. It's all so exciting."

Another clap of thunder made us both jump. Unable to just sit there and let myself get sucked back in time, I crawled from bed and reached for my robe, which rested, as it always did, on the small chair against the wall. "I'll be back," I murmured and ran to the bathroom. The shock of seeing my own face brought tears to my eyes, but when I opened the robe, a plumper me presented itself. "Hell's gates," I snapped.

I wandered through our flat, the streetlights shining a path from room to room. In the kitchen I touched the coffeemaker, the microwave. "A stove," I murmured. I opened the fridge and downed a glass of milk so cold I wanted to remember this moment forever. And water! I whirled and filled my glass with water, drinking three of them before my stomach began to gurgle. Why did all this taste so good, as if I'd gone without it for weeks even though my body had been here all along, free to eat and drink anything? How many of our desires exist only in our minds, having nothing to do with our bodies?

And there was my cell phone. I picked it up, anxious to call my mom again and tell her everything. But I didn't. I needed more time to find a way to explain it.

Finally sated of my own world and feeling the past begin to fade, I returned to bed and caressed Chris's shoulder.

"Chris, could we talk?"

"It's after midnight, babe." Chris nestled deeper into the covers.

"I know, but it's really important."

Muttering, Chris rolled over, blue eyes nearly black in the dark, face open and relaxed. She smelled of sex. She smelled of me. She plumped up her pillow. "What?"

"Could you describe everything that I've been doing since the accident in Rajamani's lab?"

Chris's eyebrows hitched halfway up her forehead. "Why?"

"Humor me, please. Let's just say I want to make sure my version of reality matches yours."

She shrugged. "You spent that day and night in the hospital, then I brought you home the next day. You were pretty out of it, as if everything around you were foreign. I had to show you how to flush the toilet, turn on the water, run the microwave. I was really worried about you because you didn't want to be touched or held. You just crawled under the covers and stayed there for a week."

I nodded. Blanche and I had both avoided reality by hiding in bed. Blanche must have been frightened out of her wits, perhaps believing she'd been transported to some sort of hell.

"Then the second week you got better. You started talking to me. You soaked up TV shows and movies like a desert soaks up water. You asked so many questions you drove me insane. Your interest in the Tudors flared up again, and you began skimming through all your books about Elizabeth I. You asked me to remind you how to use your computer and how to research on the Web."

I shuddered. Now that Blanche was back in 1560, what would she do with the information she'd learned? Would she see that killing Dudley was a really bad idea? Would she somehow harm Elizabeth and change history?

But I was impressed at the woman's quick recovery. Would I have been so brave as to embrace the strange world in which I found myself? Back in 1560, all I'd done was stay out of trouble.

"And this week?"

Chris's lazy grin told me all I needed to know about the sexual component of our relationship. "You've been amazing, babe. Insatiable." She sighed happily, and a pang of something I couldn't identify nearly broke me in two. How could I be jealous of myself?

"And then a few days ago you showed me the first three chapters of your novel. God, Jamie—oops, Blanche, I had no idea you could write." She reached for my hand. "You really took what I said to heart. I wanted you to want more for yourself, and you're doing it. You're reaching out in ways that would have terrified the old you."

"You mean the me before Rajamani's equipment zapped me nearly to death."

"That's a bit dramatic, don't you think? You got a jolt of electricity, that's all. And it was good for you. Now you're writing a novel."

"A novel." I shook my head. This Blanche was unbelievable. "And you like what you've read?"

"It's fucking brilliant. *Sleeping with the Queen* will reach out and grab everyone."

"That's the title?" I laughed weakly. How could this be happening? "Okay, Chris, I appreciate the recap, but I need to tell you something."

She waited.

"The reason I needed you to explain the last weeks is because I haven't been here."

"You were certainly out of it that first week, but—"

"No, I literally haven't been here. The instant Rajamani's equipment sparked in the storm my mind—my consciousness—was transported." I took a deep breath. "I know this sounds insane, but it's true and I need you to believe me. I woke up in the body of a woman in 1560, one of Queen Elizabeth's ladies-in-waiting. Her name was Blanche Nottingham."

Chris chuckled. "Is this the story you'll tell people to explain your pen name?"

My eyes fluttered shut. "The pen name I'm using is Blanche Nottingham?"

"I think it's cute."

I moved onto my knees, my eyes boring into hers. How could I convince her? "It's not cute, Chris. I've been stuck over four hundred and fifty years in the past, in Blanche's body. You can't bathe there every day. You have to pee and crap in a chamber pot or in a stinking little closet suspended over a pit on the ground below. Drinking water is contaminated by all the shit, literally, that runs into the Thames, so everyone drinks wine and ale and is almost always a little drunk."

Chris sat up now, frowning in anger. "Look, I know you don't think much of my interest in neurobiology, or in Dr. Raj's interest in locating our consciousness and perhaps transporting it someday, but that's no reason to make fun of us like this."

I threw up my hands. "I'm not making fun of anyone. This is the truth. This really happened." I told her about the London I'd seen, about Ray Lexvold locked in the Salt Tower, about meeting Harriet and finally having a friend. I told her about the food, which I hated, and the beds, which were uncomfortable, and about little Vincent adopting me as his own.

Chris folded her arms. "You've just read all of this last week in one of your books."

"No, I've been living it, Chris."

With a grunt, Chris rolled out of bed and grabbed her pillow and a blanket from her chair. "Look, life has been pretty great this week, and now the old Jamie has come back to spoil everything, and I don't appreciate it. You sound like a crazy person so I'm going to sleep on the sofa."

Stunned she didn't believe me, I pounded my pillow. No, wait. I tried to put myself in her situation. Of course it sounded crazy. She just needed a little time, but eventually I'd be able to convince her. I sprang off the bed and paced our small room until I saw my cell phone on the dresser and called Ashley. She could always make me feel better no matter what.

"Hey, Ashley, it's me," I said when she answered.

"Yeah, I know. The only reason I answered was so I could do this."

"Do what?" The line went dead. "Hello? Ashley?"

I stared at the phone. She'd hung up on me.

I left Red Lion Square without saying a word to Chris. I wasn't ready to talk to her yet because she slept on the sofa, because she didn't believe me, and because the sex with Blanche had been so great.

When he opened his door, Dr. Rajamani didn't look surprised to see me. "Ah, Jamie. How are you feeling?" He opened his door and welcomed me into the chaos of his office.

I took the closest chair, a wide wooden number that looked more like torture than comfort. "Dr. Rajamani, I think you'd better sit down."

The man sat and folded his hands gracefully over his belly. Sun filtered in through his dusty window, turning his purple tunic into a soft gray. At least I didn't have to worry about a thunderstorm today. "I am glad you are here," he said. "I have just gotten off the phone with Chris and she spoke to me of some disturbing physiological changes from the accident you suffered last month. I am most concerned and want to reassure you that I will find out what is causing your brain to create worlds that are not real. Your brain might have been shocked a bit too much, so I will need to take a few more scans." He smiled weakly. "Chris assures me you have no plans for a lawsuit of any kind."

I snorted. "Dr. Rajamani, you need to know a few things. First, I refuse to have any more of your scans, *ever.* Second, the world that Chris described to you isn't a fantasy. There's nothing wrong with my brain chemistry."

He tapped his chin thoughtfully. "You think it is psychological then?"

Boy, this was slowgoing. I leaned forward. "Chris thinks my brain is broken and that what I told her isn't real. But remember that you said you were hoping to one day locate a person's consciousness and then transport it?"

Rajamani nodded, smiling serenely. "I have been working toward this my entire life."

I leaned forward. "Well, you succeeded."

The man frowned. "I do not understand."

"That little accident in your lab, the one that Chris thinks damaged my brain, did something entirely different. You sent my conscious mind back in time four hundred and fifty-seven years. My mind, and that of one of Queen Elizabeth I's ladies-in-waiting, traded places. I've been living in 1560 since the accident. Blanche

Nottingham has been living here, in my body, during that same time."

Rajamani chuckled. "Chris tells me you have a sense of humor." I didn't smile. "I ran into Ray Lexvold. Remember Ray? He disappeared after his first session with you a year ago."

Rajamani straightened in his chair. "I do not remember that I shared the names of my other—"

"You didn't. I had no idea who else had participated in your experiments, except for Chris. Yet I know that man's name. He's now Hew Draper, locked in the Tower of London for practicing sorcery against one of Queen Elizabeth's friends."

The professor shook his head and shot to his feet. "You are telling me lies."

"No, I am *not* telling you anything but the fire trucking truth. I was there. My body wasn't, but my mind was."

"And now you are back?"

"Thanks to another thunderstorm. I don't know how you transported my consciousness, but it's definitely connected to thunderstorms, with lots of lightning."

Rajamani's hands began to shake as he paced. "You are not telling me lies? This is truth?" His brown eyes blazed with hope.

"Scout's honor. You did it. And even though I really want to sue your scientific ass, I need your help."

The man collapsed against a wall of books. "But I do not know how I did it! How can I duplicate what I do not understand?"

"I don't know, Doc, and I don't care because you shouldn't duplicate your experiment ever again. Hear me? *Ever again*. My life has, quite frankly, been hell, and I have no clear idea what Miss Blanche Nottingham, the 1560 chick who's put all this weight on my body, has been doing to my life. My best friend hung up on me last night, and this morning my older brother sent me a *Fire truck You* text. Lovely way to start the day."

Raj rubbed his eyes. "I have done it. I have really done it."

I stood and squeezed his arm to bring him out of his personal celebration. "Doc, here's the thing. You have to figure out a way to make sure that I don't go back there again, that I stay here. Can you do that? Can you shut off the GCA that's still in my system? Give me some sort of antidote? If your success is going to be real, you must control your results. You must be able to stop me from flipping back and forth between times like a goddamned Ping-Pong ball."

He clasped my hands. "Yes, yes, I hear what you are saying. You are right. Completely right." He began pulling at one wooly eyebrow.

"*Think*, Dr. Raj. What do you need to do first?"

He pressed his lips together. "Your intralaminar nuclei are oscillating at an incorrect speed. I must take a blood sample to determine the level of GCA still in your system."

"Let's do it." That a needle was involved no longer bothered me. Funny how wearing someone else's body can put certain fears in perspective. At least this was one less thing Chris could list as proof of my cowardice.

Raj hesitated, then leaned closer. "Did you meet the Queen?" His voice quavered with excitement, which I totally understood.

"Dr. Raj, she's amazing," I whispered. "Strong and powerful and clever, yet still as vulnerable as you or I would have been at that age."

He squeezed my hand. "Come to my lab. I will solve this problem for you before any thunder booms again."

CHAPTER FIFTEEN

Leaving Dr. Rajamani bent over some sort of blood analysis machine, I checked my watch. Bradley would be at King's Cross Station in St. Pancras about now. It was just as quick to walk as negotiate the subway, and I needed to reconnect with London, *my* London.

Soon the beautiful red and white St. Pancras appeared ahead. It was both a Victorian railway station and a gingerbread-like neo-Gothic hotel. The station connected trains arriving from Europe with the London Tube. I hurried inside and began scanning the bland tiled platform for Bradley. Had he noticed I'd been gone?

I heard him before I saw him. "Do you walking zombies know that this is the largest interchange in the entire Tube system? And do you know that King's Cross was originally known as Battlebridge because the invading Romans fought Queen Boadica right here? She was so distraught she committed suicide and is believed to be buried beneath either platform nine or platform ten of this very station." I loved how Bradley always found the juiciest bits of historical gossip.

I walked up, tossed a pound coin in his hat, and smiled. Annie was sleeping in the crook of his arm. But he avoided my eyes and, in fact, turned to the side so he couldn't see me. What? I shifted as well, forcing him to swing back again as he talked about the Roman martyr of St. Pancras, who was only fourteen years old when he was beheaded for converting to Christianity.

Confused, I backed away, then found a bench. I would wait. Hundreds of people scurried past, faces blank, cells pressed to their ears or thumbs busy texting as they walked. A few tossed coins into his hat. A homeless woman cowered against the far wall, lifting her head now and then to watch Bradley.

He finally ran out of words half an hour later, then quickly gathered up his life's possessions, but I was quicker.

"Bradley, how are you?"

His grizzled face was defiant but sad. "Oh, so now you care?"

I shook my head, sick to my stomach. "I don't understand."

"You've got the shortest memory on record, then. I saw you yesterday at Holborn. I called out but you glared at me and kept right on going."

"Bradley, let me buy you a cup of coffee and a biscuit. I need to explain."

Suspicious but lured by the offer of free food, Bradley nodded. "If you buy one for Mouse as well." He motioned to the woman sitting against the wall, and she shot to his side. "I met Mouse in Trafalgar, and she seems quite taken with me."

I sighed. "Bradley, you can barely take care of yourself and Annie. You really can't afford to take on another burden, although it's commendable."

"I call her Mouse because she's as quiet as one.'" He chuckled. "Don't try talking to her directly, though, 'cause she'll hop off faster than Annie could."

Mouse hung right at our heels, clutching herself as if desperate to keep her insides from spilling out. I could understand why Bradley felt so compelled to take her under his wing. She looked utterly lost. Her jeans and hoodie were torn and muddied, her snarled brown-blond hair hung listlessly down her back. Her pale eyes were the color of soft moss. I loved Bradley's generosity. Why did it seem that people with very little were more willing to share what they had than people with much more?

Bradley, Annie, and Mouse waited outside while I slipped into the British Library Café and bought us something to eat. I joined them out in the library's circular plaza, where the concrete benches were warm in the sun.

Mouse sat away from us, close enough not to lose sight of Bradley but far enough she didn't have to interact with us. She inhaled the cookie in two bites and guzzled the entire bottle of water in one go.

"What's her story?" I asked. Now I had two people and one rabbit to find homes for.

Bradley shrugged. "Can't get a word out of her, other than she came to London last month." He lifted the last of his biscuit. "I appreciate you giving her a bite to eat. Feeding everyone is hard on my salary."

We smiled.

"Okay, Bradley, I need to explain why you thought I wasn't being friendly yesterday. It's going to sound totally insane, but it's true, every word. That woman that you saw, who looked just like me? The body was mine, but the person inside, the consciousness? That wasn't me."

He waited, so I plunged ahead. By the time I was done, Mouse was asleep sitting up, and Annie had pooped on the concrete at our feet. I watched Bradley's face as he sat back and considered all I'd told him.

"Life is a constant battle not to lose yourself," he finally said.

"Do you believe me?"

He nodded. "I do. Living on the street, I've heard some real whoppers, but yours is the craziest. It's too crazy *not* to be real."

I slumped back against the concrete wall lining the green hedge behind us. "God's blood, I needed to hear that." I told him about Chris's opinion of my ambition, and how she wished I were bolder, braver, and hungrier for something outside my reach. Somehow telling Bradley this wasn't as humiliating as telling Ashley or Mary, both of whom loved Chris. It felt shameful, somehow, to admit that the woman who supposedly loved me more than anyone outside of my family thought me flawed and weak.

"Sounds like you can lose yourself in a relationship as easy as you can lose yourself in a war." He sniffed. "I've been single all my life, so I'm just guessing, of course."

I nodded, suddenly unsure of everything going on between me and Chris. Would we be able to weather my disappearance and the reason for it? It didn't help that she was enjoying life with Blanche.

I checked my phone for Bradley's schedule. "Look, I know where you go next....Wait, what's this?" I opened a video I didn't recognize.

Bradley leaned over my shoulder. "I gotta get me one of those someday."

I pressed play. The video was me, looking into the camera, wearing a deep purple shirt I didn't own.

"Hi, Jamie. It's me, Blanche. I thought I'd do the modern thing and leave you a video message. Writing notes is so sixteenth century, don't you think? I assume if you're watching this that you're back in your body, and I'm back in mine."

"Bloody hell," Bradley muttered. I shifted so we could both see the video.

"But, Jamie, that's not going to be permanent. I will find a way back, and when I do, I'll make sure I stay here. I love this life. I'm not wild about your body—skinny as a sick cow, with the fashion sense of a prison inmate—but it's been adequate."

I growled at the screen.

"Here's the thing. There is so much that is wonderful about this time period, of course, but I only need one word to describe the best: Money. I know what it's like to be poor, and I'm not going back there again. You probably don't know this, since there's no one at the palace who could tell you, but by the time my father died he had spent all our wealth. I lived with my best friend for a while, but then her parents decided I needed to leave. Do you know what options a sixteen-year-old unmarried woman has in 1555? None except marriage or servitude or prostitution. I had no choice but to travel to a town where I was not known and take a job as a servant in a "great house," one so pathetically small that the entire house could have fit inside my father's stables."

Blanche sat back and licked her lips, pain darkening her gaze… or rather, my gaze. Her eyes were harder, the lips thinner, but it was still my face. "My only chance of escape came when I realized

I wasn't far from Princess Elizabeth's home at Hatfield. I stole a gown and went to see her, throwing myself at her mercy and pouring out the terrible state of affairs. I amused her, so she took pity on me and brought me into her circle.

"All those lovely gowns in my trunk? The queen's castoffs. I know the others laugh at that behind my back. My jewelry? Made with paste and dye for a few quid." She leaned closer to the camera. "I will never experience poverty again, and I will not marry just for money. Here in this time a woman has unlimited options for earning her keep that do not involve servitude or shame or selling oneself in marriage."

She smiled. "I will return to claim your body."

The video ended.

Bradley let out a huge breath but I kept holding mine.

"That wasn't you, was it?" Bradley said.

I finally exhaled. "Thank you for noticing that."

"Freaky, freaky. Too freaky." He stood. "Mouse, let's get going," Bradley said softly, and the woman roused instantly.

"You believe me, right?" I asked. "Blanche made this video, not me."

He gave me a weak smile and motioned for Mouse to follow. I stepped back and watched them leave. Annie peeked at me over the edge of Bradley's open backpack while Mouse hugged herself and dropped in behind Bradley.

I stood there for a second, wondering why the day's warmth seemed to have left with my friend. Then, since I had research to do, I entered the library, presented my card, and signed up for database access. The cool air felt good after baking in the sun on the plaza. I did a search on "Blanche Nottingham" and found a mention of her as one of Queen Elizabeth's ladies. I printed off the page—proof for Chris. I then expanded my search from 1558-1563 to include any "Blanche." Found a Blanche Shepherd, a Blanche Walton, and a Blanche Maddox.

Huh. Jamie Maddox. Blanche Maddox.

What the hell had happened in 1560 after I left?

Shaking off my discomfort, I then did a search on Raymond Lexvold. Most of the entries were for a high school wrestler from Minnesota, but I did manage to find a London entry that sucked the air right out of me: *Raymond Lexvold killed by double-decker.* I checked the date: May 14, one year ago.

According to the article, Mr. Lexvold, appearing confused and agitated, stepped out in front of a double-decker bus as it came barreling down Kingsway. He was killed instantly.

I sat back, my heart pounding. No wonder Ray had been unable to return to his own body, his own time. No amount of lightning or GCA could reunite a consciousness with a body no longer alive. That meant Ray was truly trapped in the sixteenth century. The thought made me so tired I could barely sign out.

On the long walk back to Red Lion Square, I resolved to make sure I never returned to 1560 again. For if I did, and Blanche was careless with my body, I might never return.

Chapter Sixteen

By the time I wandered back to the flat, it was late afternoon. The sky was still a bright, cloudless blue, which was such a relief. If I never heard another clap of thunder, saw another flash of lightning, I would be perfectly content.

When I opened the door, the scent of patchouli drifted around me. Uh oh. Incense only meant one thing: Chris was home and in a thoughtful, pensive mood. She greeted me at the door with a hug and kiss, then she nuzzled against my neck so sweetly I couldn't help but lean into her. Maybe she'd come to believe my story.

"Babe, we need to talk."

"You think?"

She led me into the small living room and handed me a glass of chilled Chardonay. We each took an end of the sofa and nestled our feet together in the middle. "Okay, let's talk," I said.

Chris nodded. "I've thought a lot about what you said yesterday, so I did some research and talked with a few colleagues."

"Great, I'm gossip now?"

"Not at all, hon. You are the subject of much concern. Just listen to me, okay? I want to start by talking about the brain. I know science isn't your thing, but it is mine. Remember I explained the brain to you once?"

"I don't know why this is necessary," I said, "but I'm with you so far."

"The neurons in our brain are constantly changing their connective patterns every second of our lives in response to everything we perceive, think, or do. The human brain is so complex, so plastic, that it's virtually impossible to predict how it will respond to a given stimulus."

"And your point....?"

"Bear with me. Every single event we experience has the potential to upset the fragile balance of power within our brains."

"Makes our brains sound fragile."

"Well, the good news is that our own free will may be the strongest influence on our brains, and, therefore, on our lives. This means that with your thoughts, actions, and emotions, you can actually change the structure of your brain."

"Why would I need to change the structure of my brain?"

"Normal consciousness occurs when the two hemispheres of the brain—the right and the left—work together. When this doesn't happen, problems can result." Chris bit her lip, then leaned forward and took my foot in her warm hand. "Babe, there is a condition called dissociative identity disorder."

I frowned. "Never heard of it."

She massaged the bottom of my foot, my second-favorite place to be touched. "You might know it as a split personality, or multiple personalities."

My jaw dropped. "You think I'm crazy."

Chris squeezed my foot. "Not crazy. God, no. But the shock to your brain from that lab accident could have certainly split your consciousness in two."

"This is the most ridiculous—"

"Please, just listen. Dissociative disorder can be diagnosed when the person exhibits two or more distinct personalities. The person experiences loss of memory and a break in her sense of identity as a result of a trauma. To cope, the person literally dissociates herself from the situation. One way to do this is to create a second personality."

I chewed the inside of my cheek. "You think I'm making this all up."

"No, I don't. I think you've built an elaborate escape world in your mind, one in which you 'inhabit' the body of Blanche Nottingham." She made her point with air quotes, and I wanted to scream. "While you are in this fantasy world, your other personality—Blanche Nottingham—inhabits your body and runs the show. You no longer have to take responsibility or worry about things because Blanche is in charge."

I snorted. "Where is Blanche now, since I'm clearly in charge?"

"You've tucked her away somewhere in the recesses of your brain. We don't know *where* consciousness resides, and that's true whether we have one consciousness or ten."

"Does someone with this condition even know about the other identity? I know about Blanche and she knows about me."

"It's unusual, but it is possible."

I pulled my foot from Chris's warm grasp. "Here's the thing. I believe Blanche Nottingham is back in 1560, living in her own plump body, her rosy breasts about to pop out of her ridiculously tight bodice."

Chris nodded. "That's exactly what a person with dissociative identity disorder would think. Jamie, I'm trying to help you, not hurt you. You've created a fantasy world in your head, and you have lived there for weeks."

I showed her Blanche's video. I showed her the page from the library about Blanche Nottingham.

"Jamie, these prove nothing. You clearly read about Blanche before this. And the video is the Blanche part of your personality talking. The Jamie part wouldn't know anything about it."

A flicker of doubt licked at the base of my brain. This couldn't be what really happened. Dr. Raj shot me full of GCA, sent me on a magic carpet ride back to Blanche's body in 1560, and Blanche into mine. No question.

But when you logically compared my story with Chris's explanation, mine sounded like the ravings of a madwoman. I swallowed hard. "You mentioned good news. Why was that good news?"

Chris sat up and moved as close to me as she could get. "The good news is that the brain can be healed. Changing your patterns of thinking and behaving can change your brain's structure. With a disease, some neurons, which contain little electromagnetic fields, become misaligned, or 'locked' in place. If you change your behavior, you can break this lock by forcing the neurons to change connections."

"You think that if I stop talking about 1560 and stop thinking I was in Blanche's body, then my brain would heal itself and my split personality would return to normal."

"Remember, I'm still a student at this, which is why I think you need to see someone. They tell me Dr. Wendy Kroll is the best at UCL and could really help you."

"This is bullshit, but if you think it's true, why the lab accident?"

"What?"

"What if it was you who sent my consciousness running for Blanche? You really knocked me on my ass with all that ambition stuff. You want me to want more for myself, and you want it yesterday. Nothing is fast enough for you, is it? When you see something that needs to happen, you believe we must push our way there. Should I have jumped your bones the first night we met instead of wooing you for weeks? Should I have pushed Aunt Nicole down the stairs so her death happened faster?"

"That's sick."

"So is your refusal to believe me. You're on the wrong track, Chris. What happened to me was real."

"Just see Dr. Kroll, please? What would it hurt?"

More conflicted than I'd been in months, I shrugged, which Chris took as an affirmative. She handed me a card with an appointment time tomorrow. "I'll go with you. We need to solve this together, babe."

Head spinning now, I followed Chris into the kitchen and we made dinner, pesto chicken with a spinach salad. I didn't tell her about my visit with Dr. Raj since she would accuse of clutching at straws. But I wasn't. Dr. Raj sent my consciousness back in time and he was the only one who could reverse the process. Somehow my intralaminar nuclei weren't oscillating at forty hertz anymore. My orchestra was creating cacophony, not music.

After a dessert of poached pears and caramel, I emptied my wine glass and cleared my throat. "Chris, I can appreciate how crazy my story sounds. I really can. But it's true. My brain hasn't been split in two. Blanche Nottingham really exists. She's not just some creation of a troubled mind. So you might as well cancel the appointment with Dr. Kroll. I won't be going."

"But—"

"No." When I used that tone of voice, Chris knew to let it go.

❖

I spent the rest of the evening on a bench in Red Lion Square, wishing there were kids in the neighborhood kicking a soccer ball around or yelling. Anything to make my world seem more normal. But it was just a few people at the coffee shack in one corner of the park, me, and a handful of birds skittering around my feet in search of a handout.

I finally called my brother Jake.

"Boy, you got some balls, girl."

"What is going on? Ashley hung up on me, Mary's not answering, and you're sending nasty texts."

"Don't waste my time playing dumb. I can't believe you said those things to Mom and Dad. They've stopped golfing, Dad's skipped work all week, and they just sit around crying over your baby photo."

I pressed my lips together. Whatever damage Blanche had done, I could undo. My family loved me. "Look, Jake, I know this is going to sound crazy, but my memory over the last month or so has been, well, spotty."

"That doesn't change the fact that you really hurt them."

I considered telling my brother the truth, but if Chris couldn't handle it, Jake certainly couldn't. He'd tell everyone I'd gone off the deep end. "I need help here, Jake. I don't remember anything. Could you at least tell me what I said to them?"

The distance between London and Stevens Point, Wisconsin, was almost too far for this conversation. I wished I was sitting out on Jake and Amy's deck watching my nephews battle with busted light sabers. I could disarm Jake's scowl with a joke and easily get him to listen to me, but reaching him through my cell phone seemed impossible.

He sighed. "You said that family wasn't important, and that you were tired of always having to check in, to answer their stupid questions. You said that life was easier without family anchoring you, dragging you down. You told them not to call you anymore and to stop interfering in your life."

Now I sighed. "Jake, does that really sound like me?"

"Well, no, but you said it."

"No, I didn't. That was the lab accident talking. I've said some crazy things the last few weeks. Just ask Chris. Will you talk to Mom and Dad? And to Marcus?" I could actually hear his hesitation. "Please? When have I begged you for anything? Huh?" My voice shook like a trembling aspen. How could my family ever think I could say those things and really mean them?

"Okay, okay, don't start blubbering on me. I'll tell them you're sorry, that you didn't mean it, and that you want them to call you. How's that?"

"Perfect. Thanks, big bro. Hugs to Amy and the boys."

After he grumbled something and hung up, I sat there with the muggy August air pressing against my chest, making it hard to breathe. Now I really, *really* didn't like Blanche. My body could be taken over any minute by a woman who would be unkind to the people I loved. No way could Blanche really be *me* acting out a different personality.

I picked up my book on Queen Elizabeth I and scanned it for what happened in her world during the fall of 1560. I found pages and pages speculating on her relationship with Robert Dudley but nothing was said of pillow fights in the Queen's bedchamber late at night.

Then I came upon the sad story of Amy Dudley, which I'd forgotten. She and Robert married young, and he quickly tired of her. She eventually became ill with what historians believe was breast cancer. She died on September 8, 1560, from a fall down a fairly short flight of stairs. For four hundred and fifty years, the mystery has been unsolved—did she fall, or was she pushed? And had Robert Dudley played a role in this? When Amy died, Elizabeth distanced herself from Dudley to save her own reputation. She could no longer marry him, tainted as he was with rumors of murder, but she loved him too much to marry someone else. Instead, she simply flirted with men her entire life.

I watched a small pigeon peck at a bit of cracker on the sidewalk as it cooed softly. I kept coming back to this—If Robert Dudley were to be murdered, everything in English history—and the history of all its colonies—would change. If that history changed, *my* history, and that of every person I knew, would also change. My ancestors might not meet and marry, but instead marry other people. My brain struggled with the implications since it'd been a while since I'd read any science fiction. If my family line ceased to exist, then I would also cease to exist. If history changed, would I just disappear?

CHAPTER SEVENTEEN

The next week was an uneasy one. Chris spent a great deal of time at her school office, and I painted frantically to catch up on the next Froggity book. In my absence, the publisher had decided to continue the series with three more books, but those needed to be completed almost immediately in order to be part of the packaged series. Blanche, of course, had not answered any of the frantic emails or text messages Candace, my art director, had left.

I felt a need to reassure Candace, so I called her. "Jamie, I am so relieved to hear from you." Her voice was low and breathy, although since it came from smoking a pack a day, it wasn't that sexy.

"Sorry, Candace, I had an accident a few weeks ago, so I've been in and out of the hospital."

"Good Lord, are you okay?"

I made up a weak story about head injury and slight concussion, but it was enough to pacify my boss. "So I'll get right on these notes," I said, "and should have the dummies for all three books ready in about a week."

"It's going to be tight, but we'll make it work. Once I get back to you, the finals will be due in another week. I know that's a crazy schedule, twenty-four paintings in seven days."

I wanted to scream. Crazy didn't begin to describe the situation. Impossible was more accurate. "Candace, I know you're getting pressure from the production people, and it wasn't your fault I was out of commission for a few weeks, but wouldn't it be better to give me another two weeks so the artwork is the same quality as the other books?"

"Yes, but you can't believe the number of books waiting for artwork. The editorial team has finally gotten its act together and begun accepting books from the writers. Three weeks ago, we had four books in the queue. Now we have twenty-four. The Froggity books need to be finished yesterday so you can take on some of this backlog."

"And if I need to take my time on Froggity?"

Candace sighed, her disappointment clear even though we were separated by the Atlantic Ocean. "I need to hire four more artists anyway, so I'll assign them the bulk of the new books. I can give you what's left, but if you're not available to start this next project, there might not be room for you later."

Four artists? Crap. I'd never get assigned another book, since there were four of us already. "Candace, I will absolutely do the very best I can. Depend on it."

"Thanks, Jamie, I knew you'd step up. Now no more blows to the head. There's just no time in our schedule for that."

I disconnected and flopped down into my saggy green chair. Blanche probably had the painting skills, since I could play the lute in her body, but she clearly didn't want to use them. Inspired, I grabbed a blank sheet of paper, pondered the tone to take, then decided friendly would be more effective than hostile.

Dear Blanche,

If you're reading this, it means our minds have once again switched bodies. I assume you understand that's what has been happening to us. I don't appreciate the extra weight you've put on my body, but I can deal with that later. And your video threats really don't mean much—I doubt either of us can control what happens.

There is one thing, however, that you MUST do should you inhabit my body again, and that's keep up with my work. If I (or we) don't deliver the paintings on time, I'll lose my only source of income. Your nasty video mentioned your fear of poverty, so you must help. I need to earn an income, and painting is what I do best. Attached is a list of the paintings required, as well as a few samples from previous books. I know you can do this, since I've been able to play the lute in your body.

Jamie Maddox

I wondered where to leave the note. If I left it in the studio and Blanche never went there, all would be lost. I couldn't leave it lying around the flat for Chris to see and think me even more mad than she already did. For now, I folded the note and slid it into my back pocket.

The next morning when Chris and I bumped around each other in the kitchen, I aimed for casual. "Let's just say you're right, and my personality did split into two, me and Blanche. How are we different? Does Blanche dress the same way I do?"

Chris poured herself a mug of coffee. "Not really. She tends to wear what you'd consider dressy as her daily clothing. That crushed velvet jacket you bought as a joke? Blanche loves that."

I shuddered. The midnight blue jacket was so dark it could have been the background for an Elvis painting. "What else does she wear?"

"Skirts. She doesn't like wearing jeans. And she's much bolder in her color choices. She puts crazy outfits together, but they work."

That we were standing around talking about Blanche's wonderful fashion sense churned my stomach. The elephant in the discussion, of course, was that Chris must think I chose boring, less risky, less flashy clothes, which fed right into her idea that I was too cautious and without ambition. And another thing—Chris seemed to brighten whenever she said Blanche's name.

"Okay, thanks. I was just curious."

"Does this mean you'll go see Dr. Kroll?"

"Nope."

Before I left, I slipped the folded note into the pocket of the velvet jacket, even though only an idiot would wear it in the summer.

Back at my studio, struggling to bring the next Froggity story alive with a few brushstrokes, I thought about what would happen if I lost this educational publishing job. Chris certainly wouldn't let me starve, and she'd pay the rent, but she preferred to keep our finances separate. We still split everything fifty-fifty, coupled in such a way that an uncoupling could happen as fast as sliding down the emergency chute on an airplane. Yet if Chris and I were truly committed to each other, why did we still have things arranged for an easy exit? We were intimate in so many ways, yet we had no joint account of any sort. It was the most uncommitted commitment ever.

She was receiving money from her father, and she had a part-time job at UC London, but otherwise her income was lower than it had ever been. I would have been thrilled to pay more than my share, to literally feed and clothe the woman I loved.

❖

Dr. Raj still hadn't come up with anything. We talked every day, and he'd go into painful detail about this theory or that, but ultimately nothing he said reassured me that my body-switching days were over. I obsessed over the weather reports as if my life depended on them. Every morning, I raced to the kitchen window and searched the sky for cloudy wisps that might gang up and start a thunderstorm.

One day I couldn't paint and I couldn't bear to sit in the flat, so I walked all the way down to Trafalgar Square and the National Gallery. I returned to Dr. Rajamani's basement exhibit and stood in front of each of the twelve scans, staring at them as if one of them held the answer to my problem. As I moved from scan to scan, my spirits sank because each scan was nearly identical, a mishmash of red and green and blue, with slender threads of white visible at the outer edges.

Then it hit me. The scan in front of me had much more white than the others. I checked all twelve, and found one more just like it. These two had been the only ones to catch my eye the day Chris and I had attended the exhibit's opening. I called Dr. Raj, and he answered right away.

"Jamie Maddox, I am studying this. Be patient."

I told him about the huge amounts of white in the two framed scans.

I could hear his confusion. "Of course, I did notice that as I prepared the exhibit, but I could find no data to explain it. Give me the patient numbers of the two with more white, if you please."

I read off the two numbers and waited while he checked his research. "Hmm, the reason there was no more data on those two subjects is that they dropped out of the study after only one session."

Excitement pulsed through me. "I'll bet one of them was Ray Lexvold."

"Yes, one was Ray, and the other was Meg Warren."

"Dr. Raj, it can't be a coincidence that the two scans with all that white never came back. We know that Ray was sent back in time. What if Meg was as well?" I asked Dr. Raj for her phone number and address. Maybe I could track her down and eliminate her as another traveler.

I had time, so took the Tube to Meg's Soho flat. She didn't reply to my buzz from the locked vestibule, but someone leaving held the door open for me. I climbed the narrow stairs, which were clean as freshly-fallen Minnesota snow, then found number Three A. The hallway smelled of furniture polish. I knocked, but no one came to the door.

I tried twice more, with the same results, then a door down the hallway opened. An elderly woman popped her curly gray head out and glared at me. "No matter how much ye knock and disturb the rest of us, ye can't bring a person to answer her door when she isn't there."

I approached her, hands up in apology. "I'm so sorry. Do you know when Meg will be back?"

"Not an inkling."

I handed her my card. "Could you have her call me when you see her? It's very important."

With a curt nod, the woman accepted the card and closed her door.

I slid a card under Meg's door, then left. There was nothing more I could do.

That night I read about the Tudors and realized how lucky I was to have known Elizabeth, even if it had been under crazy circumstances. Then it struck me: I was the only person currently alive on the planet who had actually met her.

Elizabeth was pressured her entire life to marry, at least until she was beyond childbearing age. Her councilors were terrified that the country would erupt into warfare without a clear line of succession, since so many branches of the Tudor family could claim they were next in line.

Possible marriage candidates included Philip II of Spain, the widower of Elizabeth's sister Mary. Eric XIV of Sweden was passionate about a marriage, but the oafish Swedes were almost considered clowns in court, with their thick accents and rough clothing. Elizabeth had been courted by the Archduke Charles of Austria and the Earl of Arundel, yet she'd strung each of them along until they drifted away. She insisted on meeting each man in person, but few members of foreign royalty would consent to travel the great distance to England only to be put on display and rejected at a whim.

My heart sank into my ankles as I read more about Dudley and Elizabeth. They loved and fought each other their entire lives. She never married him, however, because of the cloud of suspicion surrounding his wife's death. Some believed that the very fact that Dudley was available after his wife died kept Elizabeth from marrying anyone else.

I put the book down. Poor Amy Dudley, in love with a man who wanted nothing to do with her, then dying so young in a tragic fall. What would it mean for the future if Winston succeeded in killing Dudley? The Master of the Horse was so handsome and charming that every man the council put before Elizabeth as husband material paled in comparison. Without him, what would Elizabeth do? I did a quick search on plots to kill Dudley and found there were two. Neither succeeded, and neither involved Winston.

On the weekend, Chris and I went to *Spamalot* at the Apollo Victoria, even though I hated its steep stairs without railings. Descending to our ticketed seats felt like a barely controlled fall. Chris seemed to have given up on the idea I had multiple personalities, and a truce of sorts settled over us. We laughed until we cried and ended up holding hands. That night, for the first time since I'd returned to my own body, we made love. At first, I was nervous, thinking she would be comparing me to Blanche, but her delighted moans told me I could withstand that sort of scrutiny.

Later, as I curled around her warm back, Chris kissed my hand. "Babe, can I ask you something?"

I nuzzled closer in assent.

"Why haven't you asked about the manuscript that you...that Blanche started writing?"

I sighed. "I guess I don't want to know anything more about her. The whole thing seems like a bad dream. I don't ever want to leave you again, Chris. And if Blanche ever came back, there's no telling what she'd do." I told her about the plot with Winston to kill Dudley, about the horrid things Blanche had said to my parents. She'd likely done the same to my friends, since neither Ashley nor Mary was letting me back into their lives. "I don't want that sort of person around you, or running my body. She could really muck things up."

"But the novel is really good. I just think you might try reading it. Maybe, given your...experience, you might be inspired to add to it."

I sat up, letting the covers pool around my naked hips. "By 'add to it,' you really mean 'keep going,' don't you? You think *I'm* writing a novel called *Sleeping with the Queen*, not Blanche."

Chris sat up as well, and we faced each other in the dark. Until this Dr. Raj mess, I'd been very content with my life, and by *content* I didn't mean settling for less but *content* as in happy. Why, in Chris's eyes, was that so wrong?

"I'm trying to respect what you believe to be true, but I also think it would be a good idea for you to step outside your comfort zone. Read what you've written. You might feel some creative spark."

"Blanche lived here, in this time, and in my body, for less than a month before she began writing. I just can't believe she could have assimilated that quickly."

"That's the thing. It's written in some form of very old English, which makes the voice totally unique. And the details are rich and vivid, so you feel as if you've stepped into Elizabeth's world."

I snorted. "I have, remember?"

With that, we slid back down into bed, pulled the covers back up over our shoulders, and rolled away from each other.

The next day dawned so hot that I was sticky with sweat even before I left the bed. Chris was already gone. I dressed in loose shorts and a baggy shirt, took a walk to get my creativity flowing, then attacked the next Froggity painting. That afternoon I would try Meg's flat again.

Candace liked what I was sending her, so my job once again seemed on firm ground. The sweat pooled at my waist and tickled the back of my neck until, five hours later, my growling stomach drove me downstairs into the pub.

"How's the artisté?" asked Sam as he poured me a tall frosted glass of lemonade.

"Parched," I said. "When is this heat going to break?"

"Oy," Sam said. "Probably about October."

We laughed and talked of politics and neighborhood scandals. The fresh salad he brought me and the iced drink were two things I'd really missed when stuck back in Blanche's body.

Something flashed against the brass railing around the bar. I turned around but saw nothing out the window. Five minutes later, it happened again. "What's that flash I keep seeing? Do you think I'm going blind?"

He shook his head. "Naught but a bit of heat lightning. It'll move on quickly, but it does give one a start to see the flash in a blue sky."

I froze, then slowly placed my glass on the bar. Heat lightning.

Another flash. I looked at Sam but couldn't hear the words he was speaking. Another flash, then darkness as I was yanked from my body and sucked up into the heavens.

CHAPTER EIGHTEEN

It was like racing down the freeway at a hundred miles per hour and driving right into a bridge support. *Sudden stop* didn't even begin to describe the sickening jolt as my consciousness exploded into a body and fought its way into the brain. I doubled over and began coughing, struggling to breathe. Why the hell was every time different? A little consistency would have been nice.

"Lady Blanche, are you unwell?" It was Lord Winston's voice.

I forced myself to sit upright as I struggled to breathe normally. "No, I am fine," I croaked out, even though I wanted to start screaming and pulling down wall tapestries and breaking ale mugs and sticking the burning candles into Winston's eyes. God's blood, I was back in 1560 again.

We sat in a room I didn't recognize. There were two other men with us, the two who'd been with Winston in the bowling green.

"Good, then it is settled," Winston said with a slap to his knee. "We will put our plan into action tomorrow night. Thanks to Blanche's intelligence, we know Dudley will be climbing the rear staircase to the Queen's bedchamber around midnight. Lady Blanche will descend and delay Dudley with idle court gossip as Charles and I come up the stairs behind him. William, you will descend behind Blanche so Dudley will be trapped. Lady Blanche, you then leave us and return to Her Majesty's chambers. We will do the rest."

Great, just great. Blanche had continued to participate in the stupid murder plot. And now, of course, I had to deal with what she'd arranged. "One question. Must we kill Dudley? Why not wound him or frighten him instead?"

Charles snorted. "My God, Lady Blanche, you change your mind more often than Her Majesty changes gowns. Do you think a man such as Dudley frightens easily? He expects to be King within a few years, for it is said his wife is gravely ill."

William leaned forward, resting his elbows on muscular thighs. Clearly, he was in excellent shape and could do Dudley bodily harm. "As for wounding him," William said, "that would only incite the Queen's sympathies and perhaps those of others in the kingdom. No, to protect the realm Dudley must die. Were he to become King, the country would split wide open, thus encouraging the French or the Scots to begin a war."

Winston stood, tugging at his breeches and gathering his cloak together. It was too warm to actually wear it, so he slung it over his arm. "We have been over this ground before, Lady Blanche. You will encounter Dudley in the back stairs tomorrow at midnight and play your role in this necessary action."

I stood, unable to think of any way to stop this plan, so I nodded weakly. Charles escorted us out onto broad brick steps lined with green hedging. Behind me, the house rose three stories, the roof holding many chimneys. At the base of the steps waited a carriage. When the footman saw me, he stepped forward and offered his hand. Thank God someone knew where I was to go. I climbed into the carriage, which rocked slightly, then settled back on worn velvet cushions. I was greatly relieved not to be negotiating the streets of London by foot again.

Within minutes, the carriage horses turned smartly, and we entered the palace grounds. After being helped from the carriage, I stood there watching all the activity. The many buildings of the palace loomed over me, and I couldn't bear to once again enter its dark hallways and rooms, some lit only by candlelight in the middle of the day. Damn Rajamani for not figuring this out in time.

Instead, I wandered around the gardens, finally landing on a marble bench near the raised bed of roses. The scent of blooming flowers and wet earth calmed me a bit, but I still scanned overhead, willing a streak of heat lightning to split the agonizingly blue sky.

I blocked out the sounds of palace life, humming to myself the Beatles' "Back in the USSR," and then, unfathomably, switching to Captain and Tennille's "Muskrat Love." What a nightmare.

Rattling metal cart wheels snapped me out of it. An elderly gardener with round shoulders, black-stained nails, and a hound dog face stopped his cart when he saw me.

"Aye, m'lady, sorry to disturb. I'll be returning later." His cart was heaped with white-flecked black soil and must have been heavy.

"No, please. Stay and work. You won't bother me."

"If the lady is sure...."

I smiled to seal the deal, tired of snooty courtiers. An earthy gardener was just what I needed. "What are you doing?" I asked.

"Feedin' the plants, m'lady. They gets so hungry they eat up all the goodness in the soil." He began shoveling soil from the cart and laying it gently along the base of the trimmed hedges. "This here is chicken dung that's been sittin' for some time. Now mind you, dove's dung is the best but hard to come by so I'm usin' fowl dung. Next best after that is ass, then donkey. Then you got your ox and cow dung, then swine. Horse is the most vile of dung, and I won't use it on Her Majesty's gardens. It burns too hot."

I smiled with interest as the man continued to expound on the various dungs. He was a welcome distraction. I wondered where sheep dung fell in his ranking.

"Lovely day, is it not, Lady Blanche?"

Before I could rise or protest, Robert Dudley himself joined me on the bench.

"Yes, it is," I said, faltering a little. If I couldn't stop it, this lovely but irritating man would be knifed to death tomorrow night.

"Ho, gardener. Leave us." He flicked a wrist, and the man bowed arthritically and pushed his cart down the path of red brick dust.

Dudley smiled, his teeth surprisingly white behind his moustache. In this era black rotted teeth signified you were wealthy enough to consume great quantities of sugar. Elizabeth had such a sweet tooth that by the end of her life, all her teeth would either fall out or be black.

"Lady Blanche, I am delighted to have found you, for I wish to speak to you on an important matter."

I adjusted my skirts so the man's knees weren't so close, since it was just too hot to touch anyone, man or woman. "Of what did you wish to speak?" I almost called him Sir Robert, but he wouldn't be given this title for a few more years…if he survived, that was.

Dudley's face was earnest as he leaned closer. "It is Her Majesty. She has so many offers of matrimony before her, and I know each one distresses her. But when I ask if she is any closer to a decision, she merely smiles and changes the subject. I would know her mind, Blanche, and you are the closest to her of all her ladies."

Kat Ashley was closer, having been with Elizabeth since the Queen was a child, but Dudley knew Kat would never say anything. Blanche, however, must have had a reputation as being less than loyal.

The breeze shifted enough I could now smell the gardener's applications. "The Queen's rule is that politics are never to be discussed in her inner chambers, so matters of state such as her marriage are not aired before me."

Dudley waved off my comment. "I know that, but surely Elizabeth speaks of matters of the heart in her chambers. That is what I am interested in." He cocked one eyebrow with such humor that I could see how Elizabeth had fallen under his spell years ago, when she was still a princess and he just a rich boy living nearby.

"You wish me to violate her trust and reveal to you the true path of her heart?"

His sheepish grin nearly won me over. "She says she holds me above all others, but what if she says this to every suitor?"

What a jerk. "I understand you wanting to know. But is there not a Mrs. Dudley awaiting you at home?"

Dudley's mirth and earnestness shut down immediately. "My dear Amy and I had several good years together, but we are in no way compatible. She abhors court, and I thrive on it. She despises the city, and I require it. Also…." And here his voiced softened enough that I truly believed his emotions. "…my wife is not well. Some infirmity of the bone has overtaken her, making her as brittle as clay baked too long in an oven. She cannot travel, even should she wish to join me here at court."

I rose and gathered up my skirts in both hands so I could launch myself without tripping. "A true husband would therefore be at his wife's side at such a time. I will not grant your wish to know Her Majesty's heart, for you do *not* deserve any affection she may have for you." And with that, I stormed out of the garden and through the nearest palace door.

I retired to my room, relieved to not have encountered the Queen and been swept up in the day's activities. Instead, I lay down on my bed and stared at the table leg where I'd been scratching the days off from the moment I'd arrived. I'd been in the past for over thirty days, then back in my own life for nine days. At least thirty-nine days had passed.

I sat up. Had Blanche gotten her period while I'd been gone? While back in the future I'd researched Elizabethan menstruation and learned the women used rags. I dug through Blanche's trunk of gowns, sleeves, and collars until I found a bundle of rolled-up, clean rags. They smelled musty like the trunk, so they'd been in there a while. They hadn't been used while I'd been gone.

I returned to the bed. The lack of a period. The nausea. The vomiting. Winston's reference to taking Blanche in the park.

Fire truck. Goddamned *fire truck*.

I was pregnant.

Chapter Nineteen

Now that I knew I inhabited a pregnant body, my desperation to get back to my own time doubled. Yet life in 1560 dragged on. After too many days of entertaining Elizabeth, we finally got a break when the Queen spent hours consulting her council over some threatening words from France. That gave me the freedom to go in search of Harriet.

She wasn't in the any of the palace buildings, so I began searching the outer areas, the woodshed, the charcoal yard, the laundry. When I finally found her in the bakery, my spirits rose. Truth be told, I'd missed her when I was in 2017.

The outdoor ovens gave off so much heat that I stopped twenty feet away, already feeling my face start to melt. I called to her and waved her over. "I need a favor. Could you come with me on an errand outside the palace?"

Harriet looked helplessly down at her wet dress, at the same time touching her sweat-soaked hair. "I am not dressed—"

"You can change your gown." I waved to the woman who must have been in charge, given the way she glared at Harriet for stepping away from the ovens. "Harriet must accompany me on the Queen's errand," I called, doing my best to sound haughty, which was how the other women spoke to servants.

I didn't really need Harriet on this errand, but I thought she might enjoy a break outside the palace. And I wanted her calm presence beside me. We were so comfortable together, as if we'd known each other in another life. She shot me a happy look, grateful for the break. While Harriet ran for her room in the building next to the bakery, I tracked down my buddy, Jacob the guard, and asked sweetly if he could take me by barge to the Tower on the Queen's business. He blushed, said I was looking lovely today, and that he'd be happy to take me.

As soon as we left the dock, Harriet thanked me for the opportunity to read for the Queen. "I hope to do it again."

"You were impressive," I said. "Latin!"

"Impressive until I fled the room without permission like a startled rabbit."

"She forgave you, but next time a storm frightens you, it would be best if you could keep your head and stay put. When I saw you later in the hall—"

She held up her hand. "Please. May we move on from that night?"

I nodded, unsure if she was uncomfortable with her fears or something else.

The Thames swans, property of the Queen and not to be meddled with upon penalty of death, bobbed and honked as the barge moved through the river. One was so close I reached out and stroked the soft feathers on her back, even though I knew swans weren't all that friendly. This one, however, didn't seem to mind, which I took as a good sign. She paddled next to us for quite some distance, even though I could no longer reach her. Her dark eyes were set in a snow-white head, her neck arching gracefully. When she veered close again, I changed places so Harriet could stroke the bird.

"I miss this," Harriet murmured.

"Miss what?"

"Touching something alive," she said. She scooted back onto the cushioned bench, not meeting my eyes.

I knew what she meant. Spending time with Chris, no matter how strained things got, had reduced my isolation a bit. "Are you missing someone's touch?" I asked softly, glancing at the oarsmen to ensure they were fully engaged in their work. Jacob stood in the bow. At the moment, we were ensnared in a river traffic jam caused by small boats launching and docking along what I called Mansion Row.

Harriet pressed her lips together. "Not anyone in specific. But since I…since I have come to the palace, I have felt the lack. My parents, my relatives, my friends were all very free and generous with their hugs and kisses. It feels as if my body has become a desert, dried up for lack of affection."

Harriet ducked her head, realizing she was confiding in me. I pulled off my gray glove and rested my hand upon hers. That slight touch sent welcome heat up my arm and into my heart. My family was touchy-feely, but with me in London I'd been cut off from that. Chris wasn't big on affection.

Harriet lost her haunted look and lowered her voice. "But I do not think you need go too much longer without affection. Guard Jacob seems smitten with you."

"No, he's not for me." I didn't say anything about Lord Winston or the pregnancy, still too shocked myself to make it real through speech.

"He is not of your class, of course, but surely a little dalliance might be fun." Her wry smile gave her plain face an impishness I hadn't seen before.

"No, I really prefer wo—" I pressed my lips together and gazed at the far bank. The river had begun to stink so we both perfumed our handkerchiefs. "I, ahh, prefer men who don't blush," I finished weakly.

When she didn't reply, I risked a peek. She looked thoughtful rather than shocked. Good. She hadn't deciphered my babbling.

The boat gently rocked us as we sat on the cushions without speaking, our hands touching lightly. Soon we slipped under the London Bridge and the high ramparts of the Tower loomed ahead.

After the barge beached itself on the muddy shore, a man ran planks from the barge to the wooden steps leading to the Tower entrance. We stepped carefully along the planks as the smell of dead fish and wet mud rose up all around us. The Thames was filled with ships creaking at anchor and men shouting.

When Harriet realized where we were headed, she froze in place. "We go to the Tower?"

I nodded. "Don't be afraid. The guards are very considerate and will treat us well. There is a man I must speak with who is being kept in one of the towers."

"You know a prisoner in the Tower?"

I couldn't tell if she was horrified or impressed. "We both lived in the same village...years ago."

At the entrance, Jacob greeted the Tower guard, and soon we were up walking along the wall. The way was too narrow for both our skirts, so Harriet dropped behind me but stuck so close to me her skirts bumped up against my own. I stopped to reassure her. "You can wait outside the cell so you don't need to go into that confining space." I waved out toward the Thames. "There are dozens of ships to watch. Please don't be frightened."

Harriet nodded, eyes wide in her pale face, but she eagerly took in the river activities. "Anything is better than staring into a boiling pot of laundry," she said.

The Tower guard unlocked Ray's cell, then he and Jacob retraced their steps to stand at a distance from Harriet.

Ray sat at his desk, bent over a notebook. When he raised his head to greet me, I nearly gasped. The man looked gravely ill. His red-rimmed eyes streamed, and his face was ghastly gray, as if coated in ash. "Jamie, how lovely to see you. Thank you so much for your gifts." He wore the blanket around his shoulders.

I clutched Ray's hand. "You are ill. Have they not gotten you a doctor?"

He chuckled weakly. "Doctors in this era know less about the human body than a ten-year-old. I will not have them draining me or attaching leeches."

We both shuddered. "Ray, I'm in a terrible mess." I explained about the plot to murder Dudley and how Blanche had gotten herself all mixed up in it.

He tugged on a sagging earlobe. "Remember, I know nothing of history, so I'm doomed to experience it as innocently as these people do. What would be the impact of Dudley dying?"

I explained the belief of historians that Elizabeth remained unmarried because Dudley was alive but unattainable. "Should Dudley die, Elizabeth may lose her resolve to never marry and let her councilors arrange a marriage. This will entirely change England's path. Because Elizabeth ruled alone, she was able to focus on the things most important to her. If you introduce a king, especially a foreign one, then the country's goals and choices will totally change. Change England's history, and you change the history of all of Europe and of every British colony, including the US."

Ray leaned back in his chair, frowning slightly at some pain. "So Dudley must *not* die."

"But how do I stop it? I could mess up this plot, but the men involved will just try again and again until they succeed. How do I dissuade them? I can't very well tell them their goal to keep England safe will only happen if Dudley remains alive. They'll ask to see my crystal ball." The astrological chart that Ray had carved into the wall caught my eye. "What about astrology? Elizabeth believes in it and often consults Dr. Dee. What if you could come up with some important astrological reason for me to give the plotters?"

"There is none." Ray stood and moved to the hearth, where he stirred the coals. "I cannot get warm."

Don't change the subject, I wanted to scream. Any change of subject could lead to discussing what I had learned about Ray Lexvold in the future.

The elderly man pulled his chair closer to the hearth, and settled back down. "God, I hate this. I'm a fucking old man, but I'm not." A heavy silence fell between us. "There have been a few thunderstorms, yet you remain in this time period. You, too, have had no luck."

I looked down so quickly that I gave myself away.

"Wait. You have been back," he said softly.

I blew out my breath so hard the edges of the notebook fluttered. "I have been back to the present. I managed to remain in our time for over a week. Do you know a Meg Warren?"

He wiped his eyes on a sleeve, leaving a trail of yellow mucus. "No, never heard of her, I'm afraid. But please, did you learn anything about me?"

"Ray, I—"

"Just tell me."

How did one deliver such horrible news? Just as there had been no way for my parents to shelter me from Aunt Nicole's cancer, there was no way for me to make this easier for Ray. I wasted a few moments straightening my skirts around me.

"Jamie, just tell me."

"The same day that you exchanged consciousnesses with Hew, and he was in your body, he must have been very confused to suddenly find himself in such a frightening place. It would seem crazy to anyone from this world, except for Blanche, who seems to have adjusted just fine." I paused for a deep breath. "Ray Lexvold stepped off the curb into the path of a double-decker bus. Killed instantly."

Ray covered his face with both hands, then released a healthy string of curses. "That's why I can't get home, even in the middle of the most violent thunderstorm."

"There is no body waiting for your consciousness to return to," I said softly.

His drawn face broke my heart. "That's it, then."

I leaned forward. "I'm working with Dr. Rajamani, so maybe he can figure something out. Maybe we could find a person who's about to die, and find a way. Raj is working on an antidote to the GCA, but what if he gave this person a shot of the stuff? Maybe you could return then."

Ray shook his head. "I appreciate the idea, but I can't imagine it would work." He stared at me through bleary eyes. "Jamie, if you can get home and stay there, do it. Don't worry about me. It might look as if these curved walls are my prison, but they aren't. It's this body that imprisons me, and there's nothing you can do about that."

We sat for a while listening to the banging and slapping of water against the wooden docks, the shouts of the quaymen as they worked. Crows cawed from the four peaks of the White Tower, not far from Ray's cell.

"Ray, do you ever wonder why Blanche? Why Hew?"

Ray shook his head, confused.

"Why did I land in Blanche's body? Why did you land in Hew's?"

"I chalk it up to fucking bad luck."

"I suppose," I said, "but there has to be more to it than that."

I couldn't imagine how Ray felt. Despondency threatened to overwhelm me daily, yet I still had a chance to get home and stay home. Ray was stuck in this world forever. I must have destroyed his last shreds of hope—a terrible thing to do to anyone.

"Maybe it's time for you to leave the Tower," I said. "I'm one of the Queen's favorites. I'm sure I could convince her to let you go. We could set you up in a small inn. You'd have a room and food prepared for you. You could roam London and do whatever you wanted."

Ray snorted. "Look at this body. Its roaming days are over." He gripped the edges of the table to stand, then waved me toward the door. "Thanks for coming, Jamie. I appreciate it."

My heavy skirts rustled against the dusty floor as I hugged Ray so hard he grunted. But he hugged back.

"Ray, I'll visit again, I promise."

He held me by the shoulders. "Don't take this the wrong way, but I don't *want* you to come back. I want you to find a way home, and I want you to stay there."

As I pulled on the iron knob, Ray held out his hand. "As for your problem with Dudley, all I can advise is to be clever. You know history, so you have a huge advantage. Use what you know." He smiled. "You'll figure it out. I know it."

Blinking back tears, I fled the cell.

CHAPTER TWENTY

That afternoon we hung around the presence chamber watching Elizabeth and some ambassadors talk. The only part of this whole scene that I enjoyed was the small band in the corner playing light and airy music with a steady beat. For some reason, this grounded me. Even when the musicians took a break, I found myself humming one of the tunes.

"Why are you not stitching?" snarled Lady Mary.

God, these women were exhausting. I bit back a retort and resumed stitching the hem of a lacy white collar. Snapping at Lady Mary seemed cruel because, when I was home and reading about the Tudors, I learned that when Elizabeth became ill with smallpox, Lady Mary cared for her until she caught the disease herself. Upon recovering, Mary was so disfigured from scars that her husband said, "I left her a full fair lady in my eyes, and when I returned I found her as foul a lady as smallpox could make her." I'd memorized the horrid words. What an asshole. (Aunt Nicole had no problem with that word; she said it reminded her of her ex-husband.)

Cecil, Elizabeth's secretary, bustled back and forth between his office and the Queen, presenting long scrolls to sign. When would I be released from this regal hell? I scanned the room for Harriet, but of course she wouldn't be hanging around the courtiers. Perhaps she was still stuck working in the laundry. Thinking about Harriet helped pass the time. I wondered about her past, and at her feeling as out of place as I did. At one particularly slow point in the afternoon, when the sun shone in on my stool, I grew so sleepy that waking dreams took over. In one, I could no longer travel back to the future. Perhaps the GCA in my system had diluted enough that it no longer electrified me. What would I do if I were stuck here? I would buy a small house for me and Harriet in one of the better London neighborhoods. We would hug each other until we no longer felt like walking deserts. Harriet's sparkling eyes, warm smile, and trusting love could reduce the pain of being stuck forever in the sixteenth century. Too bad Blanche had absolutely no money.

"Lady Blanche."

I jumped. One of Cecil's assistants stood before me. "Lord Cecil wishes a word."

Grateful to escape the hot, stuffy room, I followed him to Cecil's lair, a labyrinth of five or six rooms connected by hidden doors. Cecil sat at his desk, scratching at a document with a long goose feather. The smell of warm ink and hot dust tickled my nose.

I began to sit.

"Stand, if you please," he barked.

I did so. Cecil also stood, his deep red robe swelling over a middle-aged gut. He strolled around his desk, coming to a halt inches from me. I could not step back because of the heavy chair behind me, but the man needed an Altoid. "I know of your scheming," Cecil said.

"I don't know what—"

"You are plotting with three men. I do not know their names, nor do I know the goal of that plot. You will tell me all."

I swallowed. "I have no idea what you are talking about. I plot with no one." I wondered if Blanche had a poker face. If not, I was screwed.

"My sources tell me you have met several times. Male voices could be heard. You appear all kindness and innocence, then you change into a woman of cunning and wiles...then back to innocence. My sources are most impressed with your ability to change yourself. Her Majesty calls you her Spark, but you would more accurately be called her chameleon."

I shook my head. "I know nothing of which you speak, Sir Cecil."

He snorted, amused. "Lady Blanche, you can be a hard woman, but I can be harsh as well. Your plotting must cease. You have one day in which to reconsider. At that time if you tell me everything, I may be lenient with you."

"And if I don't give you this information?"

"I will use the Tower to get it," Cecil snapped.

I shivered, since I'd seen the Tower's implements of torture—the manacles hanging from the ceiling, the racks, and a nasty set of irons called the Scavenger's Daughter. Crap. Now what was I supposed to do? The plotting would end tomorrow with Dudley's murder. Cecil would have been thrilled to know this, since he was Dudley's greatest enemy. If Dudley were killed, Cecil would know *that* had been the plot. He wouldn't follow through with his threat because he'd hardly punish anyone who killed the man he despised and feared as the Queen's potential king. I closed my eyes. If I let Dudley be murdered, then I'd be safe from the Tower.

I didn't like any of my choices.

I nodded, curtsied, then backed out of the room. What the hell was I supposed to do?

I paced the length of my bedroom, stopping to open drawers to touch piles of elaborate collars and sleeves then closing them again. On top of one dresser was the small wooden box that I'd assumed was Lady Mary's, but when I looked at the underside, I found etched into the dark wood, "To Blanche from Daddy."

Huh. If this was Blanche's box, then it was mine now. The hinge protested but opened. The first thing that popped out was a folded piece of paper. Beneath that glittered drop earrings made of paste, along with a likely fake pearl necklace.

I opened the paper and gasped.

Dearest Jamie,

I will continue to leave messages for you until one day it will no longer be necessary. I have come back to my body to find that you have nearly destroyed all that I have built. You have affected my plans in quite an unacceptable manner.

Blanche's handwriting was narrow but firm.

My gowns fit more loosely, so I am clearly wasting away. My generous body is proof I am prosperous, that I can afford to eat well, so do not change this. Yes, I realize I eat at the Queen's merciful table, but I earn every morsel. I leave you this note only to tell you that I have nearly figured out a way to remain where you and I both know I prefer to live. When this has happened, you may emaciate the body you inhabit to your heart's content. I will no longer require it, so you may consider it, and the life that it bears, yours to keep.
Your rival of the most unusual sort,
Blanche

The bitch. She knew she was pregnant. I stalked through the apartments until I found a fireplace burning, wadded up the letter, and tossed it into the fire. As I watched it burn, I realized I had never felt so turned upside down in my entire life. No matter which body I inhabited, I was alone.

That night I managed to find Harriet and suggest a bath in the pond. After sunset, we met at the edge of the park, and Vincent led us down the dark trail.

At the pond, I flung off my dress, no longer self-conscious, and we were soon both floating on our backs. My breasts and toes rose above the water, as did a small swelling of belly. I'd never been pregnant before, and I found myself horrified and excited at the same time. I'd always thought Chris and I might one day have a child together, but she was lukewarm on the topic.

An owl hooted nearby, but otherwise the forest was silent except for the occasional rattling of leaves. I inhaled the smells of moist earth, feeling relaxed and safe in my forest cocoon. Because I ached for someone to know me as *me,* not as Blanche, it was time to tell Harriet the truth.

"This is nice," Harriet said.

Tell her, my brain screamed. *Tell* her! "Harriet, is it wrong to be content?"

She frowned as she dipped her head back in the water. "I do not understand."

"Everyone is to be driven by ambition. As a maiden, I am supposed to marry the wealthiest man I can find. I am supposed to be the best dancer, aside from Her Majesty. I am supposed to have the straightest stitches, the most graceful walk, the whitest skin, all aside from Her Majesty. Yet I often don't feel driven in this way."

"I understand what you are asking. It is a question I have struggled with all my life. In my village, women are expected to be as busy and successful as men, not like it is here, in the palace, where you are expected to do as little as possible."

"That seems to be my greatest skill," I said, drawing a warm smile from Harriet.

"In my village we are taught to always desire more than we have, to raise more sheep, bake more bread, to have the cleanest home. While I understand that striving to be better pushes people to move beyond their skills, I also understand that it sets us up to be forever discontent." She squeezed my hand. "I cannot imagine a world in which you deserve to be discontent, my dear Blanche."

"You would not think less of me should I choose to be content, rather than the best or the fastest or the richest?"

Harriet's brown eyes shone with a brightness more often seen in lighter-colored eyes. If I could only capture that sparkle in a painting. "I would think less of you only if you walked down someone else's path instead of your own."

My eyes stung. Why couldn't Chris say this to me? It was exactly what I needed to hear.

Because of that, doubt crept back into my heart. Maybe Chris was right, and all this around me was entirely the product of my imagination. Perhaps Jamie, the real me, *had* retreated to some corner of my brain to indulge in this fantasy while "Blanche," my other half, controlled my body and my behavior. Chris would insist I'd created Harriet to say what I needed to hear.

Tell her. "Harriet, there is something I must tell you."

Harriet's face was open, receptive to anything I might wish to share. But what if she, like Chris, would think me mentally whacked out of shape? My throat tightened at the thought.

"I'm pregnant," I said.

Harriet drew back, eyes wide and her skin flushed from her swim. "What?"

"I am with child."

"But...but how?"

"Do you not know of the act that brings a child into the world?"

Now her face went blotchy with embarrassment. "Bloody hell. Of course I do."

Her flash of irritation suggested Harriet had more fire in her than I'd thought. "Well, apparently, I engaged in that act."

"Apparently?"

"I'm not certain what I should do."

Harriet pursed her lips, then straightened. "You are not alone. We will puzzle this out until we have a solution and a plan. Every problem needs a plan."

We talked so long that Vincent gave up and snored beside the pond, and my fingers and toes turned into prunes.

Despite putting our two heads together, we didn't come up with a plan.

CHAPTER TWENTY-ONE

The next day, I managed to avoid Cecil and his minions, but doing so involved wandering through the outbuildings of the palace, hanging out with Jacob in the guardhouse, and hiding behind a black gilded screen in the library.

That night, Elizabeth and her ladies played cards late, while I claimed a headache so I could just sit quietly and watch. Were I not so freaked out by the evening's plans for murder, I would have enjoyed the time. Candlelight at night always softened the chamber's rough edges like a blurred watercolor and seemed to repel the frightening and strange world outside. Within Elizabeth's circle, I felt safe and secure. True, the other women didn't seem to like me much, but I had detected some softening in their attitudes. Vincent and I played a gentle game of tug on my lap with a rag, but soon he tired and curled up like a cat.

Elizabeth was by turns raucous and tender as she played. She always insisted that her ladies not let her win, so the contests were real and tense. Elizabeth, to her credit, always laughed heartily when she lost. I didn't remember history recording her as such a good sport. But of course, few of the people who wrote down the events of the day were actually in the room. Most scribes were foreign diplomats writing back to their sovereigns about the latest gossip. They were councilors who wrote letters and diaries. Within the Queen's intimate quarters, I'd never witnessed any writing, other than the Queen herself jotting notes to Cecil or Dudley.

It had to be almost midnight. Then a clock chimed from a nearby room. Twelve chimes. I tried to still the tremors running through me. *Use what I know*, Ray had counseled. I knew too much, that was the problem. The way forward felt lined with broken glass; any misstep could send history spiraling off in the wrong direction. Was I supposed to stop Winston? Was I supposed to let it play out, hoping that the men were unsuccessful? Three men against Dudley placed the odds in their favor, even thought Dudley was skilled with both knife and sword.

Use what I know. Like a zombie, I stood and forced my feet to move toward the open door. I left the room without notice and headed for the back stairway, where the dank air was cold against my skin. I lifted a wall candle from its hook, and in its feeble light I took one step down, then another.

Then I stopped. I saw with hyper clarity, in the nearly black stairwell, what I must do. The pain of it doubled me over so quickly I refluxed, then gagged at the acid burning my throat. God's bones, I would use what I knew.

I continued down the stairs, hurrying now. The candle sputtered and smoked in protest. At the first small landing, I could hear his footsteps so I stepped carefully, drawn to the sound like iron to a magnet. At the second landing, the light of our candles merged. "My Lady Blanche." We stopped, and Dudley flashed me a roguish grin. "Now I do not need a candle to see, for the glow of your beauty enables me to walk through the darkest cave."

I snorted, my candle trembling. "Robert Dudley," I said softly. "You are so full of shit."

He laughed in delight. Then I moved my skirts aside with one hand and let him pass. As he continued upward, I took a shuddering breath. That was the easy part.

I reached the base of the stairs, feeling the breeze from an open door. My candle fought for its life as two dark shapes entered the hallway. I stood in front of the stairs, blocking their way.

"What in God's name are you doing down here?" Winston hissed. I jerked free of his angry grasp.

"We only have a few minutes, so listen carefully," I snapped. "I let Dudley pass up to the Queen's chamber. William will not find him on the stairs."

"You stupid cunt," Charles growled. "You have ruined everything."

I ignored him. "Killing Dudley is not the answer to your problem. You want him powerless, no? You want him banished from the court? You think that with Dudley dead, England is safe? Not so. With Dudley dead, Elizabeth will lose heart. She will lose hope. She will accept the next proposal she receives, even should it come from King Philip of France himself. You will have led England directly into the hands of her enemies."

"That is ridiculous," Winston said. "We have been over this a hundred times. The only way to keep Elizabeth from marrying Dudley is to kill him."

"What if I told you of a way that would both humiliate Dudley and place the Crown of England forever beyond his reach?"

Jaws working in fury, eyes glancing up to the stairs in hopes that Dudley would appear, both men were only seconds from pushing their way past me.

My lips were so dry I could barely spit out my next words. "Don't kill Dudley. Kill his wife."

The men gasped. "What?" Winston snapped.

"If Amy dies a questionable death, Dudley will be so tainted that Elizabeth dare not think of marrying him. Her subjects would never accept a king who has come under the shadow of murder."

The men looked at each other. "Why did you not suggest this in our last meeting? Why wait until now?"

"Because I did not think of it until just two minutes ago. But this will be the best way to accomplish your goals, and at much less risk to you." I hesitated, feeling sick to my stomach, trying to recall the details surrounding Amy Dudley's death. "There is a fair in Abingdon soon, September eighth if I remember. Amy will be at Cumnor Place, and will likely send all her servants to the fair. This would be an excellent time to, say, push her down a flight of stairs."

Winston's eyes widened. "Murder an innocent woman?"

"Her bones are brittle. The fall will likely kill her. And it will ruin Dudley. The entire kingdom will believe he had his wife murdered in order to pursue his ambitions with the Queen. He will never be welcome in court again." That last sentence wasn't true, but my goal was to stop Dudley's murder tonight, not tell the truth.

Winston looked up the stairs at the sound of a sword scabbard scraping the wall. William appeared around the corner, clumping down the stairs and out of breath. "What the hell happened? Dudley is already in the Queen's chambers."

Winston held up a hand. "I will explain as we leave." His dark eyes were ominous above my dying candle. "We will follow your plan. But should it fail, you will not live to see September ninth."

The men's capes flared as they whirled and ran out the door like cartoon evildoers escaping into the night. My candle flared once, then collapsed into a steaming puddle of wax. As I felt my way back upstairs by touching the moist walls, I could hear Elizabeth and Dudley laughing. The man Elizabeth loved would never know how close he had come to death. I passed the room and found my way to my own bedchamber. I was alone, so I untied as much of my dress as I could, then collapsed on the bed and pulled the covers over me. Amy Dudley was going to die. That was part of history. That I had just arranged for it to happen made me feel unclean.

CHAPTER TWENTY-TWO

The next morning, I still felt sick to my stomach. I'd saved Dudley's life, plotted Amy's death, and now had Cecil to face. When Rosemary helped me dress, I asked her to not lace me so tightly. It couldn't be good for the baby.

After Lady Clinton and I had dressed Elizabeth in a gown of nut brown brocade with sleeves slashed with pink and a headpiece covered in pink beads and small shells, I lightly touched Elizabeth on the wrist. She stopped, stunned. No one touched the Queen. She did all the touching. I waited until Lady Clinton had left, then I collapsed at the Queen's feet, my skirts billowing out like Marilyn standing over the city grate. I looked up into Elizabeth's concerned face and realized how much I respected this woman. She would help me.

"Please, Your Majesty, there is no one I can turn to but you. I know you are petitioned every day for Your Majesty's grace and wisdom, but now I find myself one of these helpless beings who falls at your feet."

Her hand rested lightly on my head, spreading warmth down my neck and across my shoulders. God, I was hungry for touch of any kind. Elizabeth lowered herself gracefully into her chair. "Pray tell us what has brought you to this state."

"Lord Cecil is your Spirit, Robert Dudley your Eyes, and you have named me your Spark. Well, this spark is about to be dimmed too greatly to ever be relit." I swallowed hard. "Ma'am, Lord Cecil suspects me of something almost too horrid to even speak out loud, but I must. My lord suspects me of plotting against you." Something other than fear of Cecil crept up my throat and made it hard to talk. It was the very idea that I would do anything to harm this woman. I had already prostrated myself before her. I would not cry as well, so I rose up onto my knees and straightened my dress around me. Both of us could see that my hands shook. "He says I've plotted with three men to harm you, and that if I do not reveal the names of the men, and the nature of the plot, he will use the Tower to extract the information."

A hot tear slid down my cheek, cooling before I could wipe it away.

Elizabeth stood and graciously helped me to my feet. "My dear Spark, Cecil is our advisor, not our ruler. And if we say you are free from the taint of treason, he will have no choice but to respect that."

I bit off a strangled sob, partly in relief, partly out of love for this woman. Then I took Elizabeth's hand, pressed it against my heart, and placed my hand over hers. When the young queen's eyes widened, I struggled to breathe through my emotions. "I know you do not require oaths of your ladies, but I say this to you now: I have never, and will never, harm you or your realm. I will be your faithful and loving servant for as long as I draw breath. I will accept no advice but yours. I will live for no voice but yours." I released her hand and stepped back, only then meeting her eyes. They glistened as mine did.

"We are…" Elizabeth's voice struggled, thick and tight. "We are deeply moved by this, Blanche Nottingham, and will accept your pledge without reservation." Then she smiled shyly and touched my chest. "We know your heart, and we know it is good."

❖

When Elizabeth gave a summer party, she spared no expense even though her royal coffers ran low her entire reign. Out on one of the broad lawns between the courtiers' apartments and the forest, she had men build a banqueting house of birch boughs and ivy. Stiff canvas painted blue with white clouds formed the roof. Underneath the canvas, rows of tables groaned under pitchers of drinks and platters of sweets and fruits. The most impressive was a menagerie made entirely of spun sugar—camels, lions, frogs, mermaids, and unicorns. The banqueting house's open sides allowed the hot air to circulate, but there was still barely a breeze.

It was a beautiful day for a party, and I seemed to have acclimated to wearing all these layers of clothing. Women sat on stools and benches, while the men strolled among them. I sat off by myself, knowing that if Elizabeth needed me she would let me know. Meanwhile I held the collar I was supposed to be mending, only pretending to stitch by moving the needle up and down through the fabric. The saturated air settled over the party as if it, too, was exhausted.

Harriet's job was to keep the dessert trays full, so she'd disappear now and then, returning with another full tray. After the third tray, I wandered close, pretending to study the choices. "How was the tart?" I asked.

"What tart?"

"The one still on your face."

Gasping, she wiped her mouth with the back of her hand. We didn't look at each other, but both chuckled softly. Ladies and servants didn't share jokes together.

"Do you like tarts?" Harriet asked.

"I do."

She picked up another empty tray with a devilish grin. "That's good, because I am one."

Now I did laugh out loud. I might have been stuck in the pregnant body of a bitch named Blanche in 1560, but at least I had Harriet to add spark to my days. The look Harriet tossed over her shoulder as she left reminded me so much of my friend Mary that, for a second, Harriet seemed a contemporary, a twenty-first century tease.

"Lady Blanche."

I jumped at the male voice behind me.

"Might I have the honor of your company as I stroll around the edge of the garden?" It was Lord Winston again, my definition of a waking nightmare.

"Get stuffed," I said. He was the reason I was walking around pregnant.

"I beg your pardon?"

"Leave me alone."

Winston dug his fingers into my elbow so deeply I gasped as he pulled me away from the party. He had shed his cape, so I could see that dark stains rimmed the undersides of his billowing sleeves. The vest he wore sparkled with silver threads woven through the green.

When he felt we'd walked a safe distance away, Winston directed me to another bench. I sank down gratefully and decided to play offense. "Have you considered my alternate proposal, Sir Winston?"

"I have." The man's thin moustache twitched, and I could see that it had been dyed to better match his black hair. "And I have decided that as much as I want to harm Dudley, I am unable to harm an innocent woman."

I tried to hide my sigh of relief, but my breasts gave me away by nearly popping over the top of my bodice. By the downward flicker of his eyes, Winston clearly found my sigh fascinating. "Then I guess we will have to think of something else," I said.

Winston's tight smile made me nervous. "No, I think not. Your plan is a sound one. But instead of one of my men performing the act we spoke of the other night, you will do it yourself."

I lumbered to my feet. "I don't think so."

"Don't be coy, Blanche. You are as capable of performing this act as the most ruthless man."

I swallowed despite the lump of fear blocking my throat. "I cannot kill anyone."

"You have all but done it with your plan. Sneaking into Cumnor Place and giving Amy Dudley a push down the stairs will be nothing."

I didn't need to ask what would happen if I refused. Winston could send me to the Tower as easily as Cecil.

God's teeth. What the hell was I supposed to do now?

❖

I rejoined the other women in the shade and picked up my stitching. Damn that Winston. I tried to concentrate, but thoughts of Amy Dudley kept piercing my focus. Amy must die in order to keep the time line intact. But what if Chris was right? What if I really wasn't here, in 1560, but just playing out some weird fantasy in my mind? What difference would it make if Amy lived, or if Dudley and Elizabeth married?

None. I was either deeply mired in a struggle for the future, or I was boxing with shadows. I didn't know which, and I hated that. I needed to talk to someone. Ray. I needed to see Ray.

During a lull in the conversation, I stood and curtsied, requesting permission to remove myself from the party. Elizabeth nodded, so I walked back to the palace and found Jacob in the guardhouse. "Jacob, darling," I said. If flirting worked, I'd do it. "I was wondering if you could take me to visit Hew Draper in the Tower."

Jacob stood, scratching his unshaven cheek. "I am sorry, m'lady, but my friend at the Tower was here sharing a jug last night. Said that your friend died yesterday."

I exhaled and doubled over in pain. Jacob rushed to my side. "I am sorry to be the one to bring you the bad news. Is there anything you require?"

I stood, brushing away tears. "No. Thank you, Jacob, for telling me."

I quietly returned to the party. Poor Ray. Transported back into the past, with no way to return. Now both he and Hew Draper were gone. I stitched quietly. Selfishly, it hit me that I still had no one to talk to.

After about thirty minutes of this, I snarled my thread so badly that I couldn't keep going. "Hand it to me," Lady Mary said. But when I tried to do that, the fabric snapped free of my hand and clung to my skirts.

"What?" I tugged at the collar, only to realize that at some point I had actually sewn it to my dress. "God's blood. Today I seem to have hooves instead of hands."

Elizabeth threw back her head and laughed, a welcome sound at the edge of the quiet party. Surprised, I caught the Queen's mirth, and we both laughed until tears streamed down our faces, which helped banish, at least temporarily, my sadness over Ray. As we laughed, wagons rattled down the rutted King Street and several boats floated by on the Thames.

That's when it hit me: Living in this century—or this corner of my mind—wasn't so bad. The weather was similar to modern London. The Queen adored me and I think even depended upon me. Harriet kept me sane and grounded. I actually *liked* it here some days, even though the air was so moist my legs and arms were slick with sweat.

"Lady Blanche, how are you feeling?" Lady Mary gave me an insincere smile over her stitching.

"I am well, thank you."

"It is just that you have not seen your courses for many weeks."

The women around us gasped, and the Queen looked up from her card game with Lady Clinton and a few others.

I glared at Lady Mary. "Kind of you to notice, but they came yesterday."

"Perchance you are lying, since your rags remain in your trunk." The little sneak had looked through my things.

"Don't 'perchance' me, Lady Mary. This is none of your business."

"But it is ours." Elizabeth's chilly voice froze us all in place.

Fire truck.

The Queen waved her hands. "Be gone with all of you. We wish to be alone with Blanche." I kept my eyes on the ground as the women gathered up their skirts and headed toward a knot of courtiers, and wondered how much leeway the Queen would give her Spark.

"Who is he?"

I stammered with guilt even though I'd done nothing. "I am so sorry, ma'am. I never meant this to happen. That I have disappointed you wounds me deeply."

"You must marry this man."

Marry Winston? Perchance when Republicans supported universal health care. "I do not wish to marry."

"What you wish is of no consequence to us. You cannot remain in court unless you do. Who is he?"

"I cannot tell you."

Elizabeth stood, becoming in less than a second the haughty, to-be-obeyed monarch that she was. I swallowed hard.

Out of the corner of my eye, I saw the brilliant flash of heat lightning that yanked me from Blanche's body and shot me skyward.

Thank God. Now Blanche could deal with her own mess.

CHAPTER TWENTY-THREE

I stood, but wove on my feet as if drunk, so I took in a deep breath and let it out slowly. After a few more times, I felt better and realized I was in my studio.

Black angry splashes caught my attention. I turned slowly in a circle, moaning as I did. Every Froggity painting on the wall, the ones I'd completed for the next series, had been slashed with black paint. My books had been strewn around the room. My computer had been pounded into nothing but a pile of parts.

Growling in fury, I paced, desperate to yell at the person who had done this. It had to have been Blanche. She found my note. She chose to ignore everything I asked her to do. Bitch.

My hands shook as I gathered up my computer and carried it gently to the dust bin. Too upset to even cry, I sagged against the wall. The digital versions of the paintings had been in my computer. The backups were on a fire-engine red thumb drive, which I found stomped to bits beside the computer.

When I put my hands on my hips, *so* frustrated, I felt a lump in the back pocket of my shorts. I pulled out a piece of folded note-paper and opened it. God, would these letters never stop?

Dearest Jamie,

How dare you give me a list of tasks you require. I am not your slave to order about as you will. In fact, I am in charge of you, and of everything. I will figure out a way to take your body and your life, permanently. The idea that I would passively remain stuck in the past is laughable. The riches in this life are beyond imagining, and I intend to take all of them for myself. This includes Chris. She is a gem you have never appreciated, and has been the best guide to this world that I could have asked for. If you are reading this, it means we have once again traded bodies, but I have taken steps to ensure that the next time I return to your body, I will remain there until Jamie "Blanche" Maddox dies of old age. Fuck you.... Blanche

Shaking, I jammed the note back into my pocket, fled my office, and ran for Halsey House. My phone said it was Sunday, so Chris should be home. I banged into the flat, slamming the door behind me. "Chris? Chris? Are you here?"

She stepped into the hallway from the kitchen. "I was just about to call you. Waffles are almost ready."

"I hate waffles. Why would you make waffles?"

Chris's jaw twitched. "Because last week you told me you loved them now."

"That wasn't me," I shouted, directing my fury at Chris because Blanche was gone. "I'm Jamie, and I'm back. Look at the note Blanche left me. This is war, Chris. I'm gonna kill the bitch."

Chris took the note from my trembling hand. She read it out loud, then let the note flutter to the floor. "Jamie, this note is in your handwriting."

"God's blood, of course it is!" I shouted. "It's my body, so it'd be my handwriting."

"God's blood? What the fuck does that even mean?" Chris stepped back into the kitchen, reached for the counter, but didn't make it. Her knees folded like a wounded deer's and she collapsed against the cabinet. Her shoulders shook. I recognized the signs. Chris was a silent crier.

I knelt beside her. "Look, I'm sorry I yelled at you. It's not your fault. The God's blood thing is Elizabethan. They tend to curse all of God's body parts. I'm surprised Blanche hasn't done that. I—"

Chris clutched at my T-shirt, eyes wild. "I love you so much. Do you know that? And I'm terrified for you. One minute you're Jamie and then you're Blanche and then you're Jamie. You hate waffles, then like them, then hate them. You paint, then you write, then you paint, and I'm going crazy. I can't live like this." I took her in my arms, holding her tightly against me as she sobbed. "You need help, Blanche. Please! Please get help. We can't do this without help."

I wrapped my legs around her as she curled up on the floor. "Please," she whimpered. Tears stung my eyes as I stroked her hair. Chris had never broken down like this before.

"Baby, it's okay. We—"

"No, it's *not* okay. You need help. None of this is normal."

I leaned toward an open, low shelf, grabbed a handful of tissues, and handed them to Chris.

"Okay, okay," I crooned. "We'll make an appointment to see Dr. Kroll. It'll be okay." I kept her warm with my body, massaging her shoulders and back, until the shuddering ceased and she fell quiet.

For me to remain sane, I had to believe that my travels back to 1560 were real. Yet this was tearing Chris apart. I had no choice.

Dr. Kroll wasn't what I expected. She couldn't have been more than a few years older than we were. Her hair was unfashionably long, two thick braids brought forward over each shoulder. She wore shiny brown boots, a mid-length skirt of some sort of flimsy material, and a peasant blouse. She would have fit right into the sixties. Her office was painted a soft orange, the chairs and pillows splashing the room with a mild turquoise and pale pink.

"Fill me in, Blanche," Dr. Kroll said. "Tell me what's been happening." I looked at the small clock on the table beside her striped chair. "Don't worry," she said. "We have two hours." Chris sat in the chair next to me, hands clasped in her lap.

"First, my name is Jamie." Then I told her everything, even details I'd kept from Chris for fear of alarming her. I told them both about Winston and the plot to murder Dudley. I even confessed my own suggestion that they kill Amy Dudley instead. I told them about

Ray Lexvold. I shared that I'd made a friend in Harriet. I told them about my respect and affection for Queen Elizabeth and my joy at life with a dog by my side. I told them that I—in Blanche's body— was pregnant.

Dr. Kroll didn't write down one single word. Weren't psychiatrists supposed to take notes? Then she turned to Chris. "Now tell me what's been going on from your perspective."

"After the accident Jamie was not herself at all. It was as if the whole world terrified her. She stayed in the spare room. Wouldn't sleep in our bed. Wouldn't look out the window. Barely ate. But then she started coming back, which was such a relief. It was as if she had to relearn everything, however. She watched TV constantly, asked questions that only an alien suddenly dumped in London would ask."

I nodded at Kroll. "See? That was Blanche, struggling to adjust to life in the twenty-first century."

"One of the things that fascinated her was money and the idea that a woman could earn it herself, that she didn't have to wait for a father to dish it out."

"See, Blanche again."

Chris waved in irritation. "You knew all that stuff from your research."

Kroll leaned forward. "Chris, keep going."

"She started rereading all her books on the Tudors, and I even found her crying one morning. When I asked her why, she flung the book across the room and said, 'Dead! Everyone I ever knew or loved is dead.'" Chris shot me a look. "That hurt, I can tell you."

"It wasn't me!" I snapped.

"Then Blanche started writing, on paper at first, but then she asked me to show her how to use her laptop, as if she'd never seen it before. She pretended to be a quick study, but of course, she already knew how to do everything. Then she wrote like crazy. She only stopped when I pulled her away to eat. She let me read part of it one day." She turned to me. "I know you think painting is your thing, but your novel is riveting."

"It's not mine," I said, weaker this time. My story was lunacy compared to hers.

Chris shared a few more details of her life with Blanche. "She calls me 'her princess,' which I love. And sex with Blanche is different."

"In what way?" I snapped.

"It's hard to describe," she said. "But don't pretend to be jealous. Blanche is part of you. She is you. So it's not like I'm being unfaithful or anything." Then she finished, ending with the waffle story. Dr. Kroll steepled her fingers and stared at me like I were a ripe pineapple needing to be carved open.

I waited, my heart thumping loudly in my ears. This was it, the point where she told me I was crazy. But maybe—just maybe—she might believe that 1560 was real.

"We need to run a full brain scan," she finally said. "I want to compare the readings with any records that this Dr. Rajamani might have. And there are a few tests I would like to you to take."

Chris's hands shook in her lap. I wanted to reach over and take one in mine, but then I realized I was the one who needed comforting. It was *my* brain, *my* life we were picking apart like a Thanksgiving turkey.

Dr. Kroll shifted in her chair until she looked directly at me. "Jamie, I find your story amazing and rich and incredibly exciting. Because of what you've told me, 1560 now feels as real to me as this very moment."

My mouth went dry.

"Let me ask you one question. Have your feelings for life in 1560 changed any since you first visited that time period?"

"Changed?"

"Do you feel more or less excited about being there? Do you feel more or less calm at the idea of staying?"

I licked my lips. "Well, I hated it at first. Everything was so freaky. I kept doing and saying the wrong thing. But now when I go back, I can see the beauty in a world that technology hasn't yet dominated. Life is complicated in many ways, yet so much simpler at the same time." I didn't look at Chris. "Each time I return, I grow more…comfortable."

Dr. Kroll's eyes flickered away then returned to my face. She tried to hide her inhale, but I saw the rise of her ribcage. "Jamie, this is going to be hard for you to hear, but you exhibit all the signs of someone with dissociative identity disorder. You might have heard it called split personality. For some reason, perhaps because of a deep trauma or something in your unconscious mind, when you were shocked by Dr. Rajamani's equipment you created another identity. Think of it as allowing an unfamiliar part of your personality to emerge. These two personalities, Jamie and Blanche, are fighting for control of your mind and your body."

Chris began to cry softly, wiping her eyes with the palms of her hands.

I felt numb. "I don't believe you." Kroll didn't know what she was talking about.

"I don't want you to be ashamed or embarrassed by this. Mistakenly, mental disorders used to be associated with character flaws, but luckily, we no longer frame psychopathology in such cruel terms. Still, there's so much confusion about our psyches that people tend to feel ashamed of any problems."

I threw up my hands, still unwilling to accept anything she said.

"You have created a world with fascinating characters. You have a dog for the first time in your life. You are becoming more comfortable in the past, which tells me that your mind is trying to find some way to resolve the struggle between Jamie and Blanche. If one of your personalities can be convinced to remain permanently in the past, either Jamie or Blanche, then the other can take full control of you, here, now."

I showed Dr. Kroll the note. "Are you really trying to tell me that I wrote this to myself? That I, as Blanche, want to harm myself? That I trashed my own studio?"

Dr. Kroll read the note and handed it back to me. "The power of our unconscious mind can be frightening. You are struggling with something and this is your mind's way of resolving it. Why has this happened? I don't know."

I met Dr. Kroll's steady gaze. "I don't believe you are right, but for Chris's sake I'm willing to move forward with your suggestions."

She glanced at the clock. "I would like to do some tests. Once we have those results, we'll discuss medication options, as well as therapy to uncover the issues that might have led to this psychic break."

Chris clutched at my hand, eyes moist. "Blanche, we'll figure this out. We'll get through this together, okay?"

I pulled my hand away. "My name is *not* Blanche." I should have been jealous that Chris kept calling me Blanche, but strangely, I wasn't.

CHAPTER TWENTY-FOUR

D r. Raj hustled me into his office, then began wiping at a white board covered with calculations. When he faced me, hands clasped, I realized I was about to hear a lecture.

"Lightning. It strikes the planet twenty-five to thirty million times a year. Mortality rate for lightning strikes is between five and thirty percent. One man, Roy Sullivan, was the human lightning rod, surviving seven strikes. People rang medieval England church bells violently to keep lightning from striking the towers. Commonly inscribed on the bells was *fulgura franco*." He wrote this on his board. "This means *I break up the lightning flashes*."

"Dr. Raj," I interrupted. "All interesting facts, but could you skip to the good part, please, where you remove the GCA from my blood before another storm hits?" Dad had given me advice, years ago, that if you want to accomplish something but are afraid, you must act as if you *aren't* afraid, as if you're confident the thing you want to come true will actually happen. For now, at least, I needed to act as if 1560 were real, as if Blanche Nottingham truly was a consciousness trying to take over control of my body.

"Yes, yes, certainly. Electricity is drawn together when positively charged protons move toward negatively charged electrons. Lightning is negatively charged, the surface of the earth is positively charged, so the lightning is pulled down to the ground. Lightning happens!" He flung up his hands energetically.

I began to pace the small room. "But what does this have to do with my consciousness?"

"Yes, yes, certainly. Here is the key." He returned to his board. "As a bolt of lightning approaches the ground, an upward streamer emerges from the object about to be struck. When the two meet, the bolt from the cloud hits the earth at the same time a return bolt from the earth is shot back into the clouds."

"Wait. Lightning moves from the cloud to the ground, then back up to the cloud?"

"Precisely."

"Why don't we see that?"

"Happens too quickly. Lightning moves at 320,000,000 feet per second." Raj looked at me. "Remember the GCA I injected into your system before the lab experiment?"

My mouth seemed to have stopped producing saliva. "Not likely to forget that."

"Somehow, inexplicably, the drug changed the electrical charge of your glial cells, which *must* contain our conscious minds. Remember the orchestra I described at the beginning, the conductor being the intralaminar nuclei oscillating at forty hertz? Together the GCA and your nuclei oscillating at a different rate have created the conditions for transport. So when the lightning strikes, your consciousness is the opposite charge of the cloud and is pulled from your body and taken up to the cloud on the return bolt of lightning."

My jaw dropped. "You're telling me that, basically, I'm riding lightning?" Fire trucking insane. "Let's assume your theory is correct. Thanks to the GCA, I'm charged the wrong way. How do we recharge my glial cells so they're repelled by lightning, not attracted? How do I get my orchestra back to forty hertz?"

Dr. Raj dropped into his chair. "That, Jamie Maddox, is an excellent question." His shoulders slumped. "I do not know how to counteract the GCA."

My pulsed raced. "Wait. You said you'd solved it."

"The reason for what happened, not how to fix it."

"How long will this stupid GCA remain in my system?"

"I cannot know for sure." He checked his calendar. "It has been seven weeks since the initial episode."

My jaw tightened. "So you haven't solved anything."

"Not true!" He leapt out of his chair and returned to his whiteboard. "Why London? That one was easy—because that is where you, Meg, and Ray were when you were taken by the lightning. I assume Meg has gone to the same place as you and Ray. But why 1560? That is more interesting." He scribbled a series of numbers on the board and stood back, beaming. "Your brain has three basic types of waves—delta, which is between one and four hertz, theta, between four and eight hertz, and finally gamma, which runs from thirty to seventy, with some spikes as high as one hundred. Your gammas, however...." He tapped the board for emphasis. "Yours spiked to four hundred and fifty-seven hertz."

I winced. "Intense."

"Very! And that is the precise number of years you went back in time."

"That fits nicely, but why did Ray go back the same number of years? And what about Meg—we have no idea where she ended up. Wouldn't our brains spike at different rates? Does it have to do with the strength of the lightning?"

He shook his head. "I checked the records. You all spiked up to four hundred and fifty-seven hertz."

"But as the amount of GCA in my blood decreases, wouldn't the spikes be lower? Wouldn't I start traveling fewer years back in time?" The thought of popping up into an entirely new time made me twitch.

"Either the pattern has already been set, or the GCA stays constant for a long time."

I ran my fingers through my hair, squeezing gently. "But how does this help me stop traveling back to 1560?"

"I will solve this problem. Do not fear. Together we are making history."

I told Dr. Raj about my session with Dr. Kroll. His eyes widened. "But that cannot be true. She is trying to undercut the importance of my discovery. I am the first to locate and transport a consciousness! She cannot weaken this by throwing jumbo mumbo at my accomplishment." He slammed the marker onto his desk. "No, I will prove that your experience is real, not jumbo mumbo. The Consciousness Conference is next year in Tucson, so I must be ready by then."

I stood. "Let's focus on now, shall we? The clock is ticking, Doc. Thanks to all the thunderstorms we've been having this summer, I don't know where I'll be when."

Dr. Raj gathered together a chaotic stack of readouts. "I will solve this yesterday. You will hear from me soon."

❖

There was nothing to salvage from the mess Blanche had made in my studio. Standing there, heart breaking at the angry black slashes, I could not believe that I was Blanche. Why would I ever do this to my own work? Never, never, never.

I didn't have to replace my smashed computer because Blanche had bought her own. I found it hidden under the desk in the spare room. It wasn't password protected—thank God her computer skills hadn't progressed that far—so I could easily take the computer on as my own. Tempted as I was to open Word and read Blanche's novel-in-progress, I decided not to. Doing so would make her seem more legitimate.

Instead, I reentered the important email addresses I could remember, then sent a long, so-sorry-I-messed-up email to Candace. I claimed that vandals broke into my studio and destroyed all my work. I would have to start over on the Froggity books, but I assured her it wouldn't take long since I'd already done them once already.

Her reply was speedy, but terse. "So sorry to hear of the break-in. Send all Froggity art ASAP. We are behind behind behind. As for the new books, they have all been assigned. Our stable of artists is now quite full, so we don't anticipate any more assignments for you."

If Blanche had been standing before me, all big hair and big bosom, I would have slapped her clear across the Thames. I wanted to open her novel file and perform the equivalent of black angry slashes across it, but instead, I forced myself to close the computer, then sit down and begin sketching the first Froggity painting.

I worked all day and into the evening, texting Chris that I would be home late. She must have called Sam at the pub because a bowl of Thai noodles appeared at my door, along with a cold Mountain Dew. My eyes burned by nine p.m., so I finally shut out the lights, locked the door, and staggered home, surprised it was still light out. Working with such concentration always created in me the sense that the rest of the world had gone into some sort of stasis until I emerged from my cave. Yet men and women scurried down the short street on their way home from a day as long as I'd had.

Chris and I watched TV for a while. Neither of us talked about the tests I'd undergone with Dr. Kroll. We were waiting to hear the results.

I checked the sky before going to bed. No stars, but that wasn't unusual for London. They were hard to see even with a clear sky. The Weather Channel said the chance of anything more than a light drizzle was low.

I curled around Chris's back, and she wrapped my arm around her chest. We must not have moved an inch because when I awoke in the middle of the night we were still locked in the same embrace. Rain pattered lightly on the window. There was no wind, otherwise I would have heard the long, tubular wind chimes on the neighbor's balcony booming like a church organ. I sank deeper into the bed in relief. No thunder. No lightning.

But then a loud boom made both of us jump. A car backfiring, nothing more. But I could feel Chris's chest tighten, as if she were holding her breath.

"Blanche, is that you? Are you back?"

My heart stopped. Chris thought the noise had been thunder. Without a plan, I nuzzled the back of her neck. "It's me, princess," I said, my heart constricting with pain.

Chris squeezed my hand. "Oh, thank God. I have missed you so much." She rolled over and faced me. Luckily, it was too dark in the room to see each other. She flung her arms around my neck and began frantically kissing my face. "I can't lose you, Blanche. We have to figure something out. My whole world is gray when Jamie's in charge. But when you're here, I come alive."

I rolled away then gritted my teeth as I pulled her close behind me. If she'd seen my face, she would have known it was me, not Blanche. "Don't worry, we'll figure it out," I said flatly. "I'm not going anywhere."

Chris sighed happily and tucked her knees up behind mine. "I love you, Blanche."

Blanche, not Jamie. Not me.

Chris almost immediately dropped into a light snore, but for me, sleep never came. A fire burned so hotly in my chest that I nearly moaned with the pain of it. Eventually, the burning faded, leaving me a brittle, charred shell. I could not stop the tears now, and soon my pillowcase was soaked.

In the time it took to say one name out loud, everything changed.

Everything.

The life I'd loved was over.

It no longer mattered if 1560 was real or a fantasy. Nothing mattered anymore.

CHAPTER TWENTY-FIVE

The next morning, I woke before Chris and slipped from the bed. I showered, then used some of Chris's fixative to spike my hair. I borrowed her eyeliner and clumsily created raccoon eyes. I found a tube of lipstick Blanche must have bought and grimaced as I applied it. The wine color turned my mouth into an angry slash. Perfect.

I chose a combination of clothing that Blanche might have—lime green skirt, black lace cami, and that stupid velvet jacket. It was still hot outside, so I cut off the jacket sleeves and frayed the armholes. Standing before the mirror in the bathroom, I didn't recognize myself.

When I stepped into the bedroom, Chris rolled over and stretched, the covers slipping away to reveal the body I'd loved for so long but that now turned my stomach. Forcing myself to move, I knelt on the bed and planted a wine-kiss mark on her breast, her ribcage, her stomach, then flicked my tongue once between her legs.

She moaned. "Blanche, come back to bed, please. I've missed you."

I slid off the bed and stood. Normally, I would have yielded to any plea from Chris for anything. But today all I wanted to do was hurt. "Sorry, princess, I'm taking my laptop and going to the Coffee Stand to work on my novel."

Chris's eyes lit up. "Thank God. Jamie just lets that gem sit there. All she does is paint. If I have to look at another Froggity disaster I may slit my wrists."

Sickened by her words and by my anger, I slapped her on the ass so hard I left a pink stain. She yelped, then eyes dark, she once again pleaded with me to join her in bed. I felt close to throwing up.

"Keep that flame burning, princess," I said cheerily. "I'll be home when you're done with school."

I snatched up my pack and computer, grabbed my keys, and fled the once-cozy flat. Desperate for something real in this crazy day, I headed for Holborn Station. Friday mornings Bradley always visited Knightsbridge, an easy ride down the Piccadilly Line.

❖

I heard Bradley before I saw him.

"Do you people know that this station was built in 1906? The route twists to avoid a plague pit, where victims of the 1665 plague were buried. Grim news for such an exclusive neighborhood." His voice echoed against the concrete walls. "And do you know how this area came by the name Knightsbridge? Think back to the Crusades. There used to be a bridge crossing the River Westbourne near here. Two knights crossed the bridge on their way to the Holy Land to fight in the crusades They quarreled, fought, and both were killed. Hence the name. Violence is never the answer, remember that!"

I nodded to Bradley as he wrapped up his running commentary. He slowly lowered himself off the bench, then untied Annie from the bench leg. After I helped him collect his earnings from the filthy hat on the floor, he gave me a funny look. "Is it you?"

"Yes, it's Jamie. For now, at least, that bitch Blanche is back in her own body, but I need to talk to someone who's impartial. I—" I stopped. "Bradley, are you okay? Annie's not sick, is she?"

He handed me the rabbit for inspection so I stroked her soft ears. "No, it's Mouse," he said. "She's disappeared." Bradley's hands shook and his hollow cheeks were paler than ever.

"When was the last time you ate?"

When he shrugged, I led him up out of the station and to a window taco shop. I was desperate to explain my plight but instead managed to shake off my self-focus. "When did you last see her?"

Bradley rubbed his bleary eyes. "She's been my shadow for weeks now. I make sure she gets a bite to eat every day, but she never speaks. Then two mornings ago, I was doing my thing at Charing Cross Station and she was sleeping off in a quiet corner. I had to deal with some foreign hecklers who didn't like my uniform, and by the time I outshouted them, I turned to see her leaving the station. I ran after her, but she disappeared into the crowd." He shook his head. "She's helpless. She can't take care of herself."

"Have you checked the shelters? Maybe she got tired of sleeping outside."

"She doesn't even understand the concept. I tried explaining once as we stood outside of St. Martin's, but her face was totally blank."

I started to tell Bradley about 1560 and Blanche, but he was too worried to even hear me. "She knows the schedule," he muttered over and over. "I have to keep my schedule. Maybe she'll find me."

Finally, I gave up. "Where to next?"

"Gloucester Road. She might be there now." I gave Bradley enough coins to buy a three-day pass. "Here, you look anywhere you need to."

When he squeezed my hand, his skin felt old and papery. "Bless you, Jamie. I'm going to find her."

So much for my plan to unload all my woes onto the shoulders of a homeless man. As I rode the Tube back to Holborn, I thought about my friends Ashley and Mary. They might take me seriously, but they weren't talking to me. That was the great thing about Bradley—everything was possible. The guy was a well of hope.

On the short walk back to the flat, I called my mom. This time she answered, her voice tight with the wounds Blanche had inflicted. "Mom, I'm so sorry. Please don't hang up. I—It's…it's been really hard since my accident and sometimes I'm not myself. You have no idea how *much* I'm not myself."

I stopped walking and leaned against my building as I waited for her response. The rough brick dug into my skin.

She sighed. "Well, you do sound more like yourself than the last time we talked. Your voice was so…so harsh."

"Mom, please. The next time you hear that harsh voice, just hang up. It's not me, really. You can't trust anything that voice says."

"Jamie, these personality shifts aren't right. If I made you an appointment with Dr. Benedict, would you come home? He knows you so well, and could help us figure out what to do."

I shuddered to think of setting Blanche loose on Minnesota. Those poor people would be defenseless. "Mom, I'm getting help here. Chris found me a shrink to talk to, and they're looking at my brain scans and everything. We're near UCL Hospital, and they really know what they're doing. Not that Dr. Benedict doesn't, but really, I'm in good hands." I longed to tell her everything, but then I knew she and Dad would be on the first plane over here.

"Anything new I should know about?" I needed to shift Mom's focus.

Her happy gasp told me there was. "Marcus's fiancé is pregnant. She's really struggling with morning sickness, but otherwise she's fine."

I wanted tell Mom I knew what that felt like, but then I'd sound crazy again. "That's exciting," I said. "I assume the baby-to-be will wear The Dress for its christening."

"Of course. I've already gotten the box out of the closet. But the dress is really looking shabby."

"I could sew some new pearl beads on the front. That would really help."

My mom paused. "You don't sew."

My chuckle was genuine. "Turns out that I've picked up some new skills while I've been in London." Sewing, playing the lute, bathing in ponds, plotting murders.

We talked for a few more minutes, enough that Mom's voice finally relaxed into her usual cheerfulness. Hopefully, we could put this horrible episode behind us. "Mom, I love you guys. You know that, right?"

"Yes, honey, we know. It's just..."

"Hang up when you hear the hard voice."

I finished the conversation and entered the building's side door.

Chris wasn't home, so I was free to be myself. I tried to come up with a plan to fight off Blanche. If I were sent back to 1560 again, what would I need to get back?

Lightning. *Predictable* lightning. With an ironic laugh, I remembered that in *Back to the Future*, Marty McFly knew precisely the date and time the city's clock tower would be struck. He and Doc Brown used the information to return Marty to the future. I used to think it was a fun movie, but now that I'd actually been sent back into time, not so much. I opened my search engine and entered "lightning 1560s London." My mouth dropped open as I scanned the hits provided for the 1560s. A bolt of lightning hit the spire of St. Paul's Cathedral on April 3, 1561, a few months from the last time I'd been in 1560.

The good news was that I had a predicable way home. Bad news? It was only late August now, so the summer thunderstorm season was coming to an end. Were I to be yanked back now, I might have to wait almost seven months to ride another bolt of lightning. By then I would be hugely pregnant and likely to deliver at any minute. What if I gave birth before April 3? What the hell did I do then? If Kroll was right, the baby was just a fantasy. But if this was all fantasy, I didn't need lightning on April 3. Why did everything seem so murky? Nothing was straightforward.

I called Dr. Raj and left yet another message. "Dr. Raj, I need that shot of anti-GCA stuff now. I can't wait forever. What if I'm transported back in time, and then you give the shot to Blanche? I'll be stuck back in time, unable to come home."

I slumped down onto the sofa, spent. I'd done everything I could think of. This feeling of vulnerability unsettled me. It was as if every ounce of confidence in my body—no, in my brain, since that's where it had to reside—had been replaced with confusion. I didn't feel like myself, and that had nothing to do with the strange clothing. I'd lost my faith in my sense of direction, in my ability to make a living from my art, and I could no longer rely on Chris. I was mending things with my family, but Ashley and Mary still refused to reply to my messages and texts.

I didn't know who I was.

Was I Jamie Maddox…or Blanche Nottingham?

CHAPTER TWENTY-SIX

At the beginning of our next appointment with Dr. Kroll, Chris and I took our same chairs. Chris had been looking at me strangely for a few days, despite my efforts to be Blanche. She knew something was off.

Dr. Kroll reviewed the test results with us, all of which continued to point to some sort of trauma that had created two distinct personalities within my mind. She waited for me to comment. What could I say? That she was full of crap? That she was spot-on, as they liked to say around here? Should I tell her I believed in my friendship with Harriet, in my connection to the greatest queen England would ever know?

"Every single event in our lives has the potential to upset our brain chemistry, and thus change all subsequent events. But that elasticity is a good thing. We can restore our brains through exercise, sleep, diet, friends, action, *and* setting goals. So that's what I want you to do. Start setting goals for yourself."

I was about to reply without enthusiasm, then remembered I was impersonating Blanche. This was doing a real number on my mind—impersonating one of my multiple personalities. I leaned forward. "Okay, whatever. But what will help keep me just as I am now?" I glanced at Chris, who nodded encouragingly.

Dr. Kroll settled back in her chair. "There are many options. The antidepressants citalopram, fluoxetine, and sertraline are all possibilities. These drugs help reduce depression in some dissociative identity disorder patients."

"I'm not depressed. I'm doing great. I've made huge strides on the novel I'm writing."

Chris lightly tapped my knee with her foot. "You didn't tell me you've written more. When may I read it?"

I forced a cheesy grin. "Soon."

"There are also anxiety drugs that can help as you work through this, and in rare cases some doctors prescribe stimulants to fight depression."

I shook my head. "Once again, not depressed. What about a drug that suppresses one of the personalities? That's what we're looking for."

When Chris reached over and squeezed my hand, it took every bit of restraint I had not to scream. Fury raged like a hurricane through my veins.

Dr. Kroll shook her head. "I'm afraid there isn't such a magic drug. One option is ECT, or electroconvulsive therapy. While it would probably work, I'd like to keep that as a last resort. Our best bet for success is psychotherapy. You and I will meet twice a week and talk this out until we can identify and resolve the trauma that caused this split."

Chris shook her head. "No, we need to control it more than that. With talk therapy, how can you know which personality will end up being the dominant one? I like this ECT option."

My jaw clenched. For Chris, keeping Blanche was worth the risk of frying my brain.

The look in Dr. Kroll's eye warmed my heart. She was beginning to see the problem. "Are you saying you both prefer one of Jamie's personalities over the other?"

"Yes," I said before Chris could speak up and break my heart yet again. "I'm Blanche, and I love Chris very much. Chris prefers me to Jamie." Chris nodded vigorously. "So I'd like to ensure that I remain the dominant personality."

"But don't you see that *both* you and Jamie can have Chris? Both of you are part of Jamie. It doesn't have to be this either/or proposition. With therapy we'll figure out why you've split yourself in two. What part of yourself as Jamie didn't you like? What was missing? You might have created Blanche to fill in that missing piece."

Oh, yeah, that was missing from my life—a destructive, vindictive bitch who only thought of herself.

Dr. Kroll turned to Chris. "Wouldn't you like to have a whole person to love? Aren't there parts of Jamie you miss in Blanche?"

"Not really," she said.

Dr. Kroll scribbled something in her notebook. I could imagine the words: *spouse of patient wishes patient were different person, thereby causing the trauma that created the split.*

My emotions flatlined. The puzzle pieces did fit together alarmingly well. Chris had dropped the bomb about me not being ambitious enough for her, so I had created Blanche as a result.

Chris and I didn't speak on the walk home, but once we were inside the flat, the door locked and bolted behind us, Chris slid her arms around my waist and kissed me. "Blanche, I need you so much."

I leaned back, forcing myself to meet her eyes while I fingered a lock of her hair. "I know we've talked about this before, but sometimes it confuses me. What is it about Jamie that you don't like?"

Stupid of me to ask, of course. Why not just cut myself in a thousand places and pour lemon juice over the cuts?

Chris nuzzled my neck. "She used to have an edge, but she's gone all soft. She's too comfortable with her life, with her art, with me. Jamie's nice, but I'm tired of nice. Edginess makes me feel alive, makes me feel as if I can accomplish anything." She nipped playfully at my ear, and something snapped inside me.

I stepped back. "How's *this* for edgy? I'm Jamie. I've been Jamie since that night the car backfired and you thought it was thunder. No matter who wins the battle for my body, me or Blanche, you and I are done."

I grabbed my keys and stomped from the flat. Shaking badly, I must have looked drunk as I weaved down the street and up into my studio. I engaged the deadbolt so Chris couldn't enter. I jammed in my earbuds and turned Joan Jett up to ear-shattering, then ripped off everything on the studio wall, most of it gone already thanks to Blanche. Then with black and deep red and garish blue and shocking green, I began to paint Whitehall Palace on the wall. The paint splashed and dripped, but no matter. Fury held me in her grip, so I had no choice but to let her paint.

Chapter Twenty-seven

A phone call interrupted my painting. It was Meg Warren's neighbor. "Yeah, she came home, but I don't know if she'll call you. She's in a bit of a snit and wouldn't even talk to me."

I thanked the woman and called Meg's phone. No answer. Damn. No wonder Dr. Rajamani had given up trying to contact her.

Later that afternoon, I strolled High Holborn, then turned on Endell and worked my way through the narrow streets and tiny shops of Covent Garden. I took Long to Charing Cross Road, popped down Cecil Court, and stopped into Watkins Bookstore in search of a new deck of tarot cards for my mom's birthday. I snickered at the box of alien tarot cards. Surely she didn't have that set yet. Then across to Leicester Square and down Charing Cross Road. I stopped at the gelato shop and indulged in a double scoop of coconut. I'd gotten used to the extra weight Blanche had packed on. In fact, I felt a little healthier and didn't look so gaunt when I happened to catch my reflection in a shop window.

By the time I reached the National Gallery, the sun was weak behind a thin film of clouds, but it managed to throw a shadow or two. I don't know how long I was in the Gallery, but I spent most of my time with Vincent and with Lady Jane Grey. As I stood there, I realized what was so compelling about this work of art. Even as she was about to be killed, the nine-day-queen was still generous and kind, reaching out to find the chopping block in order that the executioner could perform his ghastly task. Her long, slender fingers reminded me of Elizabeth's hands, which made sense. They were cousins. Jane was the great-granddaughter of Henry VII; Elizabeth was his granddaughter.

A pang of loneliness shot through me. Could I actually be homesick for that strange world? The long days in the company of courtiers bored me, but I loved my quiet time with Elizabeth as we talked, just the two of us. Heady stuff, to be the confidant of a queen.

I strode next door to the National Portrait Gallery and lost myself in the paintings of Elizabeth. My favorite was a copy of the *Coronation Portrait*, the original painted in 1559. Elizabeth's red-blond hair was loose and spread across her shoulders. The painter had captured her intelligence. It hadn't taken me too long in 1560 to see how cleverly Elizabeth operated. Her council met daily, but she rarely attended. Instead, she preferred to meet with the councilors individually. This allowed her to play one faction against another, to play to each man's strengths and weaknesses.

One morning while I stitched, she met with one man and was bold and direct, to the point of nearly controlling his thoughts. He was a trembling mess by the time he left. Then the next councilor to enter the room caused Elizabeth to grow smaller, more feminine. She became the weak woman who needed help and direction, and the man was so flattered he didn't notice how she managed to turn her opinion into his own. I remember chuckling into my pillowy breasts, which nearly reached my chin. Elizabeth was so adept at concealing her opinions that few knew what they actually were. This way she managed to keep her entire council unbalanced enough they didn't know how to control her.

I loved this portrait. In one hand she held a glittering scepter; in the other a globe draped in rubies. The shoulders of her ermine and gold cape were ringed by rubies, the edges dripping with large glistening pearls. Her stiff lace collar framed her long, oval face. I smiled. I now knew how to attach that blasted collar, and it wasn't easy.

Back outside, I perched on the top step leading down to Trafalgar's main plaza and let the weak sun warm my eyelids. What the hell was I going to do? I couldn't just will myself back in time to

Harriet and Elizabeth. But I certainly couldn't continue living with Chris, especially now that she knew I could impersonate Blanche, however awkwardly.

"Jamie Maddox." The breathless voice was Bradley's. He lowered himself onto the stair with a grunt.

"You're getting old, Bradley. You need to start sleeping indoors, on a bed. Sleeping on benches can't be good for your bones."

"You may be right, but I have good news. Look!" He motioned to the figure scurrying up to sit beside him.

"You found Mouse," I said. "And she looks great." Her hair, obviously washed and brushed until it shone, curled around her face and neck. She didn't avert her moss green eyes, and actually flashed me a shy, crooked smile that was so endearing I wanted to bring her home myself.

Bradley patted her shoulder. "Someone must have taken her in, washed her up, and given her a change of clothes."

I considered the silk shirt and expensive jeans. "I'll say. And that person has a lot of money. Those clothes are not cheap."

Bradley beamed at Mouse, who ducked her head shyly and scooted close enough their elbows touched. "Poor thing used to hover just out of reach, but now she's terrified if she's more than an arm's length away. It's like she's afraid I'm going to disappear."

I shared all that had happened in 1560 with Bradley. Mouse watched me, eyes wide at my story. Bradley nodded encouragingly as I spoke, then when I finished he pursed his lips and looked out across the square. He sighed. "Didn't I say to you that life is just one long struggle not to lose yourself?"

"You did."

"You are losing yourself, my dear."

I bit my lip, alarmed at the lump filling my throat. "What do I do?"

"You accept that things feel hopeless, but you don't let that direct your life. You fight. You do what needs to happen next in order to survive."

"Is that what keeps you going?"

"Every goddamned day," he said softly.

Just then my cell chimed. "I've been waiting to hear from Rajamani," I said apologetically as I fished the phone from my pocket. "It's a text from him: *Anti-CGA serum almost ready. Will contact in next day or two. Also, Meg Warren is trying to contact me, but we haven't been able to connect.*"

I barely registered the information about Meg. Instead, I clutched the phone to my chest. "Bradley, do you know what this means?"

He gave my shoulder a quick squeeze, then scanned for police. They didn't like the homeless people touching tourists or residents. "It means if you can remain in the present for a few more days, Dr. Raj will cure you. He will stop all this flipping back and forth between centuries. That's gotta be driving you crazy, man."

I nodded, too choked up with hope to speak.

He gestured toward the phone. "Not to bring you down, but what if something does happen before the anti-stuff is ready? Won't Blanche see this text?"

"Hell's gate, you're right. Neither she nor Chris knows I've been working with Dr. Raj. I specifically asked him not to mention it whenever he ran into Chris on campus." I began thumbing a reply. "I'll ask him not to send any more texts but to wait for me to contact him." This way Blanche would be kept entirely out of the loop. There would be no threat of her receiving the injection instead of me. I was about to hit SEND when thunder rattled my teeth. I nearly jumped out of my skin. What the hell? The weak sun had disappeared, now hidden by clouds as thick as gray soup.

"Bradley, if I—"

Crack! Up, up, up I flew. Another ride on the bucking lightning.

Winston stood next to me as rain clattered on the courtyard beyond the open doorway. The other two conspirators formed a tight circle around me. "Next week Holmes will take you in my carriage to Cumnor Place. The house is in Berkshire, near the Oxfordshire border. You will dispatch Mistress Amy, then Holmes will return you to London. You will be back in Whitehall before the news of Amy's death can reach the Queen."

I bent, gritting my teeth against the need to empty my stomach. Acid pushed its way up my throat. "But—"

Crack! With a bone-crunching jerk, I was back in my own body. I stood in the square, cell phone in one hand, the other pointing accusingly at an astonished Bradley, Mouse hovering behind him. Two police officers were biking toward us. "No," I said, waving to them. "It's all right. No problem here, Officers."

Boom! I stood up, reaching for the wall to steady myself as I gagged, but nothing came up. Winston made a noise of disgust. "Clearly you have no stomach for murder, but this was your idea so you will perform the action. If you do not, Dudley will be dead by the end of the day."

Crack! My head spun with the suddenness. Too fast to recover. Too fast to even know where or when or who I was. One officer had Bradley by the arm, the other struggled to restrain Mouse, who'd gone wild with fear. "No, they are my friends!" I cried. "Stop!" The officers shot me confused looks over their shoulders.

"But you just said they were harassing you."

Crack! I was back in the heavy gown, Winston and the others walking away, their heels drumming sharply on the ceramic tile floor. I gripped the nearest hall table, bending over so low I nearly set my hair on fire with the table's candle.

Vincent stood nearby, stiff and angry, whining in alarm. "Poor baby." I held out my hand. "It's me, little guy." When he gave me a cautious lick, I sank gratefully to the floor and leaned back against the wood paneling. My mouth tasted sour, my gut ached with emptiness. A choir sang softly in the distance, perhaps practicing for the Sunday service. The music was somber, the voices harmonizing perfectly. Hot tears slid down my cheeks from the violence of the last sixty seconds, the helplessness, the frustration of not having any control.

I curled up around myself. I hadn't had time to send the reply text to Dr. Raj. Even if Blanche didn't see it, Raj would send another text when the shot was ready. Blanche would receive the text and figure out that this was the final scene between the two of us. The consciousness in control of Jamie Maddox's body—my body—at the moment Dr. Raj administered the injection would be in permanent control of me. The other mind would be forever exiled to the plump and treacherous body of Blanche Nottingham, lady-in-waiting to Queen Elizabeth I.

Any flame of hope I'd felt over Dr. Rajamani's text was gone.

CHAPTER TWENTY-EIGHT

After breakfast, I stood in the gallery overlooking one of the palace streets, the air hot and thick above the chaotic crowds—carts, horses, barrows, people. It was a sunny day, which I'd come to hate because sun meant no thunderstorm. Everyone's mood was lighter except for mine.

The last time I'd been in 1560, my Queen had commanded I reveal the father of my child. What had Blanche said? No one, not even Lady Mary, was making an issue of the pregnancy. If Blanche had kept her mouth shut, perhaps I'd dodged the bullet called "marriage."

A familiar sturdy walk caught my attention, so I leaned over the railing. "Harriet!" I tried several times, but she didn't look up, so I found the nearest stairs and hurried outside.

I caught up with her near the laundry. "Harriet," I said, gasping. "Slow down. Where's the fire?"

She turned, alarmed. "Fire? Where?"

I laughed, my hands up. "Just a saying. How are you?"

Now she looked confused. "I am well, m'lady. Is there something you require?" Her eyes lacked their usual sparkle and flash.

"Why are you acting so strange?"

"I do not know what you mean, Lady Blanche."

I dismissed her with an angry wave. If she was going to play servant, I would play the noble lady.

The week dragged on. Midweek, Elizabeth asked me to travel to Hampton Court, another of her palaces, to retrieve a piece of jewelry she'd left there months ago. When I boldly asked why she needed it, she laughed. "You know perfectly well why I need it. Now off you go."

I didn't, actually, but that knowledge wasn't required to run the errand. I requested Jacob as my coachman and insisted he sit inside the carriage with me while the driver barreled down the road. I needed a distraction—Harriet was cold, Ray was dead, I was still stuck here. Could it really be that I was doing this to myself, that all this bad stuff was just a fantasy? I grew weary of thinking the same thoughts. I'd once seen an old-fashioned record player with its arm stuck in one groove, playing over and over again. My thoughts felt just as stuck.

The sounds of horses' hooves, the jangling of their harnesses, and the creaking wheels were soothing background for our conversation. I made Jacob tell me all about his life—parents, siblings, hopes, goals. If not for the transportation mode and our clothes, we could have been two Londoners sharing a cab.

When we returned the next day, the streets around Whitehall were damp, and deep gray clouds were moving off to the east. *Damn.* I'd missed a storm.

That evening, after I'd delivered the exquisite ruby necklace to Kat Ashley, I mingled in the outer chamber with the other ladies and courtiers. Within minutes, Lord Winston had me by the elbow and was coming in for a kiss.

I leaned back so far I nearly slipped a disc. "What the hell are you doing?"

"I'm attempting to kiss my fiancé," he snapped. "You did not refuse my kisses last week when the Queen announced we are to be wed."

Crap. Blanche *had* spilled the beans, and now the Queen was going to make an honest woman out of her—or rather, out of me. That was why Elizabeth needed the ruby necklace—to wear at my wedding.

I shrugged, freeing myself from his grasp. "Bite me, asshole. No way am I marrying you."

"Lady Blanche, you vex me to no end with your inconsistency. One day you are pressed up against me, the next you cannot stand the sight of me."

What was I going to say? *Blanche likes you but I don't?*

He sighed. "No matter. I am weary of seducing court women, so I am content to wed you and give our bastard my name. And as for tomorrow, all is set. You will leave for Cumnor in the morning."

God's teeth. Amy Dudley. I pulled Winston into an empty corner of the room. "Look, I can't do it. I won't kill that woman."

Instead of getting angry, Winston held his palm against his forehead and sighed. "Lord, give me strength." He looked at me, his eyes sunken, face weary. "Do you have any idea what is at stake?"

"You don't want Dudley to marry the Queen. I get that."

He sighed again. "Where have you been these last thirteen years? Living in a cave? Did you just recently hatch?"

Close.

"After King Edward died, many of us worked to put Lady Jane Grey on the throne. Robert Dudley was among the most visible of these, and for that I respect him."

Lady Jane Grey was the figure in the National Gallery painting, blindfolded and reaching for the executioner's block.

"But once Mary came to power, the country was once again Catholic, and Mary went on a killing spree."

"I know that."

"Then why do you not seem to understand? Mary killed so many Protestants that we still call her Bloody Mary." He stopped, swallowing hard. "My brother...my brother was most outspoken in his religious beliefs. Because he spoke against papists like Mary, she condemned him to burn at the stake."

Unexpectedly, sympathy for Lord Winston closed off my throat. What would he think if he knew Mary's killing spree had been trivialized into a cocktail made out of tomato juice and a stalk of celery?

I'd never seen Winston show any emotion other than anger or disdain, but his love of country was clear from his furrowed brow. He leaned in closer. "If the Queen marries poorly," he said, "like

Dudley, the Catholics in France, Spain, or Scotland will rise up and overwhelm our forces. They will put a Catholic on the throne, and the killing will start again."

We were so close we could have kissed, but he only thought of England. "Amy Dudley must die so, as you suggested, Elizabeth can never marry Dudley because of the scandal, thus keeping the Catholics at bay, for now."

I nodded, my head as heavy as my heart. "I understand. I will do what you've tasked me to do."

He squeezed my shoulder. "Thank you."

Confused to see Winston as a genuine person instead of an evil caricature, I excused myself and fled.

That night after Rosemary helped me undress and left the room, I slipped on my servant's dress and headed across the lawn with Vincent at my heels. We avoided two groups of men passing around jugs of wine and slipped into the forest. Loneliness seeped through me like the chilly ground crept through my thin slippers. Harriet was angry with me for some reason, so I hadn't asked her to join me at the pond. I reached down and patted Vincent's soft head.

Once inside the woods, Vincent ran ahead to the pond. When I broke through the last of the bushes, their leaves damp with evening dew, Harriet was throwing a stick for Vincent. She grinned. "I knew you would be along soon when Vincent showed up." She closed the distance between us and hugged a very surprised me.

"Now we're friends again?" I snapped. "A few days ago you wanted nothing to do with me."

"Oh. I—I didn't realize. I'm sorry. When I get like that, please ignore me. You, however, have been just as inconsistent in our friendship. Most days you smile as a friend, but there have been a few days when you have looked right through me."

Now it was my turn to apologize, which I did. It killed me that Blanche was so cruel to Harriet. *Tell her*, the voice in my head urged. No. Then I'd lose her, my only friend in 1560, or my only friend in my twisted, whacked-out-brain fantasy.

Everything around the pond was dark blue and almost magical, including Harriet's face and clothing. I longed for a canvas and brush with which to capture the enchanted scene.

I was relieved Harriet wasn't mad at me because I really, really liked her. She was kind and insightful, with a capacity to care that was greater than that of all of the court members combined. She was the only person I'd met here who felt as I did, as if we didn't belong, as if everyone else was an alien dressed up in sixteenth century clothing.

I gently steered the conversation to safer topics, and soon we were both naked and in the pond. God, the water felt delicious.

Harriet asked about my health and if I'd felt the baby within me.

"Too early," I said, not knowing if that were true. For a few minutes, Vincent danced at the rocky edge, then finally belly-flopped between us. His ears spread out across the surface of the water as he paddled with great determination.

Laughing, I began dog paddling behind him, and Harriet joined me as we followed the little dog on his erratic swim around the pond. But when he brought us too close to the bank, my toe slammed against a submerged rock and exploded in pain.

"Fire truck!" I shouted, then grit my teeth against the sharp needles shooting through my foot.

"What did you say?" Harriet was suddenly right in front of me, her hair swirling in the water around her shoulders.

"Nothing," I said, massaging my wounded toe.

"No, you said fire truck, which is a long, red vehicle that contains hoses, firefighting equipment, and sometimes a Dalmatian."

We stared at each other, eyes wide. "God's knees," I breathed.

Harriet's breath was ragged. "Dr. Rajamani. 2017"

"God's knees" was all I could manage until I licked my lips and inhaled. "Dr. Rajamani, GCA injection, lightning, 2017."

And then we were in each other's arms, bobbing up and down like drunken corks. We were laughing and then crying and then laughing again. Harriet pressed her face into my neck as I kicked to keep us on the surface. "I'm not alone, I'm not alone," she sobbed.

I moved us close to the bank so we could each grab a handful of grass and hang on. We just grinned stupidly at each other until Vincent broke the spell by climbing out and shaking water in our faces. His wet ears slapped against his head.

Harriet held out her hand. "It is so nice to meet you. My name is Meg Warren."

I nodded as we shook hands. Of course she was. "And I'm Jamie Maddox."

"You left your card at my flat!"

"Why didn't you call?"

We helped each other climb out of the water and began toweling off. "I didn't call you because this whole thing has totally freaked me out. I've been here, in 1560, for over three months, then finally, last week, I got zapped back into my own body, then back and forth another time." She bent over and toweled off her hair. Vincent did a stiff-legged hop between us, caught up in our excitement.

"You've only traveled back three times?" I snorted. "You should see the frequent flyer miles I've accumulated."

Harriet, I mean Meg, threw back her head and laughed. "Such a cheeky monkey you are." Still chuckling, she pulled on her dress and settled it over her hips. "Returning to my own body was quite the shock. The woman in my body—Harriet—had been living on the street. I stunk like a trash bin. My hair was—" She stopped, briefly closing her eyes. "So gross. I had no money to take the Tube, so I walked from Kingsbridge Station all the way back to my flat. I had no key, so the manager had to let me in. He almost didn't recognize me."

Dressed now, we sat on the rocks as close together as we could get.

Knightsbridge Station. "Have you ever seen an older black man with gray dreadlocks shouting out a history of the station?"

Meg grimaced. "Yes! He started chasing me, so I ran out the station and lost myself in the crowd."

The world tipped on its axis so quickly I reached for the tree trunk. My lightheadedness wasn't the pregnancy. It was the realization that Harriet was really Meg, who was really Mouse. That was too much coincidence to be real. Dr. Kroll might be right.

"Jamie, are you okay?"

I rubbed my temples. On the other hand, coincidences *could* happen. They didn't have to be inventions of my split personality mind. "That man was my friend Bradley. He's been taking care of you…of Harriet."

We spent hours talking by the pond, with a now-dried Vincent curled up at my feet, his paws twitching with dreams. A damp cold had settled onto the forest floor, but we didn't dare have this conversation back at the palace and risk being overheard. The only ears around us belonged to the unseen forest animals skittering around in the dark.

I told her about my family and the story behind "fire truck." I told her about Chris preferring Blanche to me. The one thing I didn't tell her about was the upcoming plan to throw Amy Dudley down the stairs. Then Meg told me about her family, and about her job at the British Library, and about past girlfriends. She'd studied Latin in college as well as library science. Eventually, we drifted back to Rajamani's experiment. As we talked, Meg's true personality opened up like a blooming rose. How hard it must have been for her to not stand out; servants were to be invisible, not interesting.

"Because I live alone now," Meg said, "no one was watching out for me. That's why I must have been living rough. Poor Harriet had no idea where to go." Meg sighed. "When I got back the first time, after I reached my flat and recharged my mobile—amazingly, Harriet still had it on her—I called Dr. Rajamani. Would you believe the wanker didn't answer? You'd think he'd see my name and break a thumb trying to answer his mobile. So I hauled my arse to his office. No luck there. Rajamani's experiment was a total cock-up, but I couldn't find him to tell him that." She left frantic messages on his phone and office door. But a few days later, before she could connect with him, she found herself once again in 1560, back in Harriet's body.

We discussed the trigger for transport and could not come up with a pattern. When it stormed in 1560, we had a chance of returning. When it stormed in 2017, we were vulnerable to being pulled back in time.

"Which reminds me," I said. "You need to know about the storm on April third." I described how the wooden steeple on St. Paul's Cathedral would be struck by lightning and burn. "If we're standing in the plaza right next to the cathedral, we should be able to catch the lightning and ride it back to the future."

"I knew the steeple had burned, but not the date. Good to know. Until then, I guess I just keep slaving away and you keep being a pampered lady." Her smile took the sting from her words.

I told her about Dr. Rajamani's serum. By now we were huddling side to side, arms around each other for warmth. "This is really important," I said as our heads touched. "The instant you find yourself back in the future, run, do not walk, directly to Rajamani. If you don't have the money and Bradley is nearby, explain and he'll give his tips to you. Or take a taxi and skip out on the fare. Or hijack a car. Just get yourself to Dr. Raj as soon as possible for that blasted serum."

Meg nodded, suddenly quiet. I raised my eyes to hers and saw in them what I, too, was feeling. Not only did we need each other, but we *liked* each other—a lot.

My spine went liquid, and I leaned against Meg, nestling into her warm neck. Even after a dip in the pond, she smelled of fresh bread and lemons.

"You are the only person standing between me and insanity," I said.

She kissed the crown of my head, then we gathered ourselves up, called Vincent, and left our secret pool.

Chapter Twenty-nine

I let myself sleep in the next morning; each time I awoke I remembered Meg and daydreamed myself back to sleep. But midmorning Rosemary came in and informed me my carriage had arrived.

Hell's gate. I lay on my back, hoping she would go away. Dust motes drifted through the air like tiny fairies. The room smelled of candle wax and musty tapestries and urine. This whole world smelled of urine.

"M'lady, Lord Winston's man grows impatient."

She didn't go away, so I rolled out of bed and let her dress me. I packed a small bag and followed her to one of the palace's side entrances.

Four shiny black horses, tossing their heads and snorting, stood before an elaborately detailed black coach. Holmes, Winston's man, stood with the door open and a small stool that he placed on the ground when he saw me. The driver above murmured to the horses.

Holmes handed me in, then closed the door and climbed up beside the driver.

We were off.

Sadly, the coach's shock absorbers didn't match the elegance of the gold trim, so I nearly bit my tongue off half a dozen times. The coach smelled of wet feet and mildewed leather, so I spent the day with my face near the open window watching the countryside pass and thinking about Meg and how amazing it was that we'd found each other.

Holmes and I spent the first night in an inn, but the bedding in my room was so filthy I just lay on top rather than disrobe and crawl inside. Also, without help from someone, I couldn't actually disrobe all the way. In the middle of the night, I was no longer able to push away the thoughts of tomorrow. I lay there, eyes wide open, terrified at what I was about to do and what it meant. Murder in the moment of passion or anger was horrible but at least understandable. You got carried away. But I was traveling sixty miles, quite a journey in 1560, in order to commit premeditated murder.

As I tried to sleep, I struggled with the reality/unreality thing. Was I really saving history or just playing out a little drama in my head while Blanche continued to ruin my life and be the ambitious, edgy chick Chris so desperately wanted?

Good thing I wasn't bitter.

Winston hadn't accompanied me, of course, in order to distance himself as much as possible and be visible around the palace when Amy's death was announced. He and the other co-conspirators were, in fact, going hunting with Dudley and the Queen in one of the parks. Late the next morning, we passed through a town that Holmes announced as Abingdon, the last before our destination. I felt sick to my stomach.

Ten minutes later, we begin passing cornfields with orchards behind them. Well before we reached a small gatehouse, the driver drew the horses to a halt. The carriage rocked as Holmes descended and appeared at my window. "M'lady, we have arrived at Cumnor Place. My lord said not to announce your arrival but that you should approach the house on foot. I am to ride on and return in a short while."

He helped both me and my dress fight our way out of the flimsy carriage. I straightened my skirts, hoping Holmes couldn't hear my heart pounding. As far as he knew, I was here to extend an invitation to Amy from Robert Dudley to come to court. It was weak but the best I could come up with.

Holmes leapt back into his seat, the driver clicked to the horses, and I was left alone. The road at this point was quite wide, sloping away to shallow hills. Blue sky was dusted with little puffs of white, leaves rustled in the gentle breeze, and a late-blooming flower sweetened the air. It was far too perfect a day in which to kill someone.

I approached the gatehouse, feeling every pebble in the road through my thin soles, then passed under the slender arch. "Hello?" No one stepped out from the gatehouse, so I continued walking. Crows scolded me from the tops of the firs lining the drive. My senses were on alert for sounds of people or horses, anyone who might encounter me, since my excuse for visiting was so flimsy.

The servants would be gone, so all I had to do was walk into the house, find Amy, and push her down the stairs. Then history's timeline would continue on as it should. Too bad I was shaking so hard I couldn't walk a straight line.

And too bad that never, in one thousand years, would I push an ill, feeble woman down the stairs. In fact, I would never push anyone down any stairs. I needed a Plan B. I stopped in the middle of the road. Why was I even going to this house if I knew I couldn't do it?

I took a few backward steps then turned and huffed my way back to where Holmes had left me. I searched in vain for some sign of the carriage, but I was alone. My lungs struggled against the stupid stomacher, which I hated even more than Lord Winston. I blew out a few massive breaths to calm myself. No, I was here. I needed to find Amy Dudley and help her somehow.

The edge of a white, square building came into view, then the entire building. The estate was an odd mix of differently styled buildings connected to one another, all covered in thick ivy. At one point in our plotting, Winston had mentioned Cumnor Place used to be a monastery taken over when Elizabeth's father, King Henry VIII, changed the country's religion and took possession of Catholic cathedrals and monasteries. That explained the pointed arches on all the doorways and windows.

Squaring my shoulders, I approached as if I had reason to be there. I walked through a wide arch in one corner and found myself standing in a huge courtyard. Grass had grown up through the cobblestones, enough that seven black-faced sheep grazed there. One looked up and bleated, but otherwise they ignored me.

Which building was Amy's? Feeling faint, I rested my palms on my knees for a second. What the hell was I going to do? I retraced my steps out of the courtyard and looked for an entrance. A studded oak door with slender windows on each side seemed to be the main entrance, so I stepped up. Without knocking, I pushed open the heavy door, grateful it didn't creak. I stood inside an airy vestibule, listening for any movement, any voices. Nothing.

I began walking through the rooms. To the right was a parlor of sorts, to the left a dining room. The home wasn't elegant, but it was clean and filled with solid furniture. The stone floor shone in the sun. I was relieved that at least Dudley had ensured his wife lived in relative comfort.

When I reached the farthest room, one that looked out over a smallish lake, my legs refused to work anymore. Even though I had no idea what I would say should Amy Dudley appear, I sank into the nearest chair and squinted against the sunlight pouring through the leaded windows. A rock pathway lined with dense, trimmed boxwood led to a short dock, faded gray and listing to the left. An empty rowboat bobbed alongside the dock.

While I listened for any sound in the house, my brain spun. How could I kill Amy Dudley without really killing her? She had to disappear for about…I quickly did the math. Sir Robert Dudley would die of malaria and stomach cancer in 1688, so Amy needed to hide out for a mere twenty-eight years.

Hell's gate, how would that even work? I stared at the lake. Okay, there it was, right in front of me. First, I would hide Amy in the woods, then wait for the servants to return. When they did, I would run toward them, crying that Amy had fallen into the lake. In the confusion I would slip away, retrieve Amy, and we'd walk to safety.

I clenched my jaw. What a fire trucking idiot. Amy was too ill to walk anywhere. And I couldn't hide her until 1688. Once again without a Plan B, I rose and finished searching the main floor, ending up at a wide but shallow staircase. It rose for seven steps, turned ninety degrees, then rose another ten steps. God's bones. This was the staircase. One Tudor fan website had described it in detail. How could someone die on such a short staircase? Surely Amy Dudley had been murdered, and that man could show up at any time.

Then I heard a floor creak upstairs. "Amy? Mrs. Dudley? Hello?"

Nothing.

Lifting my skirts, I ascended the stone steps and hesitated at the top. Had the sound come from the room at the top of the stairs? I knocked softly and let myself in. Clutching my chest, I struggled to calm down. The room was empty but for a tall-backed chair facing the open window. "Amy?" I took a few steps.

My pulse raced so fast that all sound faded. All I could hear was my heart trying to pound its way out of my chest. Calm *down.*

When I looked over the chair back, I blew out a huge breath. Nothing there but an embroidery hoop holding a silk handkerchief. Okay, Amy must be farther down the hallway.

I rubbed my face for courage, smoothed out my skirt, and stepped out of the sitting room onto the landing.

"Oh!" A painfully thin woman at the top of the stairs whirled around in surprise at my rustling skirts.

"Oh!" I echoed stupidly.

The startled woman took a step back.

"Don't be frightened!" I reached toward her. "I mean no harm." But she took another step back onto nothing, and began windmilling her arms.

"No!" I cried as she did two awkward backward somersaults, arms and legs flopping like a doll's. She made no sound except for a soft moan and landed in a crumpled heap at the bottom of the stairs.

No, no, *no!* I stared down at her for a second, willing her to move. She didn't.

I scrambled down the steps. Judging by the fine dress, it had to be her. I knelt and felt her neck for a pulse. Nothing. I felt both wrists. Still nothing. I sank back onto the floor. How could someone die so incredibly fast? One second staring at me, the next second dead.

"Amy, Amy, I'm so sorry." Her eyes were wide and unseeing. Hell's gate. I'd killed her by mistake. I curled over, hugging myself.

What had I done? Ensured history's continuity? Or just killed a woman in my multiple-personality-induced fantasy? I squeezed my sides. I'd never seen a dead body before.

Shaken, I forced myself to stand and straighten poor Amy's body out so she looked more dignified. I replaced the pale green headpiece that had come undone in her fall.

I wiped my eyes and looked around. No one else was here. Did that mean that Amy Dudley really had fallen by accident, that there was no murderer lurking in the house? (Except, of course, for me.) I took in the white vase of lilies on a nearby table, a heavy basket on the floor filled with fresh marigolds. The perfect blossoms were so plump and alive it hurt to look at them. Birds chirped outside. It did not escape me that I was the only witness to an event that would confuse and confound people for centuries.

Taking a shaky breath, I smoothed the hair back from Amy's pale face, kissed her cooling forehead, then left Cumnor Place as quietly as I'd entered it.

I took two steps outside and threw up. When I was done gagging, I kicked the dirt to cover my mess, then looked back at the house. It would be demolished 250 years from now because Amy's ghost would give the locals so much trouble.

Holmes and the carriage awaited me at the end of the drive. I climbed inside and cried for a long, long time.

CHAPTER THIRTY

I have little memory of the wild ride back to London. Holmes wanted to stop at the inn again, saying it wasn't safe to travel at night because of thieves and that the road could be dangerous for the horses, but I refused to get out of the carriage.

"Keep going," I insisted, even though my ass burned from bouncing over the rough road and my empty stomach ached. I'd just killed a woman. Comfort and food were not something I deserved.

So, armed with a sword by his side, Holmes had the driver keep the horses to a walk so they wouldn't injure themselves in an unseen pothole, and we pressed on all night. I felt no desire to curl up on the velvet seats and sleep. It was as if I'd consumed a twelve-pack of Pepsi or a gallon of coffee. I wondered if I would ever sleep again.

The rising sun had just begun to lighten the dark sky when Holmes stopped the carriage beside one of the side entrances to Whitehall. My legs protested as I climbed down, waving off Holmes's help.

The palace was in an uproar. As I hurried to my room, chattering servants and scandalized courtiers buzzed with the news of Amy Dudley's death. A messenger must have ridden at breakneck speed and taken shortcuts not available to carriages.

Lady Mary sat on a stool in the Queen's outer chamber. She looked up when I walked in. "Where have you been?" she snapped.

"Visiting a cousin in Cheapside," I said. "I've been gone since yesterday."

Mary's face crumpled. "Something horrid has happened." I sank to my knees at her side, desperate to divert attention from my absence. "My sister-in-law Amy has been found dead in her home." I held Mary's hand, stunned. "You are Robert Dudley's sister?" She nodded.

"Tell me what happened."

Mary took a shuddering breath. "We know not. Amy was found dead yesterday. Did she fall and break her neck? Was she...?" Mary didn't finish. "My brother is frantic and the Queen is frightened."

"I will go to her," I said.

The Queen was in one of her private chambers, a long, narrow room with a window at the far end that overlooked the Thames. Tapestries with hunting scenes lined the walls, muffling all sound. Elizabeth was surrounded by women as she dabbed her eyes with a snow-white handkerchief. Everyone looked up when I entered. "I was visiting my cousin in Cheapside," I said before anyone could scold me. Sun reflected off the water, creating ripples of light across the ceiling above us. How could such a lovely day follow such an ugly one?

"Ah, our Spark," Elizabeth said weakly. She wasn't dressed for court but instead wore an open-necked pale tan gown that turned her skin an unhealthy gray. Free from corset or hoops, she slumped in her chair. "The world has tumbled around our shoulders and become a burden too great to bear."

"Ma'am." I sank into a deep curtsey. "Surely it cannot be as bad as all that."

Elizabeth's skin was pale and eerily beautiful, but her dull eyes and worried lips told another story. She waved everyone away. I turned to leave, but she stopped me. "Spark, you stay."

Ignoring the daggers the other women aimed at me, I waited until the room was empty save myself and the Queen. I returned to her side, sinking onto the nearest stool, and let her clutch my hand to her chest. "What are we to do?" she moaned.

I kissed her hand with much love and respect. "Ma'am, let us talk this through, shall we?"

She nodded, her headpiece in danger of coming unpinned. I took a moment to reattach it, then sat back down.

"Yesterday, I was talking with Ambassador de Quadra," Elizabeth stammered. "He made mention that Robert seemed unhappy, and I replied that he was doubtlessly thinking of his wife. Then I said she was dead, or nearly so. Why did I say such a thing? I only meant that she was quite ill. I never meant to imply that I had any foreknowledge of her fate." She moaned again. She had forgotten, in her anguish, to be the royal "we." She was just Elizabeth, the woman. "My people love me. They trust me. If I were to lose that, I would lose all my strength."

"Those who know your majesty could never believe you had anything to do with this tragedy."

"Yes, but what about my Robin? The pall of murder now covers him like a shroud. What am I to do? How could I ever choose him as a suitable husband when people suspect he did great harm to his wife in order to be free to consort with me?" Her head dropped so heavily against her chest that she looked like a very old woman. I was hit with pangs of regret that I knew her future.

Elizabeth would die an old, sick woman with most of her friends and contemporaries in the grave well before her. She would have no one but a few young men who flirted with her in hopes of currying favor. Many of her subjects would be ready for her to go so new blood could lead the country. For a brief moment, I considered staying. I could be her friend through the end of her life.

Elizabeth blew her nose. "Robin is in the presence chamber, insisting on an audience with me. I have commanded the guards to keep him out, which slices my soul to ribbons. All is in ruins. I do not know where to turn."

My heart broke at her confusion, and I had a flash of insight into how hard it must have been for Elizabeth to grow up, emotionally isolated from everyone but Kat Ashley, with the entire country knowing her father had beheaded her mother. Elizabeth had been raised by servants, away from court, and, for a while, by one of Henry's later wives, but she really had been alone, the child of a woman believed to be an adulterer who'd betrayed Henry. What a terrible burden to bear, and one that likely made all other problems in her life feel ten times heavier.

"My Queen, here is an idea. Why not give Robert an order to retire from court for a few months? It would be better if you weren't seen together. Send him to his palace in Kew. Tell him to remain there until his innocence has been determined. Treat him as you would treat any other courtier suspected of murdering his wife."

"But it will worry Robin so. He will think I no longer care for him."

I stood and took Elizabeth by the shoulders, a rare experience for her, I was sure. "Your Majesty, what matters right now is the safety of your subjects. If the French or Scottish were to suspect a great weakness in England, one of them might pounce. To keep your country safe, you must push Dudley away. Show everyone that you are not so swayed by him that you would condone murder."

"But how will I get through the day without him?" Elizabeth moaned.

I pulled the Queen to her feet. "Ma'am, you must not give up hope. Hope is your future. It is the light that will guide you for many years. I am not a fortune-teller, but I *know* you. I know your strength and your determination. You are going to hold yourself above all this marriage folderol. You are going to live a long and rich life. You are going to be the greatest queen, nay, the greatest ruler, this country has ever seen or will ever see again. Your wants as a woman will come second, or third, or even last. You are a Tudor, so ruling is in your blood. You will put aside, for now, your love of Robert Dudley. You will do what needs to be done."

I could see that she was almost there, but not quite. Then I remembered one of her more memorable quotes about being the daughter of King Henry VIII. "Ma'am, you may not be a lion, but you are a lion's cub, and you have a lion's heart."

With those words, the transformation took place before my eyes. Elizabeth straightened. She met my gaze with a fire that I hadn't seen in days, released my hands, and smoothed down her skirts. She readjusted her heavy pearl necklace and touched one slender hand to her hair, then let out a long and tremulous breath. "Blanche

Nottingham, you are wise beyond your years. Please accompany us to the presence chamber. We will receive Robert Dudley and banish him to Kew until the truth be known." Her voice was strong and royal. The Queen was back.

❖

I managed to find Meg at the laundry and pull her away. "Where have you been?" she whispered. I led her to the middle of the bowling green and sank to the ground. The grass tickled my ankles, but I ignored it because no one could eavesdrop on us out here. We were in a fishbowl, but a secure one.

I told her what had happened at Cumnor Place and the role I'd played for the sake of ensuring that events stayed true to the historical timeline. Talking about it brought some relief, but not enough. My chest still ached when I replayed the scene with poor Amy at the bottom of the stairs.

Meg clutched my hand. "I don't understand," she said. "Was someone else supposed to have killed Amy and you stepped in and caused an accident? Or were you the person who caused her death all along?"

I swallowed hard. "No idea. What if the reason Amy's death has been shrouded in mystery for centuries is because a woman from the future caused it then disappeared?"

Meg gave me a weak smile. "Now my head hurts."

I tried not to think about Chris and Dr. Kroll, but they were with me almost all the time. According to them I was making all this up for my own entertainment. "I don't know what's real anymore," I said. "Chris would say I'd even created you so I wouldn't feel so alone in my psychotically-induced Elizabethan fantasy."

Meg stroked my cheek then quickly dropped her hand. "Bollocks. Of course I'm real. I am Meghan Warren, chief researcher at the British Library. I was born in Haworth, home of the Brontë sisters, and attended Oxford. I moved to London ten years ago. You haven't made me up."

"I could have created you in my head to say that very thing."

Meg's smile lit up her small, round face. "Here's the bloody truth, my friend. I'm so amazing that you couldn't make me up. No one has that much creativity."

The world stopped for a second as we appreciated the delicious arrogance of her words, then we both broke up laughing. "Can you believe I said that?" Meg managed to get out between laughs.

An idea flashed through me. She was right about some things being too magnificent to make up. What if I could find a creative way to prove that this world was real? I clutched both her hands. "Tell me something about yourself that no one knows."

"I don't understand."

"If we both make it back—"

"*When.*"

"When we both make it back, I'll find you and tell you what you said. If you, Meg in the future, have no idea what I'm talking about, then I've fantasized this entire experience."

Meg's cheeks flushed. We watched a group of men in colorful tights and puffy velvet pants pass through the lower end of the green, neither of us wanting to speak until we were totally alone again.

"I don't like it. Then I'm participating in Chris's stupid fantasy theory."

"Humor me."

She looked off into the park and smiled. "Okay, here's one that nobody knows but my parents and my sister. My mum has a wicked sense of humor so she does this thing to my dad that cracks him up every time. She throws her arms around him and says, '*God*, I love you… What was your name again?'"

I laughed in surprise.

"My dad's so easy that it still makes him laugh after thirty-five years. Now we all laugh when Mum does it. It's been a family secret for years."

"Thank you. That's exactly what I need."

"Here's one thing I don't understand," Meg said. "How are we able to talk to these people in this time? Our English and theirs are very different."

I rolled my shoulders to release tension. "I've been pondering that. What if the bodies we inhabit somehow translate what we say into the vernacular of the time? When I say *do*, Blanche's body says *doth*. When I say *you*, she says *thee*."

"Makes some sense."

But then I shook my head. "But what about *fire truck*? You recognized that word. How could Blanche's body have not translated that into carriage or wagon or something?"

"Because *truck* exists in 1560. It's a very old word that means agree with. When you didn't agree with something, you didn't truck with it."

"Damn, you're smart."

"Kind of you to notice," she retorted. "Now I've got to get back to work before they notice their slave is missing."

I rose to my knees and hugged her quickly. The urge to do more than hug this woman nearly overpowered me, but we were in the middle of a green visible from one entire side of the palace.

Two women linking arms, okay. Two women holding hands, okay. Two women in a passionate lip-lock, not a good idea.

Still, the urge was great.

CHAPTER THIRTY-ONE

The rumors about Robert Dudley hummed through London and spread across England. And if the whisperings among the courtiers were to be believed, shocking tales of Dudley and the Queen as coconspirators blanketed Europe as well. The inquest into Amy's death ruled it a "death by misadventure." I was relieved that none of the rumors spoke of an unknown woman visiting Amy on the day of her death. Instead, the gossip focused on how Dudley hadn't visited his wife for over a year before her death, didn't attend her funeral, and didn't arrange for a memorial. And with Amy's death, Dudley inherited his late father-in-law's wealth.

Dudley remained at his palace in Kew, which meant Elizabeth was out of sorts. She was especially hurt by the revived gossip about her late mother, Anne Boleyn. People began once again calling Anne a slut and claiming that Elizabeth was just like her mother. So we were kept busy caring for her and flattering her, but for days we didn't see her smile nor hear her laugh. She was pale and restless, unable to sit still or concentrate. She held her councilors off, refusing to discuss matters of state, insisting that Cecil could take care of things for a while. That Elizabeth would willingly give up power shocked us all.

For some reason it fell on my shoulders to make her laugh. I hated doing that at the expense of others—my style was more self-deprecating—but I took advantage of any opportunity that arose. I elicited my best laugh from Elizabeth when Lady Clinton, in lowering herself onto a chair, farted softly. As my brother Jake liked to say, "Silent but deadly." While the others pressed their hands to their noses, trying not to laugh, I put down my stitching. "Oh, Lady Clinton, that was not one of your better efforts." The Queen laughed until she had to pull out a handkerchief and wipe her eyes.

Meg and I worked hard to see each other at least once a day. After a week of snatched moments in hallways, we managed to escape into a far garden one afternoon. We sat on a bench, our hips as close together as my stupid dress would allow.

"What I don't understand," I said, "is why Blanche Nottingham?"

"And why Harriet Blankenship?" Meg asked, stretching out her short legs.

"We must be connected to these women in some way, otherwise this is just entirely random and stupid."

Meg groaned. "Give me a laptop and access to the library database, and I could figure it out for you." She started listing the best databases and how to access the paper records from the sixteenth century, but my mind started worrying about another problem. Finally, Meg bumped my shoulder with hers. "You must think I'm dull as dishwater. Where did you go?"

I made a face. "I'm worried about Blanche. She's so determined to stay in the future that I'm afraid she's going to outsmart me. What if she figures out a way to stay?"

"Then we'll just have to be smarter," Meg said. "The next time one of us goes back, we'll research the hell out of both Blanche and Harriet. When I find out what happened to each of them, we can make a plan." She groaned and slumped forward. "Sadly, finding material about Blanche will be easier because she was someone, but Harriet's just a servant. The chances of learning anything specific to her are depressingly low." Meg straightened. "But I'm glad you're talking about the future as real, instead of all that dodgy split personality muckety-muck."

I toed the loose gravel at my feet. "I'm not convinced either way. It still could be true."

She snorted.

"Seriously, Meg. You think this is real, but what if you're in the same boat? What if you are really running around London with Harriet's very confused consciousness in charge, and you're tucked away in your brain somewhere imagining all this."

"Rubbish."

"You've invented me so you won't feel so alone. You're punishing yourself by having to do unpleasant jobs like the laundry."

"A city *full* of rubbish."

"Did you have any sort of emotional trauma in the months before Raj's experiment?"

She pursed her lips together and stared up into the apple tree above us. "My favorite cousin, who was my age, died suddenly in April."

I flung up my hands. "I knew it. You might have created this fantasy as an escape from the pain of losing your cousin."

"But why are we both having the same fantasy?"

I rubbed my temples. "That's the thing. We aren't. You could have created me in your 1560 world, and I could have created you. You can't trust anything about this world." She was shaking her head, so I touched her arm. "Just think it through, Meg. Give it a minute."

We sat there watching a bumblebee struggle down between the petals of a red snapdragon. After a few seconds, the bee backed out and flew to the next flower.

"Bloody hell," Meg finally muttered. "That would mean we're both mad as a bag of ferrets."

I laughed. "We crazies need to stick together. I could ask the Queen if we could set up house in one of those old cottages at the edge of the park. We could sit by a cozy fire all winter drinking ale and reading to each other. We could go off our trolleys together."

Meg's eyes sparkled. "Smashing. Two nutters from the future setting up house." Then she gave me a smoldering look that curled my toes. "Might be fun, though."

Laughing, we strolled back through the garden, across the bowling green, and back to our lives. As I watched Meg disappear around the corner of the palace, my heart swelled.

Chapter Thirty-two

Despite my constant efforts, Elizabeth continued to mourn the loss of her horse master. We encouraged her to eat, but she only picked at her food. Her cheekbones became too prominent, and her skin took on a gray hue. She rarely called for a dance or for musicians to play for her. I managed to draw out a chuckle or two every day, but it wasn't enough. Soon the rest of us slowed down, as if the same heavy cloud blanketed us as well.

I finally sought out Meg at the laundry. Her face and bare arms were red as she stirred a huge pot full of sheets. She winked at me as I approached, an innocent moment that revved my pulse into high gear.

The other women were working far enough away that we had some privacy, but the steamy area, smelling of burning wood and soap, sent perspiration running down my forehead and neck. I motioned her away from the heat.

Meg dipped into a half-hearted curtsey with an insolent grin. "What may I do for you, m'lady?"

"Oh, stop," I said with an answering smile. "I need your help." I described the Queen's mood. "Do you have any ideas? I'm out of them. She won't even listen to ten minutes of Harry Potter before she rises and wanders away."

Meg nodded thoughtfully. "I do, actually. I know lots of kids' games."

"These are grown women."

"No matter, Blanchy, I've got a great idea."

"Seriously? Blanchy?"

She gave me a gentle push. "Off with you. I'll only need a few hours."

True to her word, Meg showed up in the Queen's chambers after we'd eaten a lunch of soup and thick bread.

She approached Elizabeth and curtsied, a real one this time. "Ma'am, I respectfully need your help, and the help of your ladies."

Elizabeth managed to muster enough attention to ask "What sort of help?"

"I am returning to my village for the fall festival soon, and it is my task to bring a game for all of the village to play. But I have not yet tried out my idea, so I do not know if it will be a fun game or a boring game."

I bit my lip and felt my eyes fill as Elizabeth's face lightened up. She loved games. "Pray, tell us about this game."

"I call it a scavenger hunt, ma'am. If Your Majesty and the ladies could form three teams, then I will give each team the same list of items. The first team to find all of the items shall be declared the winner."

Elizabeth's competitive streak flamed to life. "And where shall we find these items?"

"Anywhere on the palace grounds. You may not pay for them, nor steal them, but only ask to take them temporarily. Some items will be found in the park, so those may be taken freely."

Elizabeth stood and barked off five names, including mine. "We shall form the first team. What shall we call ourselves?"

"The Lion Cubs," I called, and the Queen clapped her hands. Then she formed two other teams, each of which chose a name— one was the Ferrets, the other was the Swans.

Meg handed the Queen and the two other teams scrolls of grayish white cloth that must have a been an old sheet she ripped up. She'd managed to find ink and a quill and had written the same items on each list. The Queen took one look at the list and said, "Let us begin!"

As we raced to follow her, Meg called out, "The first team to bring all items to me in the west knot garden shall be given a prize."

"A prize!" the Queen chortled as she ran. I threw Meg a grateful look over my shoulder as I hurried after Elizabeth. This was exactly what we all needed.

We collected a book written in Spanish from one of the Queen's libraries. We found a child's shoe in the servants' quarters, assuring the small, nervous woman that we would return it. We found a chunk of charcoal under a laundry pot, and a guard's red hat from Jacob, who looked at me as if he'd give me the clothes off his back if I'd only ask.

As a result of this silly game, my heart now was as light as the Queen's, and I felt, for the first time, as if I could cast off my guilt over Amy Dudley's death.

We collected oak acorns from the park, a wooden pin from the bowling green, and a handful of blackberries from the kitchen gardens. When Elizabeth, excited and hungry, ate them all a few minutes later, she sent me back for more while she and the others went in search of a fork. Good luck with that, I thought as I backtracked and let myself into a narrow alley that led to the walled gardens.

"Jamie!"

I whirled to see Meg running, her short legs moving fast as she crossed the street and entered the alley. "Maybe you should call me Blanche if you're going to shout it," I said with a smile.

We were standing in the shade, walled in on both sides. The palace was far enough from the garden that no one could see us. Meg's chest heaved and her eyes were dark with an emotion that took my breath away. Holy crap. I swallowed hard.

Meg turned, closed the six-foot-high, solid wooden gate, and latched it. Breathing heavily through her nose, she nodded toward the gate at the other end of the short alley. Body buzzing with the possibilities, I managed to walk the twenty steps and latch the gate into the gardens. Now we were locked in...or more importantly, everyone else was locked out.

We met in the middle and stared at each other. Then she slid her arms around me and we clung to each other for a moment. After feeling alone for so long, being held was marvelous. Meg murmured something into my hair, and I turned my head slightly to see her eyes were dark with arousal. Hell's gate. Heart pounding, I moved until our lips slid together naturally.

The kiss was tentative at first, gentle, but then the taste of her silky lips aroused me to a state I hadn't felt in months. Urgent now, we clung to each other as our hungry mouths took control, melting against one another's.

Everything clicked into place. This was what I'd wanted since I'd realized Meg was so different from Chris. As we began exploring each other's bodies, my heart raced. God, I needed this.

Meg pressed her mouth against my neck. "What color are your eyes?"

"What?"

"I see your soul shining through Blanche's eyes, but I want to know what your real eyes look like."

I struggled for breath as we nuzzled and nibbled each other. "Light hazel. They've been called amber, if that helps."

"It does." Then our kisses deepened to the point I could barely breathe, but that didn't matter. Only her mouth mattered. I stroked her breast with my thumb.

Meg pulled back and slumped against the brick wall. "Bloody hell."

"What?"

"What are the ethics of this situation?"

I was trying not to pant like an over-eager Vincent. "What do you mean?"

She sighed. "This isn't my body. It's Harriet's. And you're in Blanche's body. Is it right to be doing this?" She leaned in for one more kiss. "Maybe. But to go further? Is that really ethical?"

"But they aren't here. They'll never know."

She gently stroked my cheek. "That doesn't make it right. You say you're done with Chris, but Blanche is there, right now, possibly making love to Chris with *your* body."

I slapped my forehead, suddenly furious. "Oh God, you're right. I hate the idea of ever touching Chris again! Which means we shouldn't do anything in Harriet's and Blanche's bodies!"

We reached for each other's hand, then smiled.

"Fire truck," we said at the same time.

We gave in to one more kiss, then she unlatched the gate. "See you in the west knot garden," she murmured.

I stood there, numb, as she left the alley. How does this stuff happen? You couldn't make it up. Did I travel 457 years into the past in order to find my future? I headed for the exit then stopped. The blackberries! In just a few minutes I picked a large handful, then popped a few of the plump ones into my mouth before leaving the garden. The baby inside me said it needed more berries, so I ate more, luckily stopping myself before consuming them all.

As I began searching for the Lion Cubs, an unfamiliar emotion settled over me. It took a few seconds but I managed to identify it. I was happy for the first time in a very long time.

After fifteen minutes of wandering through the grounds, the sound of women shouting and laughing helped me find Elizabeth and the others. All three teams were running up from the shore of the Thames, the Queen in the lead waving a swan feather. "To the knot garden, my spark!" Elizabeth cried. "We have our last item!"

At first I thought the other teams were letting Elizabeth win, but the women were red-faced and puffing, so no, the Lion Cubs would win, fair and square.

I joined them as we dashed—perhaps not the most accurate of terms, since in our heavy skirts the best we could do was shuffle quickly—around the walled kitchen garden, past a cluster of court-iers gossiping in the shade, and into the west knot garden.

Meg was waiting for us.

Lady Mary had used her outer skirt as a container, so Elizabeth proudly pulled out each item, including a fork. She'd found it in a room full of gifts she'd been given after her coronation. "We have no idea why the King of Sweden thought we would need a fork, but we are glad we kept it."

I added the blackberries to the pile, and Meg declared us the winning team. My emotions were such a mess I couldn't sort them out. Lust from our kiss. Gratitude for this game. Relief that the Queen was more herself than she'd been for days. Confusion over what it meant to fall for a woman living in another woman's body. Wasn't my life messed up enough already?

Meg opened a box of white cakes topped with swirls of yellow frosting. The Queen squealed in delight. After her subjects and Robert Dudley, sugar was her favorite thing. As the defeated teams watched us, Meg then revealed two more boxes that contained enough cakes for everyone. As the Queen laughed and helped distribute them, she told Meg she'd like her to come read for her again. My chest swelled with pride.

If I were stuck here forever, I could be happy as long as Meg was here with me.

Chapter Thirty-three

The next week was painful as I felt close to bursting. I either couldn't find Meg or we had to pass on the grounds without talking as I attended the Queen. We communicated with our eyes—amazing how much one can say with just a few facial muscles—but I longed to hold her again, wondering if it would feel as good the second time.

Finally, Meg appeared in the Queen's chambers one morning, having been summoned to read to Elizabeth. I sat on a nearby stool, trying to focus on my stitching instead of on Meg's animated face, but I only managed to stitch the collar onto my skirt again.

I didn't hear a word of what Meg read, instead scrolling through a "book" in my head of all the things I wanted to say to her, all the things I wanted to ask her. We knew so little about each other.

When Meg finished, the Queen once again thanked her for the scavenger hunt. "We felt more joy in those few hours than we have felt since the crown has been weighing down our head."

Meg curtsied. "If it please the Queen, perhaps you would like to take some fresh air by way of the palace balconies. You could make a tour of the balconies, stopping to enjoy each one."

Elizabeth nodded. "Yes, that would be something new. Come, ladies, we shall make a journey without leaving the palace."

Meg winked at me as I followed the group. What was she up to now?

At the fourth balcony, as we looked out across the jousting arena, Lady Clinton bent over the railing and pointed to the ground two stories below. "What, pray tell, is that?"

We all gathered at the railing. A number of white rocks had been placed on the brown, crushed stone walkway. "The rocks appear to have been laid out in the shape of an eye," Elizabeth said. "How unusual."

At the next balcony, Lady Mary pointed to the ground. "Now here is a heart made of the same white rocks," she said.

Eye. Heart. I love. My hands and feet began to tingle.

At the next balcony, we all rushed the railing at the same time. "J!" Elizabeth cried. "Eye heart J. I love J. But who is J?"

I struggled to keep my expression neutral. Meg loved me. The thought brought tears to my eyes, and I looked away to hide them, only to come face-to-face with Meg herself.

She curtsied to the Queen. "If you will allow me, ma'am, J stands for James. He is a new earl come to court."

Elizabeth tilted her head. "We have not met any James. Who is this man?"

Meg was clearly trying not to laugh. "He has not yet been presented to you, ma'am, but I have heard the others talk about him. He is the Earl...the Earl of Doonesbury."

The others murmured at this news. My jaw was clamped as tightly as possible, and I pinched the back of my hand to hold off the laughter.

"Yes, and I am told he is quite handsome, tall and well-bodied, with eyes the color of amber."

More murmuring now. "In fact," Meg added, "I just saw him a few minutes ago. He was heading to the Great Hall and seemed the most masculine of men."

That was all it took. The Queen led the way and the women followed. I hung back, met Meg's eyes, then pulled us both behind the heavy drapes lining the door to the balcony. The kiss was long and hot and weakened my knees. Then we pulled apart.

"Don't stop," I whispered.

"If we don't stop now, we won't be able to." Meg sweetly kissed the corner of my mouth. "What would Blanche and Harriet say to that?"

"I don't care."

We kissed again, then Meg stroked my sides, tapping her knuckle against my stomacher. "You must wear this all the time?"

We kissed again. "It's kind of like the Elizabethan version of Spanx."

"Ahh, the knickers that hold in all your flabby bits." Then she pushed me deeper into the drapes and kissed me so hard my knees did finally collapse. She pushed against me to hold me up.

"Goddamn it, Meg. Maybe Blanche and Harriet wouldn't mind."

Groaning, she stepped back and let me go. "Another minute with you and I might abandon my ethics."

Once outside the room, she headed left with a happy wave, then I turned right to join the search for James, Earl of Doonesbury.

After more days of catering to Elizabeth's every whim, which included daily walks, requests for games and dancing, and under-the-cover discussions about either Dudley or Harry Potter, I was worn out. At least Elizabeth was back to her normal self, thanks to Meg.

Distracted by my thoughts of her, I didn't notice the change in weather until Lady Mary pointed to the sky. Slate gray clouds rolled toward the palace like a team of out-of-control horses. Thunder cracked sharply in the distance. We picked up our skirts and began running toward the palace, Elizabeth laughing as fat raindrops plopped onto our heads and shoulders.

Once I was safely inside, my mind spun. Where would Meg be? I ran to the maids' storage room, but she wasn't there. "Gone to the cellars," one woman called.

I'd never been there, so I ended up racing through three wings of the palace until I found someone who could point me to the stairs leading into the cellar. By now my heart pounded faster than was healthy. How much time did we have? Thunder boomed directly overhead, and hard rain drilled the gravel streets.

I found the stairs and descended, ducking my head to avoid the low ceiling beams. The bricked walls and dirt floor reeked of mold and damp.

Meg was in a far corner helping another woman with a crate of bottles. "Meg—I mean Harriet, I need you to come with me."

The other woman glared at me. "She be helping me now. You can have her when I'm finished."

"The Queen has sent for you to read to her, Harriet. She hates to be kept waiting." The sounds of the storm didn't reach the cellar, so Meg didn't know.

With a mumbled apology to the woman, Meg followed me up the stairs. We were halfway down the hallway when the thunder rolled through again. "Holy shit!" she snapped. "This is our chance!"

We ran out the door and into the nearest flower garden. The rain beat against our faces and blew off my headpiece. "Fire truck, this hurts," I yelled. We stood huddled together against the bruising rain.

"Why does rain have to be so cold?" Meg shouted against the thunder. Her teeth chattered, but she was grinning. "We're going home, Jamie."

"Don't forget. No matter where you are, get yourself to Dr. Rajamani immediately and demand the serum. That's the only thing that will stop us from coming back during the next storm." Soaked now, my entire body trembled from cold and excitement.

"Okay," she said. "Let's meet at his office."

"Deal!" I shouted over the thunder.

The sky crackled like a downed power line, and I flew through the air. But instead of riding lightning, I slammed against the ground in the middle of a flowerbed. The rain pelting my face forced me to sit up. Aching, I climbed to my feet. "Meg!" She lay crumpled in the path ten feet away.

I tripped over my sodden skirt, fell to my knees, and ended up crawling. Just as I reached her, she sat up and rubbed her forehead.

"Are you okay?"

She frowned, then winced at the driving rain. She looked down at her skirts and examined her hands. "Thank you, Lord Almighty, for your forgiveness."

"Meg, look at me. Are you hurt?"

She shook her head. "Lady Blanche, I am Harriet. And God has seen fit to answer my prayers and return me to the world."

My heart soared and plummeted at the same time, which I'd never thought possible. I was thrilled that Meg had made it back into her own body, and horrified that I hadn't.

❖

Meg left me on October 10. That was when I stopped notching my table leg calendar. The only way to survive was to shut down emotionally. I waited a week for another storm. Then two weeks, then three. When I asked one of the male servants about the weather, he said that October was always the rainiest month. And it did rain. And it even stormed twice. But I was still here. A tiny part of me wanted to believe that Meg had gotten the serum from Dr. Raj, but then I stopped thinking about Meg as a real person. Believing that time travel was possible was just part of my mental illness.

After four weeks, the truth had settled into my soul like pneumonia. Chris and Dr. Kroll were right. This was all in my head. I'd created Meg/Harriet and Ray so I would have some allies in my private fantasy. I'd created the entire Elizabethan experience from what I'd read or movies I'd seen.

I'd created Kat Ashley, and Lady Mary, and Jacob, to remind me of my friends Ashley and Mary, and my brother Jake. I'd even created little Vincent.

I wasn't actually *in* the body of Queen Elizabeth I's lady-in-waiting. I was in my own body, my own time, locked somewhere deep inside my own brain while "Blanche," my alter ego, ran the show. Clearly, she'd managed to talk Dr. Kroll into the electroconvulsive therapy. She won.

I had done all this to punish myself for not being the woman Chris wanted. I had dissociative personality disorder, and there was nothing I could do about it.

Fuck.

CHAPTER THIRTY-FOUR

Just as in that first week in my 1560 fantasy, I stopped getting out of bed. That first week was because I kept expecting the nightmare to disappear. Now it was because I knew it never would.

Lady Mary told the Queen I was ill, then harassed me ten times a day to get up, since it was clear I wasn't sick. Vincent spent most of the day on my bed, only running off to visit the kitchen for food and outside to relieve himself. Not even when he nudged me repeatedly with a wet nose did I rise.

"Mary," I said one morning as she was about to return to the Queen. "We aren't friends, thanks to you ratting me out about being with child, but when the Queen becomes ill in a few years, I will care for her instead of you. Since none of this is real, why should I let you become disfigured by smallpox even if it's just in my head?"

She made a sad sound in her throat, shaking her head. "Perhaps you have a fever."

I sighed. "No, I've just let Blanche take control of my life."

I slept nearly all the time and refused most food. What was the point of eating in a fantasy? For three months, I'd believed 1560 was real. Now I knew it wasn't. Perhaps I could starve myself, die, then wake up in my own body again. I tried not to think of the life growing inside me...no, the life I *imagined* was growing inside me. My middle had widened considerably, and while I lay there quietly, I could sometimes feel a funny flutter inside. I no longer battled nausea, so that was nice. While I had no idea how the various stages of pregnancy progressed, I was doing a fine job of making it up. And because there was no water, I drank mug after mug of ale, which can give one a nice buzz on an empty stomach. Probably not too good for the baby, but that was made up as well.

And what was the point of all that Dudley drama? Me trying to keep Robert Dudley alive, me causing Amy Dudley's death. That bullshit was all something I'd read somewhere. Why fight to keep history accurate when history hadn't even been involved? I was a pathetic weakling trapped in my own mind because I lacked the strength to face the real world. I had let Chris's comments so freak me out that I retreated into my mind and created Blanche. Pretty sick.

I tried to imagine what was going on with the body I no longer controlled. Did Blanche have Bradley and Mouse arrested? Was Blanche still charming Chris? Had the bitch finished writing her *riveting* novel?

Hope was a funny thing. I knew it could come and go, advance and retreat, but I didn't know others could rob you of it. Chris took my love and perverted it, forcing me to create Blanche as a desperate measure to keep Chris. Bradley had said life was one long battle not to lose yourself. Well, I had lost. Blanche was in charge now. She had access to my cell phone. One text from Dr. Rajamani and Blanche would be knocking at his door to receive the serum. In fact, she'd likely done that weeks ago.

I laughed so suddenly Vincent jumped to his feet and barked at me, scowling in alarm. What was I still doing thinking that the serum and time travel were real? I hadn't been transported back in time to 1560 by riding the lightning—God, what a stupid explanation. And no thunderstorm could transport me back into my own body.

I was already there.

❖

After a week in bed, boredom got me up, washed, dressed, and back in Elizabeth's entourage. Of course I punished myself for this by "scheduling" the marriage to Winston for the following Saturday.

That day dawned bright and clear. Tubs were brought in and filled with hot water. The Queen and Kat Ashley bathed first, then I as the bride was able to go next so the water was still lukewarm. I sank down into the tub and moaned with pleasure. Someone behind me began washing my hair, so I dropped my head back and relaxed. Pain shot through me when I realized it wasn't Meg. It couldn't be. I'd created her to fill a need.

Once out of the bath, a servant brought me a note. I carefully unfolded the thick, coarse paper and ignored the poor spelling:

Dear Blanche,
Do not do this. You have not been yourself for weeks. Where is the Blanche who fights back, who refuses to compromise, who always puts herself first? Are you so desperate about being poor again that you will marry this stuffed fish? You have another choice.
With respect, Jacob

Huh. Nice. This "note" from Jacob was clearly my twisted mind trying to give me a way out. But by now I was four and a half months pregnant and visible. I needed to do something for the baby.

Yet while I let the others fuss over me, dressing me in a cream gown shot through with gold thread and making the necessary adjustments, I already knew I couldn't do it. So once my bridal cap had been fastened onto my head, I found Elizabeth, curtsied, and asked if we could have a moment alone. She waved the others away.

"My dear, the spark has totally gone out of you. Mary tells us you eat less than a bird."

I lowered myself carefully onto a stool, feeling lightheaded, grateful for Jacob's note. "Ma'am, I realize that you cannot have an unmarried woman with child in your court. The scandal would be too great. But please, I beg of you, don't force me to marry Lord Winston. We are ill suited. He is not kind and he brings out the worst in me."

She tipped her head back, glaring down her nose at me. "Then what would you suggest? We know your purse is light, in great part thanks to your late father. If you do not remain in court, where would you go?"

I blew out my breath. "There is an old cottage at the edge of the park in which the gardeners store tools. What if I were to take up residence there until the child comes?"

"Live alone in a run-down shack?"

I nodded. "Yes, please. You won't even know I'm there. No one will. And I could work to pay for it. I could clean or do laundry."

"Do not be ridiculous. You shall not work."

Elizabeth chewed thoughtfully on her lower lip. "We do understand the pressures of being expected to marry someone you do not like. Our councilors have been at us to do this very thing since the day we were crowned." She leaned forward and rested a hand on my shoulder. "If you really cannot manage to marry Winston, then you may have the cottage until the birth of your child. After that you will find a wet nurse to take the child and return to us at court."

I nodded, pleased that I'd managed to steer the fantasy in the direction I preferred. "And, ma'am, I intend to stay away from court to avoid causing you any embarrassment. You should not be seen with an unmarried woman in my condition."

She frowned, then sighed long and loudly. "So it will be."

I never heard how Winston took the news, and frankly, I didn't care, since none of this was real.

Vincent and I passed the winter quietly. I would sit in my chair by the fire and read while he would snore and snuffle and chase mice in his sleep. Some days the only sounds I heard were my own voice and the clicking of Vincent's nails on the stone floor. Every few days a servant would bring a plate of cold food and another jug of wine. I had no problem drinking while "pregnant" because the fetus wasn't real. I kept the fire burning and was only cold in the mornings when the fire had died out. Soon my clothes, hair, and skin smelled like campfire. Even Vincent's ears smelled of smoke when I nuzzled him.

Jacob kept me supplied with firewood but he didn't say much. I thanked him for his note, but he didn't reply. For weeks, he glared at me as if I were a total stranger. Perhaps his crush had been crushed by my growing pregnancy.

The long winter months were, not surprisingly, free from thunderstorms. I no longer needed them to switch places with Blanche; I would live in this fantasy, and she could have my life.

One morning, I remembered something funny. Queen Mary, Elizabeth's sister, had been desperate to give birth to an heir once she married France's King Philip. Eventually, she announced that she was with child and would give birth in May of 1555. When the announced date arrived, the country celebrated to hear of the birth...except that there had been no birth. It was just a rumor. Mary remained secluded through May, then June, then July, insisting the baby would come soon. Finally, by August it was clear to even Mary that the pregnancy hadn't been real. That was likely why I'd created my own false pregnancy. Instead of a child swelling my belly, it was probably just gas.

By mid-December, I could tell I'd gained at least ten pounds. I was exhausted all the time. By January, I carried a basketball under my loose dresses. My skin itched, my legs cramped constantly, and I found it hard to breathe. I managed to visit the pond a few times, gasping at the shock of cold as I sank into the water. But after a while I decided that staying clean didn't matter and stopped going. Besides, it was lonely there without Meg.

I slept well. But now and then, when a howling wind rattled my windows and reached cold fingers through the slender cracks in my walls, I would lie awake and try to conjure up Meg again. This was *my* fantasy, damn it, and I wanted her back.

The very next day came a knock on my door that I knew would be food. When I opened the door, there stood Meg, bundled up in a heavy coat and hat! My heart leapt into my throat until I realized— No, not Meg. Harriet.

She entered and put the bowl and jug on the table. "Do you require anything else, m'lady?"

The voice was the same. The body was the same. But the spirit, the soul, the *spark* of who Meg was, had disappeared. Despite that, I frantically searched for a topic that would keep her with me longer.

"Harriet, you have been to a different place, haven't you?"

Her eyes skittered around the room. "Different place, m'lady?"
"Different than here. A place where things move very quickly and people dress differently."

Her face crumpled in anguish. "How did you know?" she whispered. "Have you been to Hell as well?"

"Hell?"

"My mother always told me that I was an evil child. She said I was a sinner and would go to hell." She hiccupped in fear. "And then one day she was right. I was in Hell for months and months." She put her palms together in prayer. "Then the Lord Almighty chose to forgive me and return me to my home. But I must have done something wrong because he sent me back to Hell again. Then he changed his mind and once again brought me home. Every day I fear he will send me back."

Poor thing. "What was your Hell like?" I asked.

She wiped her eyes. "Beasts that move very fast. So much noise. Women who dress like men. Life is very hard for sinners in Hell. We have no money and no place to live. Our punishment is to live outside with nothing. We must watch other people live with wonderful food and fancy homes and nice clothes, things we do not deserve." Her voice flattened. "That is my Hell. I must be very good or the Lord will once again send me there."

"Harriet, you might be wrong. I don't think that was Hell. There is something between Heaven and Hell called Purgatory. I think you were sent there, accidentally, and God finally realized the mistake and sent you back. You weren't in Hell. You would never, ever be sent there."

As her face relaxed a little, I touched her lightly on the shoulder. "You are a good person. You have had a glimpse of the future that no one else in this life has had. Consider it a gift and move on."

"Many thanks, m'lady." Her folded hands were white from clutching each other too tightly. She needed to flee.

"Thank you for the food."

With a dip of her head she was gone, letting in a blast of cold wind that nearly froze my ankles. I pulled Vincent onto my lap and wrapped us both in my blanket.

❖

Time passed. I no longer kept track of the date, so I had no idea where in the year I was. All I did was eat—quite a bit, actually—and oil my growing belly. The baby kicked me all the time now, and my joints felt loose, as if with one good shaking I'd come undone. The baby pressed against my bladder so I had to pee approximately every two minutes. Sometimes I felt like a walking aquarium with a little human sloshing around inside me. The physical reality of this baby-to-be had forced me to accept it as real, at least in the fantasy world in which I lived.

I did receive a large slice of cake with a lion made of spun sugar on the top when the palace celebrated the second anniversary of Elizabeth's coronation. That told me it was the middle of January.

Jacob continued to help me, and Lady Mary brought me books from the Queen's library. Once, Mary suggested I visit the Queen, but I claimed to be ill since I didn't feel like giving any more energy to that part of my fantasy. It was a relief not to attend chapel or to sit among the courtiers and try to look interested in the men's constant chatter and gossip.

However, I did miss Elizabeth. By now Dudley was surely back at court and once again charming the Queen. Jacob assured me, however, that the word on the street was that Elizabeth could never dare marry Dudley now. Her people would not have her consorting with a man suspected of murdering his wife. Apparently, Dudley would not let go of the idea he could be king, so he rashly approached the Spanish ambassador to ask if Spain's King Phillip would support Dudley's marriage to Elizabeth. Cecil found out and began spreading rumors that Catholic Spain wanted to take over England. The fear of a Catholic leader roused the citizens to anger and shut down Dudley's plan.

Of course this happened because I'd read it in one of my books, and my fantasy was driven by my knowledge. In my lighter moments I wished I could create a fantasy in which Elizabeth *did* marry her Robin. They would have had many children, all surviving to adulthood, and she would rule happily until she died of old age, surrounded by her family. But since my fantasy was designed to punish me, I couldn't give the Queen a happy ending either.

A midwife began visiting me, I assumed on the orders of the Queen. The plump woman pressed at my belly and asked how my breathing was. "Easier," I said.

"Good. That means the baby has settled. You have more room to breathe." She briskly gathered up her things. "Won't be long now."

I'd estimated that the baby was likely due in early April, so that meant we were probably at or past that stupid deadline I'd created—April 3, the storm that burned down the steeple.

That would explain the warming weather and bluer skies. I'd survived the winter in a leaky cottage in my head. I was surprised I hadn't punished myself with a few Minnesota blizzards.

Jacob brought another cart of wood. He'd grown more comfortable with me and would sit on my bench and talk. His tales of guarding mishaps made me laugh.

One day after his stories, he tilted his head and all laughter left his eyes. "You have changed so much," he said.

"For the good or the bad?"

"You are kinder and calmer, but…" He pressed his lips together until I encouraged him to continue. "But I miss the feisty Blanche. She was…astonishing."

Lovely, just lovely. The whole fucking world preferred Blanche, no matter what the year.

As he stood to leave, I touched his arm. "I am curious, Jacob. Do you know the month? The date?"

He grabbed the handle of the empty wood cart. "Methinks it is the first of April, Lady Blanche." Then he waved as he headed back toward the palace.

The event hadn't happened yet. In two days, lightning would strike.

Who the fuck cared?

Not me.

CHAPTER THIRTY-FIVE

That afternoon when Lady Mary brought me books, she also brought me a mirror, her not-so-subtle way of telling me I looked like shit. After she left, I stared into the cracked hand mirror. The body, swollen with child, was Blanche's. The hair, limp and unclean, was Blanche's. The face was Blanche's. But the eyes were mine—I could see myself in the eyes.

Then I laughed at my stupidity. What did it matter what I saw in my eyes?

At dusk, I could hear a commotion outside, so I looked out my window. Elizabeth, with four guards and no ladies, was walking down the path to my cottage. I ran to the door and flung it open, wishing I'd washed my hair sometime in the last month.

"Blanche, good morrow! Make way. Spring is here. We have come to visit." Elizabeth strode into the cottage, her skirts brushing the dust into swirls she was kind enough to ignore. I swept the books off the only chair and offered it to her. With a gracious nod, she sat and motioned me to do the same on my bed. I sat there, waiting, as she examined me.

"You, my dear, look as if you've just been let out of Bedlam."

"Apologies, ma'am."

"Why have you not come to see us? It's been months."

"As I mentioned when we last spoke, I did not want to be seen in this state." I motioned to my belly.

"Yes, you could not be there as one of our ladies, but you certainly could have come to call. I meant to send for you, but the needs of the realm these last months have been great." She waved her hand. "But still, we are cross with you because you left us hanging with Harry about to do battle with that horrid wizard whose name can never be spoken."

I smiled, guessing that J.K. Rowling would be pleased to know her Harry was a hit even in 1561. "Ma'am, I apologize. Once I am delivered of this child, I would be honored to resume the story."

Elizabeth folded her hands and looked around the cottage. Bird song came through the open windows, and the guards talked quietly outside. "We are most concerned about you, Blanche Nottingham. There is no sparkle in your eyes. You are white as milk."

I gazed at her, unsure what to say but admiring her skin. It was clear and flawless, cheeks slightly pink from the walk to the cottage. In reality, that skin would not last, for she would emerge from her smallpox battle scarred. For the rest of her life, she would not leave her chambers without covering her face, neck, and chest with a mixture called "Spirits of Saturn" that was made of white lead and vinegar. My beloved queen would slowly poison herself over the years with lead. That she would make it to age sixty-nine was a miracle.

I shook my head. No, damn it. This was a fantasy. I could have the Queen recover without scars and not rub lead into her skin every day. If it took all my energy, I would find a way to force this fantasy to follow my wishes.

I sighed, then chuckled softly. "My dearest Queen, I appreciate your concern, but you need to know that my health doesn't matter. This will sound very strange to you, but none of this is real. You're not real. Whitehall Palace is not real. We are all tucked away in a tiny corner of my brain. I'm having the mother of a fantasy, and you're part of it."

She tsked loudly. "Perhaps you truly do belong in Bedlam. Of course this is real. Do not be a fool." She leaned forward. "Ever since last August, you have changed, and for the better. Before this, when we looked into your eyes, we were not sure of you. Your eyes gave away nothing. But since August, your eyes have shone with such—what did you say your Harry Potter had? Oh yes, your eyes have shone with spunk. We love that, but you have lost your spunk. You have lost your spark."

Spunk. My eyes welled up, and I looked away, desperately homesick for my family, whom I would never see again as myself. Blanche could be standing in front of my mother right now, hurting her feelings, and I would have no idea. I could do nothing to stop her.

Elizabeth stood and strolled around the small room. "Do you remember when Amy Dudley died and we were despondent over what to do about our sweet Robin?"

I wiped my eyes. "Yes."

"Your words helped me so much that my gratitude continues to this day. So I will say those words to you because now *you* need to hear them."

She knelt at my feet, which caused to me to leap up in horror. "Ma'am, no!"

"Sit down and hush. I am talking to you." She took my hands and squeezed hard. "You have lost your hope, which you cannot do. You must find it again. Hope is your future, Blanche. It is the light that guides all of us through this uncertain life. You must *hope* that matters will change. You must hope that life will improve."

I curled over my belly, suddenly exhausted. "Yes, I have lost all hope."

Elizabeth rose and sat next to me, her lavender scent tickling my nose. "Then let me give you some of mine." She held me close and I began to cry, horrified to be sobbing in the arms of Queen Elizabeth I. But I couldn't stop. It was as if all my uncertainties and fears and confusion poured into a raging river. My fury at Chris and Blanche. My sadness over Meg and Ray and never seeing my family again. My self-loathing at creating this stupid situation in the first place.

Several handkerchiefs later, I finally stopped. My eyes stung and my nose was plugged. The baby hadn't liked the crying bout, so it was actively kicking.

Elizabeth stood, straightening out her skirts. "We will leave you now. But we want our Spark back, and soon." She winked at me. "That is an order from your queen."

I smiled weakly and rose to see her out.

Then I sat on the bench outside the cottage and thought about what she said. Hope. That used to be part of my backbone. I had let Chris steal it from me because she was so sure I was lying about 1560. She had undermined my confidence. No, I had *let* her undermine my confidence. I'd been so blind that I'd given her more power to influence me than I should have. She said I was both Jamie and Blanche and she wanted Blanche, which actually no longer bothered me. Kind of a relief, actually. I'd spent ten years pursuing something in her she was never going to give me—approval. Meg gave me that in five minutes.

As I replayed the Queen's words, it hit me that she'd used the first person when talking to me about hope. The words hadn't come from the royal Queen; they had come from Elizabeth Tudor, not even thirty, who'd taken on the burden of leadership. For all those years leading up to her accession to the throne, Elizabeth didn't know what would happen—would she ever be Queen? Would her half sister have her beheaded to remove the threat of a Protestant uprising? Yet through all that uncertainty she had hope. She acted as if she would survive.

What if *I* acted as if I could survive, as if I had enough hope to change my fate?

Hope. The one thing everyone needed in order to not lose themselves to the chaos of life. Something that had died in me.

A tiny spark of something flared in my chest. Was it hope? I breathed slowly, fanning the glowing ember until it flamed into an emotion I could keep alive. What I'd lost, along with myself, was the hope I could get my life back. I no longer wanted a life with Chris, but a life in the present with my family and friends? Yes, I *did* want that. It hit me that hope wasn't something people could take from you unless you let them. Hope was a candle you lit every morning when you awoke.

The spark in my chest became a warm glow. I would act as if this world—1561—mattered to my real world. No, I would act as if *both* worlds were real, and if I believed that, I could find my way home.

I stood, ignoring the baby's kicks. Shouldn't I at least give it a shot? What if I really could affect my fate? I pressed a hand over my pounding heart. The lightning would strike tomorrow. Maybe I owed it to myself and to Meg—if she were real—to use some of the hope Elizabeth had shared with me.

CHAPTER THIRTY-SIX

There was so much to do I didn't know where to start, so Vincent and I walked through the forest until I had a plan. But before I could put it into action, Jacob arrived with a cart of wood. I thanked him and told him he'd make someone a fine husband some day. He blushed so fiercely I feared spontaneous combustion. For some reason I cannot fathom, I said, "Jacob, what is your full name?"

"Jacob Peter Maddox."

I sat down so suddenly my teeth clacked together. "Maddox?"

He smiled shyly.

Jamie Maddox. Blanche Maddox. Jacob Maddox. I started to laugh when I realized what I needed to do. I would do this for Blanche's sake since she would never do it for herself.

I stepped close, then put both my hands on his chest. "Because I am with child, it is very unlikely that you would agree to this, but…Jacob Maddox, would you marry me?"

Jacob's eyes nearly popped out.

"I realize my personality has changed, but what if I once again became the 'astonishing and feisty' Blanche? Would you have me then?"

He swallowed several times. "I have loved you since you were a girl, but you've never been interested in a commoner like me."

"I have been blind, but now I see clearly." I patted his cheek. "You will be good for her…I mean, me. But we must get the Queen's permission."

He hugged me so hard I grunted, then he kissed me like a man desperate for oxygen. "Oh," he said as he jumped back. "The baby. Pray forgive me." Then he sprinted down the path toward the palace to see the Queen. I thought about following, then realized it was too much. I'd begun feeling odd, vaguely unsettled, as if something were happening in my body. Great, just great. Watch me give birth before I could reach St. Paul's.

Thirty minutes later, Jacob returned, flushed with success. We would marry that afternoon. He kissed me again, leaving me a little jealous that Blanche was so passionately desired.

"Do we require a license?" I asked.

"Yes!" And off he ran again.

That afternoon, most of the court was hunting; they'd passed my cottage, noisy with laughter, the horses tossing their heads and snorting. So I felt comfortable roaming the palace until I found an empty desk with paper, pen, and inkwell. I pulled out one sheet, dipped the tip into the black ink, and began....

Dear Blanche,

Writing this note may be a total waste of time and paper, but it's important to me. If things go as I hope, by now I am back in my own body, my own time, and you are back in yours. I will make sure we both remain where we are, where we belong.

You are likely to give birth very soon after you return to this time. You are married not to Lord Winston but to a palace guard whom you have known for years—Jacob Maddox. While he is not the rich lord you'd hoped for, he's a very good man. He loves my dog, Vincent. I know you have been cruel to the dog in the past, but I would reconsider this if I were you. You don't have many friends in this world. In fact, Vincent is currently your only friend besides Jacob. I know you think being ruthless and selfish will hold off the poverty you fear, but you no longer need to do that. Jacob loves me (you), and will never let any harm come to you...if you treat him right. Treat him and Vincent badly, and you will find yourself poor and alone.

Of course, what is now 1561 could all be in my mind. When I regain control of my body, where do you go? Do you inhabit my 1561 fantasy? While that's what I wish, it may not be so. Perhaps you've created your own fantasy world. God knows what that looks like.

Why did this happen to us? Are you a part of me that I created to make Chris happy? Are you a part of me, long buried, that's come to life?

I'm not sure I'll ever know the answers to any of these questions. All I want is to wake up in my own body. I want to hug myself, see my face in the mirror, hear my parents' voices. Chris and I are over, but I am ready to move on. I need to find out how much of me is Jamie, and how much is Blanche.

Signed,
Jamie

I blew on my signature to speed the drying, then folded it and tucked it into my incredibly tight bodice for Blanche to find.

The April 2nd ceremony was small and held inside my cottage. I wore my drab blue gown, the only one that fit. Jacob and I stood together, with two of his guard friends behind us as witnesses, Vincent by my side, and the vicar before us. It was over in a few minutes. Blanche—if she really existed—would be furious to find herself married to a mere guard, which made my heart soar. I did worry about her future treatment of Jacob, but I'd seen enough of his character to know he would be kind and patient with her until she came around. Surely Blanche would be smart enough to know she needed his support to raise a child.

After we lifted our glasses and toasted with ale, I once again took Jacob aside. "Because we are now married, and this is legally your child, I would like to go to St. Paul's tomorrow, early in the morning, in order to pray for the health of our child. Would you take me?"

He took my face in his hands and kissed me like he meant it, leaving me a little lightheaded. Blanche had better be grateful. "Yes, I will take you, even though Westminster is much closer."

"It's St. Paul's for me," I murmured.

An hour later when Jacob's friends folded themselves into deep bows, I turned toward the open door and sank into a curtsy as Elizabeth walked into the cottage. I gasped as I began to sink too low, weighed down by my belly. Thoughtful Jacob caught me and helped me up.

Elizabeth took both my hands. "Our Spark has made a most unusual marriage, but we wish you both good health and many children." She motioned with one finger, and a servant dashed forward with a small box. He handed it to me.

"We wanted to give you a gift," she said, "as a token of our affection."

I opened it to find an exquisite baby gown, ivory with pearl beads stitched onto the front panel. It was The Dress. Too choked up to speak, I just stared at the delicate, brilliant white piece of my life nestled into the box.

"Ma'am, it's lovely," Jacob said.

The Queen and I exchanged happy looks.

Then it hit me. This would be the last time I would see Queen Elizabeth I alive. If the lightning returned me to my own time, all I would see of Elizabeth again would be her tomb. I would squeeze through the narrow entrance at the left side of the Henry VII Chapel in Westminster Abbey. I would stand next to her tomb, with its black iron railing surrounding the tall columns that supported an elaborate platform. Beneath this platform would be her marble effigy, reclining on a marble bed and wearing a large neck ruffle and beautiful crown. She would be holding a scepter in those long, elegant fingers. In the coffin beneath this cold white sculpture would be Elizabeth's bones, long since turned to dust.

I swallowed hard to fight back tears.

"Oh, dear Spark, you are moved by our gift. Pray, it is nothing. Now do not forget. When you have delivered this child, you shall find a wet nurse and come back to court. I long to hear the rest of Harry's story."

I blinked through my tears. Elizabeth was just at the beginning of her reign and had so much ahead of her—Sir Francis Drake and Sir Walter Raleigh would explore the world. Elizabeth's navy would defeat the Spanish Armada. She would meet and encourage Shakespeare. And the religious turmoil boiling through the country would calm under her leadership. For more than a second, I was tempted to stay here, living in this fantasy, so I could watch it all unfold.

Elizabeth was still holding my hands. She gave them a slight squeeze, then gathered up her skirts and swished away. I turned away so Jacob would not see my tears.

After our evening meal, Jacob chose to sleep in his own quarters because I was so large and the bed so small. Relieved, I lay down to rest, and Vincent hopped up. He barely fit, but as usual, he curled up behind my legs and kept me warm. I was going to miss him.

❖

I could not sleep and soon began to feel restless. My legs ached. My back ached. Maybe I just needed to walk, so I stepped outside and paced around. The sun had long since disappeared behind the trees, leaving the cottage shadowed, but the path still visible.

Would my plan work? Would the lightning take me on the morrow? Would I end up back in my body, or remain stuck in this time period?

Vincent stopped, staring into the trees as I gasped at a cramp in my lower back. I tried massaging it out, but the cramp moved south. God's knees. I could not have this baby yet. It was Blanche's baby to have, thank you very much. But what if the child were to be born *before* the lightning strike tomorrow? Could I give birth then leave the baby behind?

"No, I couldn't," I said to Vincent, who was whining at something. "Once he or she is born," I said, "I'm not sure I trust Blanche to take care of the baby." Since hope and I had reconnected, the life I carried within in my body had become real.

A twig snapped behind me. Ears flying, Vincent leapt toward the sound. When I turned, two men stepped out from behind the trees and grabbed my arms. I struggled, but one of them put a cloth over my mouth, and my knees went limp. Vincent barked frantically, and one of the men yelled out in pain. I fought to stay conscious but failed.

❖

When I came to, I was lying on the bottom of a boat that smelled of fish and feet and mold. Oars splashed regularly into the river. I curled up, holding my stomach protectively. This was not part of my plan. Whatever had been on that cloth to knock me out made me sick to my stomach.

The sounds of revelry somewhere along the bank penetrated the blanket the men had thrown over me. Slowly, so they wouldn't know I was awake, I moved my head to the gunwale and peeked out from under the blanket. Lantern reflections danced all around us, but I couldn't tell where we were. Then the boat turned to the left toward a stone arch directly over the water. Two metal gates swung open toward us.

Fire truck. It was the Traitor's Gate, the way prisoners could be slipped by boat into the Tower of London at night. Princess Elizabeth had been brought in this way when her sister had her arrested.

Two lanterns walked down the stone steps as our boat bumped against the wall. Then one of the men in the boat dragged off the blanket. "Ah, the little fishy we caught is awake."

They helped me out of the boat, then two men each grabbed an arm, squeezing so tightly I knew they'd leave bruises. The lantern barely lit the cobblestone street so I stumbled, but the iron grips kept me upright. I considered screaming, but I was in the Tower of London. No one would come to my aid. My jaw tightened as the men dragged me up the stairs and along the walkway. If this was really happening, then I was screwed. If this was all in my head, then what kind of wacko gives herself the hope she'll escape only to then create men who capture her? Sick, sick, sick.

They led me into the Salt Tower, Ray's room. The two men who'd kidnapped me waited until the guard muttered to himself, then dug out some coins and tossed them each one. Without a word, they left.

The guard stood in the doorway. He wasn't the one who'd let me visit Ray. "Bed's there. No wood for a fire. Food comes midday on the morrow. Be quiet and you won't be harmed."

I stood as tall as I could. "I am Blanche Nottingham, and I demand to be released at once. The Queen will be very upset to learn her favorite has been wrongly imprisoned."

He snorted. "Don't be daft. You yourself arranged this, so don't be bringing the Queen into it."

"*I* arranged this?"

"Last fall, ye dropped the coins in my very hand and said to throw you in the Tower the night of April second and that I was to keep you there for one night and one day, no matter what you said."

I closed my eyes. Blanche, while I'd been back in my own body, had been very, very busy while in hers. She'd known about the lightning strike tomorrow. While she might have won this round, I was not giving up just yet. "I'm with child. Are you prepared to deliver a baby in the Tower?"

"Won't be the first time, m'lady. Now get some sleep. If your time comes while you be here, I'll see to having a midwife sent around."

The heavy door clanked shut and a key turned the lock. The guard shuffled away, coughed, and spit.

When an intense cramp hit my back, I stumbled to the bed and slowly lowered myself. The cramp disappeared, but twenty minutes later, it returned, stronger than before, taking my breath away.

Excellent. I was locked in the Tower of London and going into labor.

This just could *not* be happening.

But it was.

CHAPTER THIRTY-SEVEN

For most of the night—the longest night of my life to date—the contractions remained at twenty minutes apart. I knew because I counted. I managed to sleep a little between contractions. Finally, a tiny glow of daylight appeared in the window slots.

I worked my way to the door and pounded on it. "Hey! Hey! Let me out!"

My hand began to hurt so I somehow got my shoe off and banged it against the thick wood. "I do not belong here! Let me out! I am in labor."

Finally, shuffling footsteps neared the door. "M'lady, please. You're frightening the other prisoners." The asshole chuckled to himself.

"I need a midwife."

"I'll see to it sometime today."

Idiot. I waddled back to the bed.

But by midmorning, the contractions were ten minutes apart. Clearly, this was *not* a false pregnancy like Queen Mary's but the real thing. I lay on the bed, sweating with each contraction, furious I was going through this instead of Blanche...or furious because I'd put myself in this position in my fantasy. Why hadn't I thought ahead and put something in place as Blanche had done? No wonder Chris preferred Blanche—she was smarter.

I tried telling myself I was okay, but I wasn't. I was in labor, locked in the Tower, with no one to help me. I was going to die, and the baby with me.

I nearly cried with relief when a key jingled in the lock and turned. I rolled to my feet and tried to stand. Would this be the midwife?

But when the door creaked open, it was Harriet standing there with the key in her hand.

"Harriet?"

"Good God, woman, you're as big as a house." The brown eyes twinkled.

"Meg!" In two steps we were in each other arms, me crying and Meg comforting me. I struggled for control, since the next contraction would soon hit. "What the hell are you doing here?"

"Long story, but basically I let one of the Tower guards cop a feel in exchange for the key. Not one of the more pleasant memories I'll have to look back on, but still worth it. C'mon, we've got to get to St. Paul's."

I grabbed her hand and bent over. The intense pain moved up my torso and down my legs. "I'm in labor."

"Sorry, love, we still gotta go."

When the contraction ended, I sort of stood up. Meg threw her arm around me and helped me out onto the walkway. The sky was steel gray, with heavy slate clouds galloping in from the west. The wind was cold on my sweaty skin.

I managed to reach the next tower in the walkway before doubling over again. I tried to breathe into the pain, huffing like I'd seen in movies, but it really didn't help. "This is never going to work," Meg muttered. The tower room was cluttered with gardening tools, chairs, and tables…and a wheelbarrow in the far corner. "Perfect."

"I can't get into that."

But in less than a minute, I was sitting in the wheelbarrow, clinging to the sides while Meg pushed me to the end of the walkway. She helped me out of the wheelbarrow, then bounced it down the stairs, leaving it there to come back up for me. "Down the stairs, then we just walk down the street and out the gate."

We stopped on the stairs for another contraction. "*Fire truck*, this hurts," I said, gritting my teeth. Then I was back in the barrow, moaning in my discomfort. Pain truly was not my thing.

Two guards approached us from the gate.

"We need help," Meg said. "This woman is giving birth. I need one of you to deliver the child and the other to deliver the placenta and cut the cord. I hope you don't mind getting a lady's private area blood on your uniforms."

"Hell's gate," one of the men muttered. They both stepped back as Meg pushed me out onto the street. I would have laughed if the pain hadn't been so distracting.

"Now what?" I said through chattering teeth.

"Give me a minute."

"Meg, if the baby comes before the lightning strike, I have to stay here for the baby. I can't trust Blanche to do the right thing."

"Yes, you can." Then Meg jumped out into the middle of the street and waved her arms. A stately black carriage, decorated with gold tassels and being pulled by four stunning bays, came to a clattering stop. By now I'd sort of fallen out of the wheelbarrow and onto my feet.

Meg yanked the carriage door open. "Okay, everyone out."

"What is this? What right have you—" sputtered the gray-haired man sitting with two women.

"You're being carriage-jacked, my friend." She grabbed his arm and yanked him out. "Ladies, I don't mean to be cheeky, but I'm putting a pregnant woman on the floor of this carriage and she's going to give birth in about thirty seconds. If you'd like to get blood all over your nice slippers, then by all means keep your big bottoms planted on the bench."

The carriage rocked as the two women nearly fell out the other side. That's when the rain started lightly tapping the dusty street.

Somehow, Meg got me up into the carriage, where I knelt on the floor and rested my face and arms on the smooth leather seat. Then she climbed up onto the driver's bench and yelled in the guy's face. "I will cut your penis off if you don't take us to St. Paul's immediately."

Then she was back inside with me and we were moving. "I bribed him with some cash. The threat was just for his boss's sake."

Another contraction hit, nearly making me scream. I clenched my teeth. "How did you know I was here?"

"You kept wondering 'Why Blanche? Why not some other woman?' So as I said I would, I did my research, and I found out that you actually *are* related to Blanche Nottingham."

My hot, wet skin stuck to the seat, but I didn't care. "Please don't tell me I'm carrying my own ancestor." How else could The Dress have ended up in my family? I could barely hear myself over the rain pounding sharply on the carriage roof.

Meg rubbed the base of my back, which helped my breathing slow down, then leaned close. "No, you're carrying the *brother* of your ancestor. Blanche and Jacob Maddox go on to have five children. You're descended from the last one, James, so that's why you can relax about this baby. Blanchy and Jacob will take good care of Paul."

"Paul. Cute. But that still doesn't—" I gasped.

"Breathe, Jamie, breathe."

I did my best, huffing until the contraction passed. My entire body felt limp as a noodle, and my wet skirts clung to my legs... wet from the rain and from when my water broke during the wheelbarrow ride.

"Your contractions are getting much closer together, aren't they?" Meg's breath was warm on the back of my chilled neck.

I sighed. "This is a nightmare. Aren't we there yet?"

Meg pulled away and looked out the window. "No, too many carriages clogging the street, despite this rain."

"How did you know where I was?"

"You were worried that Blanche would find a way to outsmart you. Then it occurred to me—what if she had? I checked the Tower records from September 1560 through April 3, 1561 to see if that had happened, and there you were: Blanche Nottingham Maddox, imprisoned April 2, 1561, for treason. Congratulations on the marriage, by the way."

We giggled like girls until the next contraction. I powered my way through that, then wiped my eyes. "So even though Blanche got the jump on me by having herself locked up, I got the jump on her by raising questions that you answered."

Meg kissed my ear. "Precisely. Hang on, this stretch of the street is going to be bumpy. Then we'll be there." By now the rain could barely be heard over the thunder. This storm was nasty.

"And you? Who is Harriet to you?"

Meg laughed. "That was harder. History isn't interested in re-cording the lives of the little people, but luckily, Harriet did some-thing that was recorded, and I managed to find it. With some help of a genealogy organization and a few very large leaps across time, we managed to learn that yes, I am a descendent of Harriet Blankenship."

"What did she do?" I cried out as the carriage bounced like an inflated play toy, then bit my lip. I pulled Meg down close behind me, and I fell back into her lap.

"She published a brilliant and descriptive treatise on her visit to Purgatory. Both Protestants and Catholics lapped it up. She wrote of metal birds in the sky, and metal rats racing down roads. Of huge metal towers and people who did nothing all day but follow the small, flat box everyone held up in one hand. She even mentioned the London Eye as a turning wheel with people trapped at the end of each spoke."

I was glad for Harriet, but then doubled over in pain. "Christ, this hurts. But why are you here? Didn't you get the serum?"

"I did." She nuzzled my hair. "But you never showed up. So Dr. Raj gave me your address. I hung around until a woman matching your description came out—you are so *cute*, by the way—and you were right. Her clothes could have come from my mom's costume box. I ran up to her and said 'Jamie!' She just sniffed and turned away. Then she yelled at me over her shoulder, 'That bitch is dead, so you might as well accept it.'"

"But you didn't."

"Of course not. I just kept track of Blanche all winter, watching and waiting for the clothing to change, but it never did. And then I thought to do the Tower research and learned you wouldn't be able to get to St. Paul's on your own. I've been trying since then to ride the lightning back, but not until this morning did it happen."

I closed my eyes and moaned at the next contraction, strug-gling to breathe. "If you came back, that means the serum doesn't work," I managed to whisper.

Meg held me tight against her chest. "The serum does work. In order to come back and help you, I took more GCA."

For a few seconds I was too choked up to speak, but then managed to form words around the lump in my throat. "Dr. Raj let you do that?"

"No, he refused. But I knew where he kept the GCA and the serum, so one day I borrowed a syringe of each and injected myself with the GCA. I strapped the syringe with the serum to my calf so I can take it immediately when I return to the future."

"But what if Harriet doesn't understand and takes it off?"

Meg's eyes sparkled. "I wrapped a note around it: *If you take this off, you will die.*"

My eyes teared up. "I can't believe you came back for me."

The carriage rumbled over another rough patch. "I'm counting on a long and wonderful life with you," she whispered against my neck.

I kissed her wrist. "I think I want kids."

"Done."

The child inside me began banging so insistently on the door to be let out that I moaned with pain. Sweat stung my eyes. "Good, but you can carry them now that I know what this feels like."

"St. Paul's," the driver called.

Meg helped me up, and we managed to exit the carriage without tripping on our sodden dresses. Gray clouds swirled like angry gods, and a flash of cloud-to-cloud lightning blinded me for a second. Then an intense cramp hit me and I collapsed on the wet churchyard green.

I could hear Meg talking, but at this point it wasn't sinking in. My body demanded all my attention. I felt an opening, sort of like the opening I'd felt in my mind when Dr. Raj had first administered the GCA. Only this door wasn't closing until a baby kicked its way out. I struggled back into the moment. Concentrate!

Meg was instructing a young boy to find the nearest midwife and bring her here as fast as he could. She gave him a coin and promised more.

My heart pounded with excitement.

This was it.

I was about to give birth.

Or I was about to be swept back into my own body.

Or I was about to be killed by lightning.

One of these three things was going to happen. Maybe all three. Meg helped me back to my feet. I lifted my face to the rain. If I really did have multiple personalities, for some reason, lightning was my trigger to regain control. If I truly was in 1561, lightning was my only ride home.

The rain now felt warm against my skin. Thunder banged through the clouds and lightning flashed off in the distance. A crowd of men had formed at the cathedral entrance to stare at us. Poor Blanche was going to have an audience when she delivered this baby.

I suddenly felt that hope was a tangible thing, something I could grasp in my fist and never again let go. I licked my lips, tasting the delicious rain, water untainted by city life. The air became charged as more lightning flashed. The hair on the back of my neck stood up, even though I was wet as an otter. I reached up, stretching like a cat, as if I could climb into the sky on my own.

I no longer cared if I was living a fantasy or in 1561. I'd managed to find my hope again and I'd never let someone like Chris take it away from me.

I raised my arms, rejoicing in the rain running down into my sleeves, and grinned at Meg. "We're back in the saddle again!"

"Ride 'em, cowboys!" Meg shouted.

I sent a silent good-bye to my little Vincent, to my ancestor Jacob Maddox, and to my Queen. Then Meg and I exchanged confident smiles as a seam of lightning ripped open the sky.

CHAPTER THIRTY-EIGHT

I gripped the lectern as I struggled to settle back into my body. I glanced down quickly to make sure—yes, it was my body, but Blanche had dressed it in pink leggings with white polka dots, and some sort of filmy, voluminous purple thing with two camisoles underneath. The outfit was topped with a white cashmere cardigan. God's teeth.

I lifted my gaze to meet about one hundred expectant pairs of eyes. Bookshelves clued me in that I stood in a bookstore. On the lectern was a fringed purse, ugly as sin. Next to it was my cell phone and a book, *Sleeping with the Queen*, by Blanche Nottingham. Stuck to the book were two Post-its: *Sleeping with the Queen* in tenth week on New York Times Bestseller E-book List, and Two More Books in progress: *Anne Boleyn's Girl* and *The Horse Master's Murder*. Blanche had been busy.

I touched my flat stomach and missed the baby with an ache so deep I wondered if I would ever recover. Then I grabbed everything off the lectern, jammed it into the fringed disaster, and leaned into the microphone. "Thank you very much for coming."

As I fled, the murmurs followed me. "But she didn't say anything. How could she be done?"

A lightning-fast taxi ride under the thin April sun brought me to Dr. Rajamani's office. "Serum!" I shouted as I blasted through the open door. Where was Meg?

He leapt to his feet. "Only if you pass the test."

"What test?"

"Wait while I prepare the injection."

I tapped the floor with anxiety. "C'mon, Doc, hurry it up." Until London, I'd never given much thought to my own sanity. But now, sitting in the doctor's office waiting to get my shot, I finally got it. Sanity was a fragile mix of hope for the future and an unwavering belief in yourself. I'd lost them both, but never again.

Also, occupying two bodies—or *thinking* that I did—had scoured me so raw I no longer knew who I was. I wasn't Blanche Nottingham, but I also wasn't the same Jamie Maddox. As I waited for the doctor, I chewed on the puzzle that was me. From now on, with every thought I had, every word I spoke, I would probe myself like you'd probe a broken tooth. Did that phrase or thought come from me, or from Blanche? Was I some weird blended personality?

I frowned impatiently at the doctor. "Could we get this over with?" I wished Meg had met me here at the office, but with the serum strapped to her leg she wouldn't need the doctor. But she had to know I'd be here and wondering. Of course, there was still the possibility that I'd made her up.

Dr. Rajamani finally turned toward me, syringe at the ready. "Blanche came here a number of times trying to get this shot, but she didn't answer my questions. She returned with answers from Chris, but they were not the correct answers. So now I ask you: Why were you reluctant to participate in my experiment?"

"I hate needles."

"Because needles are your…." He waited.

"My kryptonite."

Humming happily, Dr. Rajamani injected me with the serum. Chris had been standing right next to me during the kryptonite conversation, but she hadn't listened. I wonder if she ever had.

"Are you missing any GCA or serum?" I asked. Meg could still be the product of a split-personality-induced fantasy.

He shrugged. "I do not keep exact records of the quantity I make."

As the serum flowed through my veins, I relaxed. The nightmare was over. But to determine whether my battle with Blanche

Nottingham had all been in my head or not, I needed Meg. If she didn't know me or what had happened these last months, then everything had taken place in my head and Dr. Kroll had been right. If Meg *did* know me, then I had truly been the confidant and "Spark" of Queen Elizabeth I of England.

When I thanked Dr. Rajamani for developing the serum, his whole body lit up like a scoreboard. "No, thank you, Jamie Maddox, for pushing me to develop it. I will soon be as famous as you!"

"Me?"

He typed something into his phone and showed me the results: *Blanche Nottingham is the pen name of the literally overnight sensation Jamie Maddox, author of one of the best-selling e-books in the twenty-first century.*

"Fire truck," I said. I didn't know whether to laugh or cry since it had been Blanche's success, not mine. But I let it go in exchange for thinking about what to do next if there really was money in my bank account. Instantly, I knew I'd find a new flat, one without Chris in it. Then I would set up Bradley and Annie in their own flat. Then I'd fly my entire family, and Ashley and Mary, to London to help me get to know the new Jamie.

"We will both be famous!" It was impossible for me to remain angry with the goofy doc in the face of such enthusiasm.

We shook hands, then I covered both of his with my own. "No more experimenting during stormy weather. Agreed?"

His shake was vigorous, his voice sincere. "Agreed."

Feeling lighter than I had in months, I left his office, and stood outside, my face raised to the heavens. Now it wouldn't matter if the sky were blue or gray or black. I was staying here. I was done being Time's plaything.

And there was no Meg. Clearly, I'd made her up. I inhaled deeply, disappointed that she wasn't real, but I knew I would be okay. My spunk was back where it belonged, holding my vertebrae together. I would find a way to stay in London. I would rent a new flat, visit an animal shelter, and adopt a dog with silky ears and serious eyes. And of course I already knew the name I would give him.

Half a block away, a taxi screeched to a halt and Bradley popped out with Annie cradled in one arm. "Jamie!"

I ran for the taxi, reaching it just as a woman exited from the other side and paid the driver.

It was Bradley's friend Mouse. Her long hair shone, and she looked adorable in a pair of baggy gray sweats and a form-fitting black T-shirt. We were about the same height, but she had more curves than I did.

"Meg Warren?" I asked, my voice trembling just a little.

Her gaze flicked down my body then back up. Her voice was cold. "Blanche Nottingham. What the fire truck are you doing here?"

Bradley clutched Annie so tightly she squeaked, and his voice was just as high when he said, "This is Blanche?"

I looked down at my body and laughed. "No, I'm not Blanche. I have much better taste than this."

Bradley wasn't sure what was going on, so he introduced us. Meg and I shook hands, then stood there.

Hope flashed across Meg's face as I considered what to say next.

"Meg…" I looked into her moss green eyes and recognized the impish spark I'd seen in Harriet's eyes in 1560.

Then I knew exactly what to say. "*God*, I love you… What was your name again?"

"Jamie," she whispered. "Thank God."

She pulled me into her arms and we kissed for the very first time.

—End—

Author's Note

Years ago I read Jane Resh Thomas's book, *Behind the Mask: The Life of Queen Elizabeth I,* and have been fascinated with the Tudors ever since. In *Spark* I've tried to stay as true to the known details of Queen Elizabeth's life as possible, so I've surrounded her with mostly real people, like Kat Ashley, Lady Mary, and William Cecil. Robert Dudley and his wife Amy also came straight out of the history books. (There were several attempts on Robert Dudley's life, but none succeeded. And to this day, no one really knows what happened that September day in 1560 when Amy Dudley was found dead at the bottom of a shallow flight of stairs.)

The mysterious Hew Draper actually *was* imprisoned in the Tower of London for upsetting Bess of Hardwick. In fact, if you visit the Tower of London you can see the astrological chart that Draper carved into the wall of the Salt Tower cell. Once he was released from prison, however, he disappeared from history.

Lightning did strike the steeple at St Paul's in 1561, but it was June 3 instead of April 3. I hope readers will forgive me—I needed to move things up or Jamie would end up suffering an eleven-month pregnancy.

I've posted some images and photos of the people and places in *Spark* on my website, catherinefriend.com.

About the Author

Catherine Friend is the author of romantic adventures: *The Spanish Pearl*, *The Crown of Valencia*, *A Pirate's Heart*, *The Copper Egg*, and *Spark*. She's also written memoirs, nonfiction, and several children's books. She's won a Minnesota Book Award, the Alice B. Readers Appreciation Award, an Independent Book Publishers Association award, four Golden Crown Literary Society Awards, and has been a Lambda Literary Award finalist. She's narrated two of her books for Dog Ear Audio: *Hit by a Farm* and *A Pirate's Heart*.

She lives in Minnesota with her wife of many years, and is delighted that after all this time they still really, really like each other. They have dogs, barn cats, and lots of bees. Her past lives include economist, technical writer, bookstore employee, packer of cheese gift boxes, and sheep farmer. Her current day job is writing nonfiction for an educational publisher, which is more fun than it sounds.

Books Available from Bold Strokes Books

Canvas for Love by Charlotte Greene. When ghosts from Amelia's past threaten to undermine their relationship, Chloé must navigate the greatest romance of her life without losing sight of who she is. (978-1-62639-944-0)

Heart Stop by Radclyffe. Two women, one with a damaged body, the other a damaged spirit, challenge each other to dare to live again. (978-1-62639-899-3)

Repercussions by Jessica L. Webb. Someone planted information in Edie Black's brain and now they want it back, but with the protection of shy former soldier Skye Kenny, Edie has a chance at life and love. (978-1-62639-925-9)

Spark by Catherine Friend. Jamie's life is turned upside down when her consciousness travels back to 1560 and lands in the body of one of Queen Elizabeth I's ladies-in-waiting…or has she totally lost her grip on reality? (978-1-62639-930-3)

Taking Sides by Kathleen Knowles. When passion and politics collide, can love survive? (978-1-62639-876-4)

Thorns of the Past by Gun Brooke. Former cop Darcy Flynn's heart broke when her career on the force ended in disgrace, but perhaps saving Sabrina Hawk's life will mend it in more ways than one. (978-1-62639-857-3)

You Make Me Tremble by Karis Walsh. Seismologist Casey Radnor comes to the San Juan Islands to study an earthquake but finds her heart shaken by passion when she meets animal rescuer Iris Mallery (978-1-62639-901-3)

Complications by MJ Williamz. Two women battle for the heart of one. (978-1-62639-769-9)

Crossing the Wide Forever by Missouri Vaun. As Cody Walsh and Lillie Ellis face the perils of the untamed West, they discover that love's uncharted frontier isn't for the weak in spirit or the faint of heart. (978-1-62639-851-1)

Fake It Till You Make It by M. Ullrich. Lies will lead to trouble, but can they lead to love? (978-1-62639-923-5)

Girls Next Door by Sandy Lowe and Stacia Seaman eds.. Bestselling romance authors tell it from the heart—sexy, romantic stories of falling for the girls next door. (978-1-62639-916-7)

Pursuit by Jackie D. The pursuit of the most dangerous terrorist in America will crack the lines of friendship and love, and not everyone will make it out under the weight of duty and service. (978-1-62639-903-7)

Shameless by Brit Ryder. Confident Emery Pearson knows exactly what she's looking for in a no-strings-attached hookup, but can a spontaneous interlude open her heart to more? (978-1-63555-006-1)

The Practitioner by Ronica Black. Sometimes love comes calling whether you're ready for it or not. (978-1-62639-948-8)

Unlikely Match by Fiona Riley. When an ambitious PR exec and her super-rich coding geek-girl client fall in love, they learn that giving something up may be the only way to have everything. (978-1-62639-891-7)

Where Love Leads by Erin McKenzie. A high school counselor and the mom of her new student bond in support of the troubled girl, never expecting deeper feelings to emerge, testing the boundaries of their relationship. (978-1-62639-991-4)

Forsaken Trust by Meredith Doench. When four women are murdered, Agent Luce Hansen must regain trust in her most valuable investigative tool—herself—to catch the killer. (978-1-62639-737-8)

Her Best Friend's Sister by Meghan O'Brien. For fifteen years, Claire Barker has nursed a massive crush on her best friend's older sister. What happens when all her wildest fantasies come true? (978-1-62639-861-0)

Letter of the Law by Carsen Taite. Will federal prosecutor Bianca Cruz take a chance at love with horse breeder Jade Vargas, whose dark family ties threaten everything Bianca has worked to protect—including her child? (978-1-62639-750-7)

New Life by Jan Gayle. Trigena and Karrie are having a baby, but the stress of becoming a mother and the impact on their relationship might be too much for Trigena. (978-1-62639-878-8)

Royal Rebel by Jenny Frame. Charity director Lennox King sees through the party girl image Princess Roza has cultivated, but will Lennox's past indiscretions and Roza's responsibilities make their love impossible? (978-1-62639-893-1)

Unbroken by Donna K. Ford. When Kayla and Jackie, two women with every reason to reject Happy Ever After, fall in love, will they have the courage to overcome their pasts and rewrite their stories? (978-1-62639-921-1)

Where the Light Glows by Dena Blake. Mel Thomas doesn't realize just how unhappy she is in her marriage until she meets Izzy Calabrese. Will she have the courage to overcome her insecurities and follow her heart? (978-1-62639-958-7)

Escape in Time by Robyn Nyx. Working in the past is hell on your future. (978-1-62639-855-9)

Forget-Me-Not by Kris Bryant. Is love worth walking away from the only life you've ever dreamed of? (978-1-62639-865-8)

Highland Fling by Anna Larner. On vacation in the Scottish Highlands, Eve Eddison falls for the enigmatic forestry officer Moira Burns, despite Eve's best friend's campaign to convince her that Moira will break her heart. (978-1-62639-853-5)

Phoenix Rising by Rebecca Harwell. As Storm's Quarry faces invasion from a powerful neighbor, a mysterious newcomer with powers equal to Nadya's challenges everything she believes about herself and her future. (978-1-62639-913-6)

Soul Survivor by I. Beacham. Sam and Joey have given up on hope, but when fate brings them together it gives them a chance to change each other's life and make dreams come true. (978-1-62639-882-5)

Strawberry Summer by Melissa Brayden. When Margaret Beringer's first love Courtney Carrington returns to their small town, she must grapple with their troubled past and fight the temptation for a very delicious future. (978-1-62639-867-2)

The Girl on the Edge of Summer by J.M. Redmann. Micky Knight accepts two cases, but neither is the easy investigation it appears. The past is never past—and young girls lead complicated, even dangerous lives. (978-1-62639-687-6)

Unknown Horizons by CJ Birch. The moment Lieutenant Alison Ash steps aboard the Persephone, she knows her life will never be the same. (978-1-62639-938-9)

boldstrokesbooks.com

Bold Strokes Books

Quality and Diversity in LGBTQ Literature

E-BOOKS

SCI-FI

MYSTERY

EROTICA

YOUNG ADULT

Romance

W·E·B·S·T·O·R·E

PRINT AND EBOOKS